MARLENE,
the trespasser, froze.
Someone was in the house, *her* hiding place.
When she saw him, her mind reeled with cold terror:
"Dear Lord in Heaven, it's a nigger!"

A black intellectual from the North and a near illiterate white girl from the South are driven to a common refuge through sheer necessity. That they hate each other is an accepted fact; that they will gradually, grudgingly, grow to trust and love one another is a fact, too, but quite incredible in either of their worlds.

Other SIGNET Novels You Will Enjoy

My
Sweet Charlie

DAVID WESTHEIMER

A SIGNET BOOK from
NEW AMERICAN LIBRARY
TIMES MIRROR

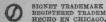 SIGNET TRADEMARK REG. U.S. PAT. OFF. AND FOREIGN COUNTRIES
REGISTERED TRADEMARK—MARCA REGISTRADA
HECHO EN CHICAGO, U.S.A.

SIGNET, SIGNET CLASSICS, MENTOR, PLUME AND MERIDIAN BOOKS
are published by The New American Library, Inc.,
1301 Avenue of the Americas, New York, New York 10019

FIRST PRINTING, OCTOBER, 1966

    12 13 14 15 16 17 18 19 20

PRINTED IN THE UNITED STATES OF AMERICA

To Dody, Fred and Eric

1

Marlene slid tight as she could against the car door, trying desperately to appear as if her sudden movement had nothing to do with the moist, doughy hand now lying flaccid and palm up, like something killed, on the seat a few inches from her thigh. Its owner peered ahead in an excess of concentration as he steered the car down the placid Southern highway in the September sun.

She stretched her plaid schoolgirl skirt over her shrinking knee as if trying to wrap the length of her naked shin in inviolable wool. She was breath-holding still, as if hiding from some questing predator. She stole a glance at the driver, moving only her eyes, not breathing, and caught the sullen edge of a glance as stealthy as her own. An angry glance, disappointed and filled with righteous guilt.

That nasty old thing, she thought. Old enough to be my daddy. My daddy.

She saw again, as if it were burned into the back of her eyes, her father's contorted face, biblical with outrage, and the vengeful lifted hand. A hand not like the one on the seat beside her now but horny and terrible, a farmer's hand, poised to strike but not falling, hanging in eternity, the threat more terrifying than a blow.

She resisted the memory. She had another problem now. Do I show that much already? she wondered. Daddy could tell because he saw me naked and throwing up, but now I'm just fine and got on my pleated skirt. Does that nasty old thing sitting there know what I done? Is that why he thought he could . . .

She squeezed her thighs together, guarding something already irretrievably and damningly lost, and pressed her slender arms along her sides, feeling with her biceps the hard breasts that had betrayed and undone her. And she remembered yet another hand.

If I just hadn't let him put his hand . . . But he was such a

7

sweet boy and so nervous-like and beseeching until I let him
put his hand . . . And he got so wild and awful and I couldn't
stop him. And then I didn't want to and I . . . we . . .

The doughy hand beside her came alive and raised itself to
perch on the steering wheel beside its doughy mate, wrest-
ing her from her familiar torment. She watched, repelled,
the play of sunlight on the row of coarse black hairs march-
ing from the thick wrist to the first knuckle of a finger shaped
like a roll ready for the oven.

A finger roll, she thought. Four finger rolls and a thumb
roll on a hand bun.

She giggled at the notion and stopped abruptly, aghast at
having made a sound and betrayed her presence. She shrank
back inside her refuge of wary terror. But it was too late. He
turned his round doughball of a face and looked at her, his
mean blue eyes pretending not to brush her outline and his
lips forming a spurious paternal grin.

"Well, now, young lady," he said, as if addressing a child,
"what was it your name was? Lena?"

He's trying to trick me, she thought. He knows I ain't no
little girl. I saw how he looked at my titties when I climbed in
his car. I shouldn't of got in. I should of told him I was waiting
for my daddy like I did those boys that tried to pick me up.

She folded her arms across her breasts and stared at the
knee he had touched. The skin no longer crawled but the
moist, ugly feeling of his hand lingered.

"What's the matter, little miss? Cat got your tongue?"

His own grayish tongue stole out through his grin and she
stared at it sidelong.

"Marlene," she answered with what felt like her last living
breath. "Marlene Cha. . . Smith."

She emphasized the last name.

"Marlene Smith," she said again.

"That's a right nice name, Marlene. Right nice. Ah got me
a little girl 'a my own 'bout your age. Fohteen."

"I'm seventeen."

"Is that a fact? Who'd of knowed it?"

You know it, all right, she thought. You nasty old thing.
I know what you was wanting when you touched me and you
old enough to be my daddy and ugly to boot. Ugly. And fat.
Like you been eating dough. Until you turned into dough your
own self.

And she thought of his thing, doughy like his fingers, and
shuddered and held herself tighter.

"You ain't cold, Marlene? Not in this weather? But if you are, Ah can turn on the heatuh. Ah got me a fine heatuh in this ole car."

"No, sir, I ain't cold. Not at all."

They drove in silence for a while, his eyes turning now and again from the highway to study her.

"Her name's Bobbie Jo," he said after a while. "My little girl. Aftuh me. Mine's Bobby. Kinda cute, ain't it?"

"Yes, sir," she said, thinking, No, it ain't cute, not one bit, and you ain't, either.

"You don't have to sir me, Marlene. Just call me Bobby."

The request increased her apprehension. He's going to touch me again if I don't watch out, she thought. And she thought again of his doughy thing and of his dough-fed body and the disgusting enterprise he wanted her to submit to.

She scanned the highway ahead of them as if searching for something familiar. On the left was the Gulf of Mexico, cat-fish gray and ruffled where the breeze plucked it. On the right they were just then passing a small stand of pines, edged by palmettos, from which a tan and white cow gazed at them, immobile except for its slowly moving jaw. There was something sadly human in the arch of its neck.

Up ahead, on the right side of the highway, was a boxlike building with an old-fashioned round gasoline pump in front. On the left, in the far distance, a small peninsula curved out into the Gulf. Marlene could barely make out the tops of houses among its trees. They were the first habitations she had seen in many minutes.

"Up there, mister," she said, pointing.

He looked at her, grudging and disappointed.

"Where you say you was goin'?"

"My aunt's. Like I told you, mister?"

"Your Aint Donna don't live there, little miss. Ah can tell you that for sure. Ain't nobody lives in them houses. Least not this time 'a year. No, sir. They move out 'fore the big storms, ever' last one, and they don't come back 'fore school's out. All them fine houses just goin' to waste all that time . . ."

He gave her a sharp, trapping look.

"Hey, how come you ain't in school yourself? You ain't graduated, have you? Just seventeen? Maybe you just quituated."

He laughed at the old joke. Marlene wondered if the creases in his face would stay set, the way dough did, but they came out again when he stopped laughing.

"Oh," she said. "Oh. Well, us, my Aunt Donna, she don't 'xactly live right there. She, uh, she's sposed to, you know, pick me up? At the store. That one right up there."

"Looks like she ain't there yet, to me."

"She said . . . My Aunt Donna told me if she wasn't there for me to just wait till she did get there. So if you'll just let me out up there . . . She said for me to just wait."

When he gave no sign he had heard her she feared he intended to keep going, but the car slowed as it neared the store and she slumped back from the brink of jumping out, faint with relief. He drove to a grudging half-car width off the highway and waited, making no move to reach across her to open the door, for which she was grateful. She turned to take her cardboard box from the rear seat, her body clenching itself against the gaze she sensed assaulting her from behind, and twisted quickly to open the door. Only when she was safely outside did she thank him.

"Glad to be of help," he replied, not looking at her.

He cleared his throat and turned toward her, a strange, sad, apologetic expression transforming his doughface into human flesh.

"Listen, little lady . . ."

Marlene waited politely for him to finish. He cleared his throat again.

"You take care of yourself, heah?" he said lamely.

Then he was gone, hunched over the steering wheel of the old sedan as if in flight, and she was alone beside the highway wanting to call out to him to come back and really take her to her Aunt Donna but it was too late. She bent without thinking and touched the cardboard box, touching her mother's face and all that remained of home.

Oh, Mama. And it seemed as if it were only moments before that she had seen her mother peering fearful and dry-sobbing from the kitchen, shrinking involuntarily from the undelivered blow Floyd Chambers aimed at her child, and waiting there, cowering, until his bony shoulders were out of the door and his angry feet had picked their way down the broken steps he was always going to fix but never had. And creeping out as near to crawling as a person could while still standing on her two feet and putting a shy arm around her shoulder for the first time since Marlene was a little girl but not saying a word. And darting away wordlessly leaving Marlene rooted to the heel-marked linoleum floor, brutally sick at her stomach as if something stigmatic were trying to rend its way out.

And her mother thrusting the twine-bound cardboard box at
her and shoving a limp mass of small papers into her fist
and saying, "Here's your thangs, Marlene, and all I got in
the house, fourteen dollars. You better be gone afore he
comes back like he told you and go stay with your Aint Donna.
Tell her . . . tell her your daddy moved into town to work days
a piece and I went with him to do for him and you need to
stay with her for a little while. And maybe your daddy will
change his mind afore long and I'll come after you."

And then her mother had looked beseechingly into her
face and said, "You bound and determined not to tell who,
sugar baby?"

"Oh, I couldn't, Mama," she had cried. "Not even if I
never see you again in my whole life. He said he wasn't the
only one and he would get the others to say so but he was,
Mama, I swear and hope to die he was and oh, Mama,
Mama, what'm I gonna do?"

Tears squirted from Marlene's eyes without warning. She
stopped them abruptly, wiped her eyes with the backs of her
hands and turned slowly to face the store, its planks rotted
at the bottoms where water had eaten at them in wet seasons.

A deep-eyed, hard-jawed man in a white shirt and clean
work pants stood in the doorway looking at her without particular interest.

"Mister?" she said.

He did not answer but grew attentive, as if he had only then
realized she was not a part of the landscape.

"Is there a bus goes by here?"

"Ah reckon."

The question seemed to have evoked an old grievance
and he worried at his cleft chin with fingers as horny as
Marlene's father's, staring blankly past her in silent contemplation of some inner rue.

"Right on by," he said bitterly, a failed cotton farmer mas-
querading as a storekeeper and failing at that, too. "Fulla'
niggers goin' to spend their money with the town Jews."

"It don't stop here?" she asked forlornly.

"Oh, it stops, all right, if they's somebody waitin'. But
not to let the niggers off and spend their money. Why, Ah
even got a *toilet* Ah'd let 'em use out back," he added in tones
of outrage. "But naw, it just goes right on by."

He came outside the store into the sun and looked up and
down the highway, his hands thrust in his pockets. Then

he turned to Marlene as if seeing her as a person for the first time.

"Where you headin'?" he asked politely.

She tried to think of some place far off.

"Uh, New Orleans. I'm goin' to New Orleans."

"They's one by here goes thataway. Your folks is there?"

"Oh, yes, sir."

"Ah was to New Orleens a time or two. Long time ago. Times Ah think Ah might just up an' . . ."

He let the sentence trail off hopelessly.

"When's it come by?" she asked. "The bus."

"Eleven tonight. If it's on time."

"Not till 'leven?"

"Don't you let that bother you none. You won't have no trouble hitchin' a ride 'fore then."

"I don't expect I'd want to do that, mister. Hitch a ride."

He nodded approvingly.

"Tell you what. You want to, you can sit inside the stoah and when somebody stops for gas, Ah'll ask foh you."

She shook her head.

"Thank you just the same. Is there a sooner bus for somewheres else?"

"You mean goin towards New Orleans?"

"Yes, sir," she said quickly, nodding.

"Well, now. They's several'll carry you part wayse. One just went by less'n an hour ago. Next one's after seven."

"Oh, shoot," she said, biting her lip.

"You can wait in the stoah, less'n you change yoah mind about hitchin' a ride. Ah'm open till nine." He scowled at no one in particular, the world, perhaps, and added, "Not that nobody comes in that time 'a night."

"I don't know," she said uncertainly. "I guess I better be gettin' . . ."

"You et today?" he demanded abruptly.

"Sir?"

"Ah said, you et today? You lookin' sunk-eyed."

She had not eaten. She had not even thought of it until now, and now she was hungry but something held her back from admitting it.

"I really better be gettin' on," she said.

"Walkin'? Seein's how you won't take no ride. You come on in and Ah'll fix you a baloney sandwich and a Doctuh Peppuh. Less you'd like sardines bettuh."

"A baloney sandwich would be right nice," she admitted, surrendering to hunger and kindness.

He led her inside the dim cluttered store and sat her down on a five-gallon milk can. He ripped open a package of white bread and made her a thick sandwich of baloney, mayonnaise and sweet pickles. Marlene took a ladylike bite and followed it with a long, grateful draught of sweet, prune-tasting Dr. Pepper.

"Good, ain't it?" he said.

She nodded, almost as ashamed of having been observed enjoying her food as if she had been seen in her underwear.

"Ah'm Mr. Treadwell," he said. "Ah own this no-'count stoah and thuhtty-five acres of the sorriest land you evuh seen out there in back. Ain't 'nough to work even if Ah could get the niggers to do it."

Least he calls himself Mister, Marlene thought. Not like he thinks he's courtin' age or nothin' like that.

She felt easier than she had since she stumbled out into the darkness and picked her way over the furrows to the highway, hoping she might die before she reached it or find some other miraculous form of deliverance.

"What's yoahs?" Treadwell asked.

"Sir?" she replied through a mouthful of baloney.

"Yoah name?"

"Marlene. Marlene Smith."

The lie came easier now that she had learned to say it.

"You runnin' away from home, ain't you?"

She gaped at him, looking in his face for disapproval but not finding it.

"Oh, no, sir. My mama and daddy moved to New Orleans and left me with my Aunt Donna till they found a place."

"Is that a fact, Miss Marlene Smith?"

She flushed and hung her head. Though she had lived a lie at home for over a month, she still had not become accustomed to falsehood.

"Well. It ain't none of mah business. You say you're Marlene Smith an' yoah daddy's waitin' in New Orleens, then you're Marlene Smith an' yoah daddy's waitin' in New Orleans."

She lifted her head gratefully and finished the last bite of sandwich and last swallow of Dr. Pepper, making them come out even and feeling a small glow of triumph at the achievement.

"Ah'll fix you anothuh sandwich," he said. "To eat on the way."

Marlene fumbled in her yellow plastic purse and took out a limp dollar bill.

"How much is it?" she asked hesitantly.

"Seein's it's you, 'bout five dollahs."

Marlene was stunned. And he'd acted like he was so nice. Then she saw the smile and knew he was teasing.

"Lemme tell you somethin', Marlene. In this world, 'fore you take anythang from anybody, you find out first how much they 'spectin' you to pay foh it. Ah mean, anythang. From anybody."

"Yes, sir."

"Ah ain't gonna charge you nothin'. Ah *invited* you. Ah ain't like them town Jews drag a nigger in his stoah an' then sell him ever'thang in sight. Not that you're no nigger. But whenevuh somebody *invites* you, don't you nevuh ask how much."

"Yes, sir," she said contritely.

She rose reluctantly, hating to leave the kindness but feeling she must be going, not getting someplace but leaving someplace, home, where her father and her shame were. She wondered if Mr. Treadwell would be so good to her if he knew about the awful thing she had done.

"They's a nice clean . . uh, place in mah back room," Treadwell said with unexpected delicacy. "If you need to . . . anythang."

Now that he had called her attention to the need, she realized she did have to go to the bathroom but she shrank from doing anything so personal in the same house with a strange man.

Even if he is right nice, she thought. He wouldn't think nothing ugly but he would know what I was doing in there and he would know I knew he knew it.

Her face grew warm with embarrassment at the thought of being half-naked and doing something a little disgusting just a closed door away from a man who knew what was going on. Even at home she tried to wait until her father was gone. She thought about the place behind the store. But if he let niggers use it . . .

And she had to be moving on, away from people, even kind people like Mr. Treadwell.

"I expect I better be goin'," she said.

"Changed yoah mind 'bout hitchin' a ride, have you?"

"Yes, sir."

She hadn't, but she did not want him to know she only wanted to keep moving.

"That's smart. Just be careful who you ride with. No wild boys."

"No, sir," she said, thinking, Or no old men, neither, at least not like Mr. Doughface. You couldn't tell just by looking, so the best thing was just to not get in with nobody even if you had to walk all day.

When she bent to pick up her box, he said, "Just hold yoah hohses, Miss Marlene. Ah promised to fix you anothuh sandwich."

She waited, fighting back her need for the room in the back, while Treadwell made another sandwich and put it in a brown paper sack with a licorice whip and a handful of jelly beans. The need subsided, and she felt relief and the same glow of triumph as when she had made the sandwich and the Dr. Pepper come out even.

Treadwell took the end of a licorice whip between his teeth and began munching it, drawing it in with his lips.

"You sure you don't want to wait here foh a ride?" he asked, talking through the licorice.

"No, sir, thank you anyhow."

She picked up her box and faced him awkwardly, not knowing exactly how to make her departure.

"You get to New Orleens, you look around foh a nice place foh a little stoah an' you let me know, heah?" Treadwell said, half seriously.

"Yes, sir. I sure will. An' thank you for the sanwich an' all."

Treadwell nodded, the last of the licorice disappearing into his mouth like a worm's tail.

"Well," she said, "I guess I better get me that ride."

When he did not answer she felt free to leave at last and went out into the sun. Its warmth felt good after the dankness of the store. She started walking and, sensing a presence behind her, turned to see Treadwell standing in the doorway and looking out, but not at her or at anything else beyond his discontent. She waited until he sighed and went back into the store, then walked along the side of the road. After a few minutes the false solace of movement drained away and she was frightened and terribly alone.

Maybe I ought to do like Mama said and go to Aunt Donna's, but I couldn't stand for her and Uncle Harold and Fay Marie and Joe Tom to find out because Daddy ain't never goin' to take me back and I'd just have to leave before I got so big they could all see and know what I did. If I went back, maybe that Mr. Treadwell would let me work in his store. He wouldn't have to pay me any money. But where would I stay? And then when I got big he'd know, too, and he wouldn't stand for having me around, and anyway, there wouldn't be anything for me to do in a little bitty store like that.

She walked more and more slowly until she came to a dead stop. She looked around blindly, clutching the box to her chest until it hurt, and taking bitter comfort from the hurt.

There ain't no place I can go, no place at all. Because what's in me will get bigger and bigger until I can't hide it no matter where I am. If I could just stand right here for ever and ever.

Utter hopelessness engulfed her. Her eyes brimmed with tears and she said aloud, "Oh, Mama, what am I goin' to do?"

2

Marlene had been walking hardly an hour but already she felt emptied of strength and all resolution. Despair had drained her, and the slick awkward stubbornness of the cardboard box.

The curving peninsula she had seen from the car was half a mile or so up ahead. Among the mossy live oaks and scattered pines she could make out the tops of four houses set irregularly a little distance apart. She sat down on a culvert to rest and studied the housetops nestled among the trees like oddly shaped eggs in the Easter bunny nests her father had made of moss when she was little. She wondered longingly, but without envy, what it felt like to be rich enough to own a house in which you did not even live all the time.

She took off her scuffed saddle shoes, her good pair, and rubbed her sore feet through her cotton socks, luxuriating in the pain as she had when she clutched the box to her chest. She looked down at her stomach, where her doom lived, even now relentlessly growing toward the day when it would bring her shame out in the open for everyone to see. Despair and self-pity made her cry again, and she put her shoes back on and resumed walking.

The sun was low and weakening when she drew abreast of the crushed oyster-shell road leading into the peninsula. She was numbingly weary and had to go to the bathroom. She crossed the highway and walked along the shell road toward the houses, now hidden by trees and underbrush except for the corner of one showing at a curve in the road. She hoped she would find a door or window open so she could get to the bathroom. It was private property and even the thought of going inside made her feel guilty, but her need was great.

It was a frame house, painted white, with green shutters on the windows. The porch was strewn with windblown leaves

17

and the empty chains of a swing dangled from its roof.
The door was locked, as were the front shutters. She walked
around the house through the tall grass, fearful of snakes,
and tested the other windows and the back door without
success.

The next house was also securely locked but the rear
screened porch of the third house was open. Marlene crossed
the porch and tried the locked back door, then a window
which lifted easily. Her relief turned to doubt. Once inside
she was the same as a burglar, even if she did not intend
taking anything. But she could not wait much longer.

She took a deep breath and crawled through, finding herself in the kitchen. Her urgency and sense of trespass did
not permit exploration and she hurried through in search
of the bathroom. She found it at the end of the hall just outside the kitchen.

When she emerged the house was full of shadows though
there was still a tinge of day among the trees. She had one
leg out of the kitchen window when irresolution stiffened
her. It would be almost night by the time she got to the road,
and what if the seven o'clock bus passed her by in the darkness? She would be stranded on a strange road full of cars
driven by strangers.

I don't know why I just don't stay here tonight, she thought.
I don't belong here and it'll be scary but not as scary as being
out on the road.

She drew her leg back inside and tried a light switch.
Nothing happened. She rummaged guiltily through drawers
and cabinets, finding tableware, canned goods, dishtowels and,
in the last wash of daylight remaining, a sheaf of thick white
candles. She lit one of them with a kitchen match and
anchored it in a saucer she selected because it had a chip in it.

The candlelight cast wavering shadows which filled the room
with ominous movement. Marlene shivered. The darkness
had brought a chill with it. She felt a burning in her feet and
a kneecap began jerking with the tension of exhaustion. She
went looking for rest and refuge.

She found a bedroom next to the bathroom and went no
further. It had a double bed with a coverlet handmade of
different colored knit woolen squares. She put the candle on
top of a bureau beside a mirror-bottomed tray on which rested
a comb and brush, a plastic bottle of suntan oil, a nail buffer,
several bottles of cologne and a small manicure scissors. There

were a few long hairs in the brush, mingled gray and dark brown.

Marlene's own light brown hair felt tangled and itchy, and she hesitated a moment before deciding she was too tired to get her own comb and brush and brush it out.

When she folded the spread back and found a bare mattress she looked through the bureau drawers for sheets, feeling like a burglar. She found women's underwear, large size; women's socks; stockings, casual summer clothing, and half a pack of stale cigarettes but no sheets. There were no sheets in the closet, either, but she did find summer shoes, a dress large enough for two girls her size, a terry-cloth beach robe and a bright rayon kimono.

With reluctance she took the candle and saucer and continued her search in the hall. There was a linen closet next to the bathroom and in it she found sheets, pillowcases and towels. She hurried back to the bedroom with sheets and pillowcases.

She tested the mattress with her fist. It was the softest she had felt, and for a moment a fleeting wash of pleasure covered the cold, the darkness and her despair. After she made the bed she reached for the snaps of her skirt, then changed her mind. To take off her clothes in somebody else's house would be almost like taking them off in public. No telling who might be coming in. She shuddered.

Why did I think that? There ain't nobody coming in. There better not be. Nobody comes here, not this time of year. That's what that old Mr. Doughface said. He acted kind of like he was sorry for acting ugly. Maybe I should of . . . Oh, well, I didn't and here I am.

She sighed, took off her shoes and slipped between the sheets. They were cold where they touched the bare flesh of her arms and legs. She felt gooseflesh forming and pulled her knees up against her stomach.

This is the way a baby sleeps, she thought. And the way a baby's curled up inside its mama's stomach. The way my baby's going to be curled up inside me.

She straightened quickly, not liking the comparison, and then, as abruptly as if she had plunged into a murky pool, fear engulfed her. Shadows lifted and dodged just outside the light of the candle and the shapes of things changed in the corners of the room. She was aware of ominous noises, of creakings and sighings and furtive raspings and rustlings. And then, very close, an eerie gurgling. She went stiff with terror and held her breath. The gurgling came again, and she realized it was her own stomach and that she was hungry.

She thought about the sandwich Treadwell had given her for the trip to New Orleans. It was in her box in the kitchen. She lay torn between terror and hunger, thinking about the tartness of the mayonnaise and the crispness of the pickle.

Hunger at last overcame fear and she ran to the kitchen with the candle and brought back her box and another candle to have ready if the first one went out before she fell asleep.

She ate the sandwich in bed, sitting up. Her mouth was dry with fear and tension but she could not bring herself to get up a second time and go for water. She somehow got the sandwich down and, though swallowing was difficult, she thought it tasted even better than the one in the store and she longed for the pruny sweetness of a Dr. Pepper or a cup of good hot coffee with two heaping spoonfuls of sugar and almost white with evaporated milk.

And thinking of hot, sweet coffee she thought of home and her mother, whom she would perhaps never see again, and of her father who hated her now and thought she was wicked and would never speak to her again. And she thought of his hand raised to hit her—smite, the Bible said—and hanging there over her, not falling, and she squeezed her eyes closed to shut out the image, which only made it sharper and more immediate so that they flew open as wide as they could and stared at the unknown terrors wreathed in the shadows of the room.

She closed her eyes again and turned on her stomach with the pillow clutched over her head to shut out whatever threatened in the murk pressing in on the candlelight. And she thought, inevitably, about why she was here.

If I just hadn't . . . I'd be safe at home with Mama. I can't let nothing like that happen again and I don't want to, not ever, because it's not beautiful like they try to tell you but ugly and awful and ruins your life and they lie to you and about you and they don't really love you, and you get a baby inside you and they hate you like it was all your fault, not theirs, and not just them hating you, but your own daddy, too, and then you get to believing they must be right and you hate yourself, too. And the baby. You hate the baby worse than anything because if it wasn't for him, or maybe it will be a girl, you wouldn't be all alone and scared and hungry with no place to go and nobody to help you.

Forgetting the lurking terrors of the darkness she turned on her back and pummeled her belly with mindless frustration and then hit herself between her legs with the side of her clenched fist until the pain brought her to unwilling understanding of the uselessness of her self-punishment.

I wish it was him I was hitting there, hitting him before he could do what he did, him acting so sweet and all until after and then saying he wasn't the only one. But he was and Mama believed me but nobody else would and what could Mama do against Daddy and everybody and what's the use? What's the use of anything?

She fell asleep crying.

Marlene did not open her eyes immediately when she awakened but lay snuggled in warmth, as yet unaware of where she was and why. It was as if she were home on her own bed but more comfortable than home, and it was the awareness of this which at last wrested her back to reality. She opened her eyes and lay there, not moving, examining the surroundings.

The room which had been so terrifying the night before was now revealed as cheerful and comforting in the strong morning light streaming in the shutters. It was sparsely but brightly furnished with the cream-colored bed and bureau, a comfortable chair upholstered in orange, a rocking chair with a round cushion covered in bright blue, and a small table on which stood a lamp with an umbrella-like shade of small panes of many-colored glass. The wallpaper was a design of pink roses and green leaves. Across from the bed, two shuttered windows extended from the floor to the high ceiling.

She propped herself on one elbow and saw on the floor a woven grass rug, dark brown, and next to the bed a woolly yellow throw rug. Never before in her life had there been anything beside Marlene's bed to step on but bare wooden floor or linoleum. She slipped out of bed and slid her feet over the throw rug, then removed her socks to feel the soft woolly texture against her bare itching soles.

There was a wide swivel mirror at the back of the bureau and, looking at it, Marlene saw with distaste her tangled hair and rumpled clothing. She pulled and straightened her skirt and blouse but they looked undeniably slept in. She wondered if there were an iron in the house. But even if there were it wouldn't be any good without electricity. She looked in her box and ate the jelly beans and licorice the storekeeper had given her and then slipped on her socks and

padded to the kitchen through the now bright and unintimi-
dating hall.

Still painfully conscious of her status as a trespasser, she
selected a jelly glass from among the better glasses in a
cabinet and got herself a drink of water from the sink. It
tasted stale. She emptied the glass and let the water run
awhile before refilling it. They must have forgotten to turn
the water off when they left, she thought. She remembered how
her cousin Fay Marie had once showed her how to cut off
the water at a little round hole in the lawn covered with
an iron lid. Marlene had reached down into the hole to feel
the knob for turning off the water and instead had touched the
cold squishiness of a frog. She screamed and Fay Marie
had rolled over and over on the grass laughing at her because she had known about the frog and had tricked her.

That was a mean thing to do, Marlene thought, then she
laughed to herself remembering how the frog had felt,
and her terror and the laughter of Fay Marie. Marlene wished
Fay Marie was here right now even if she had tricked her
about the frog and then was glad she wasn't, remembering
how a girl had been expelled from high school for being pregnant and how the other girls had talked about her.

Marlene wondered if anyone knew why she was not in
school and if they missed her, wondering if he had boasted
about making out with her and said there were others to keep
from being blamed, and her face grew hot with the shame of
her friends knowing what had happened to her. Well, she
would never see any of them again. That was one consolation.
The only one.

She looked around the kitchen. She really should be getting
out to the highway to catch a bus and go somewhere she could
get a job. Because that's what she had to do. But she was
hungry and she could not face the day and its problems on
an empty stomach. She eased open a kitchen cabinet and
looked longingly at the contents, her tongue protruding just
past her lips in concentration. There was instant coffee and
lump sugar and can after can of Carnation milk. A cup of
coffee with lots of sugar and evaporated milk was just what
she needed to help her through the day, and eggs and bacon
and hot biscuits and real butter or anyhow oleomargarine
and mustang grape jelly.

She licked her lips in indecision. It would be stealing if
she took anything. It was bad enough to slip in the house
and sleep in the bed, but at least it wasn't taking anything

that wasn't hers. If she had come to the house when the people were home and asked for a cup of coffee they would have given her one, not that she would ever do a thing like that, but if she did they would give her a cup, she was sure of that. She wished there were someone at home for her to ask because if there were she would do just that, knowing she really would not and was acting so brave because there was no chance of it really happening.

Maybe if I paid for it, she thought. I could leave a dime.

But she had no change. Only fourteen one-dollar bills worn limp and soft as cloth. A dollar bill was too much to leave for just a cup of coffee. That Mr. Treadwell had sure given her a turn when he said the sandwich was five dollars. He was a nice man.

Maybe if she took something to eat with the coffee it might be worth a dollar, that and the use of the bed and the sheets, although when she folded the sheets and put the bed back the way it was it would be the same as if she hadn't even been there.

Having made up her mind, she popped a lump of sugar into her mouth and sucked it while she made her choice for breakfast. She selected Post Toasties and a can of whole greengage plums, reluctantly passing over a box of biscuit mix sitting temptingly near an open jar of homemade blackberry jam turning to sugar around the edge.

Not worth a dollar, she thought, even if there was bacon and eggs and butter instead of just Post Toasties and plums, but a bargain was a bargain.

She filled a saucepan with water and lit a match. Nothing happened when she turned on the gas. She got down on her knees and looked behind the stove for the shut-off valve, turned it on and lit the burner under the saucepan. While the water was heating she poured Post Toasties into a bowl, opened the plums and with an icepick punched two holes in a can of evaporated milk, one of them so it could breathe.

She put three lumps of sugar and instant coffee in a cup, added water when it came to a boil and poured in evaporated milk with a lavish hand, watching the pure white thread dissolve into the dark liquid. She took a tentative sip, then closed her eyes and drank ecstatically, not caring how it burned. It was the best coffee she had ever drunk even if it was not regular coffee, just instant. Then she sat down and ate deliberately and with total concentration, alternating her attention between the cereal, the coffee and the plums, which she ate from the can with a long-handled iced-tea spoon. She ate slowly, in small bites, and while she did so thought of nothing but the food. She was at the table almost half an hour and when she was done, though she was full, she pushed back her chair with reluctance.

A little morning chill still lingered and she moved her chair into a pool of sunlight spilling in through the back porch window and sat there basking in a sort of torpor, her troubles beneath the surface for the moment. She felt as if she never wanted to move again, nor was there any need to. She was perfectly content where she was, doing nothing. After a while she rose with a sigh and began cleaning up. She wanted to leave the kitchen exactly as she had found it.

She did not know what to do about the open box of Post Toasties and the remaining plums. If she took them with her it would be stealing, if she left them they would spoil, and she could not bring herself to throw food away. That was something her father was set against, wasting anything, especially food and, after that, money. Not that they had ever had any of that to waste, she thought.

She washed and dried the utensils and put them away, putting off her decision about the unused food. Then she changed into her dress and carefully folded her wrinkled skirt and blouse before putting them in her box, thinking longingly of a soaking bath in the tub but having no intention of being naked in a strange house in broad daylight.

She stripped the sheets from the bed, folded them exactly as they had been before, being careful to follow the creases, and put them at the bottom of the stack in the linen closet. The room looked exactly as it had before she used it. Except for the opened food containers and the dollar bill she put under a cup in the kitchen cabinet no one could tell she had been there. There was nothing left to do but leave.

But she could not, not just yet. She could not face the prospect of getting out on the highway again heading for some unknown and no doubt unpleasant destination with leering men trying to pick her up or having to spend money on bus fare. She would wait a little while, until the sun was higher and she was in a better mood for traveling.

Marlene went out on the back porch, and looked into the yard. The grass was high and ragged, with here and there a clump of Johnson grass. There were fruit trees and a tall pecan, all nearly leafless now, and two small round flower beds enclosed by flaking whitewashed automobile tires and containing only dry stalks and more Johnson grass.

Seeing opened blackish-brown nut cases on the pecan tree, she went out into the yard and searched through the long grass for nuts without success. She found a stick and threw it into the branches, hoping to knock down any pecans which might still be clinging to the cases. She knocked down several of the petal-like cases but no nuts. She was disenchanted by her failure. She had wasted enough time here, she thought.

It was full day now and there was no reason why she should not be on her way. She had to get settled somewhere as quickly as possible so she could get a job and save enough money to keep her when she was too big to work, and to pay a doctor if there was a doctor who wasn't too disgusted by a girl having a baby when she was not even married.

What had the girl done who was expelled from school? Someone said she had gone to another town to have it cut out of her, and someone else said no, she had gone to a place where they looked after you while you had your baby and then took it away from you and gave it to somebody who wanted a baby but couldn't have one. It wasn't fair, to have a baby when you didn't want one when there were people who wanted one and couldn't have it.

I wish I could give mine to somebody right now, she thought. I wish there was some way to give it to them right out of my stomach into theirs and let them be the one to get so big people would know what they had done.

But there ain't any way and that's that. Maybe when I get to a big town I can get a job as a carhop or a picture show usher where there's lots of nice boys and I would meet this boy who's out of high school and everything, with a good job, and it would be love at first sight and he would right away ask me to marry him and I'd do it and when I had my baby he'd think it was his and we'd drive right up to Daddy's house in his car and I'd march right up on the porch and knock on the door and say, "Daddy, I want you to meet my *husband*, he's got this big job in a plant and if you want to move into town he'll put in a good word for you and maybe you can get a job there, too, even if you're not a high school graduate."

She smiled, thinking of her triumph and happiness, and hugged herself, only to be called from her daydream by the realization that before she could meet any nice boys or get a

job she had to start walking. Reluctantly, she went to the bedroom for her box.

She paused at the bedroom door with the box in her hand,
took a last, sad look at the room and said, "Thank you for
inviting me to spend the night, Miz . . . Miz Rich Lady, and
for breakfast and all, and some time you come visit me in
my house, hear?"

In the kitchen she folded down the paper lining in the
cereal box, hoping that would keep the Post Toasties from
getting stale, and ate the remaining plums.

She took the can with her when she left and when she
reached the shell road threw it as far as she could into the
underbrush.

It was almost as hard to leave the house as it had been
to leave home two nights before, because there she had
known a kind of security for the first time since she realized
she was pregnant. There was no one there to pry or ask
questions or say mean things. She trudged along the shell
road, forlorn. When she came in sight of the highway she
stopped involuntarily and looked back in the direction from
which she had come.

Why was she in such a hurry to be on her way to nowhere?

She thought with longing of the privacy of the house,
with no one to tell her what to do or when to do it, and
of the comfortable bed, forgetting the terrors lurking in the
shadows of the room. She was still tired from the day before
and she needed more time to think things out. Why couldn't
she spend just one more night in the house where she could
make up her mind what to do in peace and quiet without any
Mr. Doughfaces trying to pick her up and do ugly things?

Cheering up immediately, she settled her box more comfortably on her hip and walked briskly back to the house,
entering it now almost as if she had a right to be there.

She went to the bedroom and, before putting her box under
the bed, took out her comb and brush, her scalp prickling
with anticipation.

She moved a kitchen chair to the sunny part of the back
porch and combed and brushed her lanky, tangled hair
until her scalp tingled and her arms ached. When she was
done, she felt gloriously alive and clean. And that night,
when she was in bed, fewer terrors lurked in the shadows.

3

After breakfast the next morning she put a second dollar bill with the first under the cup and giggled at the thought of someone finding the money next summer and wondering how it got there. She did not feel nearly so guilty about the second night as she had about the first.

Knowing she had to be moving on and uncertain when she might get a chance to bathe, she lit the pilot light of the water heater, made sure the back door and windows were locked, locked the bathroom door and filled the tub. She lifted a corner of the pull-down shade covering the bathroom window and inspected the back yard before undressing, even then feeling someone was looking. At home she had never had any feeling of indelicacy stripped for the tub, since she was not ashamed of her body but only embarrassed by the thought of another seeing it—even the boy had never seen her completely naked—but being undressed in someone else's house was different. It was as if the owner of the house would have the right, if he were here, to come into the bathroom even though she was naked because it was his house and she was a trespasser.

She stepped quickly into the smoking tub and covered her loins with her hands in an involuntary gesture. The warm water seemed to reach inside the length of her body, untying knots she had not realized were there. Again she wished her frequent wish, that she could stay exactly where she was and as she was and never move.

When this passed, she inspected her stomach. It was still flat and she wondered how her father had been so sure just because she threw up. As far as she could see there was no evidence of the enormous and terrible change from being a virgin to being a girl in trouble.

She bent her neck at a sharp angle and inspected her under-sized breasts, then felt them tentatively. They seemed larger and firmer than they had been before. Maybe that was

27

how Daddy knew, she thought. But he didn't look at them that good. At least not at first. He didn't know I was naked when he heard me throwing up in the bathroom and he looked away real quick and started out, but then he turned and looked at me real good, not like he wanted to but like he had to and that's when his face got funny and he told me to get dressed right away and come on out to the front room.

Yes, it could have been her breasts that helped betray her to him, just as they had betrayed her into sin and ruin. She hated them, and yet she had a sneaking pride in them in their, to her, new and perilous beauty. The boy had teased her about how little they were but if he could see them now, she thought smugly, he wouldn't say they were too little, not that I'd ever let him touch them or even see them again and if he tried I'd hit him where it hurts a boy the most.

But if she was a married woman it might be all right for a boy, if he was her husband, to see and touch them and everything else if it made him happy. She lay back in the warm water and closed her eyes and thought about the tall fair-haired boy she was going to meet when she got her job as usher at the picture show. Despite her nudity and awareness of her body, she did not think of being naked with him but of standing beside him in a white wedding dress with a veil and hearing the preacher's deep voice and driving up to her daddy's house in the boy's car, still in her wedding dress and veil, and saying, "Daddy, I want you to meet my *husband*."

"My husband," she whispered aloud and dreamily and, when the sound of her own voice ended her reverie, realized she did not really want to get married to anyone but only wished for it because it was one way out of her trouble. What she really wanted was to be a virgin again and be with her mama and daddy exactly as it was before and she would never again feel deprived at being poor and living on a farm and not having a new dress any time she felt like it, at least not until she finished high school and took business and got herself a good job in town, not as a carhop or usher but as a private secretary who could send money home to her mama and maybe later move her into town.

But next to that, and even more than marrying some nice boy, she wished she could stop time and the growth of what was inside her and just stay quietly in the house until everything was, somehow, all right again and she could go home as if nothing had happened and her daddy would forgive her and she, and the thought took her completely by surprise, would forgive him. But she couldn't do that, of course, any more than she could stay here.

She washed herself quickly with the hardened bar of soap overlooked in the soapdish, dried with the towel she had brought from the linen closet, put on clean underwear and slipped into her dress. She washed out the underwear she had removed and hung it on the shower curtain rod over the tub. It would take longer to dry than out in the sun, but she did not want to chance anyone seeing her brassiere and underpants hanging outside on the line.

She could not leave now if she wanted to, she thought comfortably. She had to wait until her things dried.

She changed from her dress into her wrinkled blouse and a pair of shorts her mother had put in the box and went outside to explore. There was a thick, salty tang in the air and she threw back her shoulders and filled her lungs with it. It was the smell of the sea. The Gulf of Mexico was across the road behind the trees. Suddenly she had a longing to see the water from close by. She had not seen the Gulf, except for day before yesterday, since she was a child. She had always lived inland on some small farm or other.

She walked through the ragged grass alongside the house, painted white with blue shutters, through the overgrown oakshaded front yard and along the oyster-shell road past the last house, the closest one to the water. In front of it a wave-lapped pier extended more than a city block into the Gulf. Fiddler crabs and scorpion-like amphibious creatures scuttled for safety along the driftwood-littered beach at her approach, frightening her a little.

She walked out midway on the pier and stopped, filled with unease by all the water around her. The pier creaked and moved and seemed to her dangerously unstable. There was water in front of her, behind her, on both sides and below her. She was frightened of so much water, being unable to swim and not knowing the Gulf of Mexico was only two feet deep where she stood. She retraced her steps, almost running, and did not feel completely at ease until she stepped off the end of the pier and planted her feet firmly in the sand. Though she feared the sea she loved the beach with its soft, warm sand.

She sat down in a heap, as if she had tumbled there, snatched off her shoes and socks and worked her feet into the sand, finding it cold below the surface. Then she ran along the beach at the water's edge, dodging away laughing from the lapping waves. When she could run no more she walked sedately beyond the reach of the wavelets, picking her way around driftwood and looking for fiddler crabs.

After a while she went back to her shoes and sat down with her head between her knees and let the sun warm her back. Lulled by this, she sat motionless for a long time and then, restless, picked up a nearby stick and began digging a hole in the sand. Tiring of this, she rose to her knees and built an elaborate sand castle, dug a moat around it and scratched a channel to the water's edge to fill the moat.

She felt alone but not lonely. The creak of the pier, now that she was not on it, was companionable, and between the Gulf and the trees she was completely cut off from the outside world. She could not see anyone and, what was better, no one could see her. It was as if this particular spot was hers alone. As she had done so often the past two days, she wished she could stay exactly where she was forever, never having to move.

With a sigh, she picked up her shoes and socks and, balancing first on one foot and then the other, brushed off the sand before putting them on. She walked back to the house through the trees instead of taking the road.

Palmettos bristled among oaks and pines, and here and there the way was clogged with shedding blackberry brambles. Spanish moss trailed low from the oaks, and Marlene pulled loose a handful of tendrils and twisted them into a green-tinged gray mask, which she held in place beneath her nose by wrinkling her upper lip.

She pulled down a larger clump and fashioned herself a mustache and full beard by poking a hole for her mouth and drawing back tendrils over her ears under her hair to keep it in place. She wished she had a mirror so she could look at herself.

The closer she came to the house the slower she walked, knowing she had no excuse to remain longer but reluctant to leave this haven of comfort and tranquillity. When she reached the road she removed her moss beard lest someone see her playing a child's game, although she really did not expect to meet anyone and would have been disappointed and frightened if she had.

When she reached the house she went straight to the bathroom, put on the beard and studied herself in the mirror.

Just like Santa Claus, she thought, and said aloud, "Ho,

ho, ho," giggling self-consciously then and sticking her tongue out at the bearded imposter in the mirror.

Her underwear, as she had expected and, secretly, hoped, was still damp. So was the towel, which should be dry before she folded it and put it back in the closet or it would mildew. She simply would have to spend another night in the house, she decided. There was no way of getting around it.

She was hardly frightened at all in bed that night, having become familiar with her surroundings and feeling more comfortable physically than she ever had in any bed before. In the morning she prepared breakfast and cleaned up as if it were a familiar routine and added a third dollar bill to the two under the cup.

She was disappointed when she found her underwear and the towel had dried overnight.

Now I've really got to leave, she thought.

She folded the towel and put it away, put her underwear in her box, tucked the box under her arm and marched resolutely to the kitchen. Going down the back steps, she felt a small itching on the ball of her left foot. Normally she would have thought nothing of it but now she sat down on the step and took off her shoe and sock. She found a small scratch there where she had stepped on a broken shell on the beach the day before.

She could not start walking Lord knew how far with a cut foot, she thought. She might get blood poisoning. Her mama was always warning her against blood poisoning and lockjaw from cuts and scratches, and telling her stories about little girls who hadn't tended to cuts and had lost their arms or even their lives or whose jaws locked so they couldn't eat and just starved to death.

Hers was a small cut, to be sure, but that was the most dangerous kind because you were tempted to neglect it. She couldn't take a chance on getting blood poisoning when there wasn't anybody in the world to look after her, and especially in her condition.

She hobbled back to the bathroom, being careful not to touch the floor with her sole, and daubed on iodine from the medicine cabinet. Another day, she thought, and the foot would be healed enough to travel on. Gratefully she took her box back to the bedroom and passed the day playing on the beach and just sitting.

Next morning, huddled in a shivering ball, she awakened to the sound of rain. At first she thought it was still night,

the room being in semidarkness, but when she went gingerly
to the window across the cold grass rug, forgetting to limp
on her scratched foot, she saw it was day. Rain was plunging
down from a spongy grayness which seemed to hover just
above the trees, and water dripped in large scallops from the
drainless eaves.

Her first reaction was one of disappointment. She loved
the sun, and rain made her melancholy except those times
it broke dry spells when it was badly needed for crops. When
she realized she could not leave the house in such weather,
her mood changed. She sat on the bed, shivering and hugging
herself but pleased despite the cold and gloom of the day. She
realized she was humming a tune and cocked an ear to listen,
as if the sound were coming from somewhere outside herself.

When she realized what it was she was humming, melancholy far greater than that prompted by the rainy weather
surged over her. It was a song her daddy sometimes whistled
or sang, though it was seldom he did either, and the only song
she had ever heard him attempt, except hymns in church.

"Oh, I'm thinking tonight of my blue eyes," it began. It
was a sad song, she had always thought, though her daddy
sang it without particular emotion, or even awareness of the
words. She had always been puzzled by the words because her
mamma had brown eyes, as she had herself, and when she
was a little girl had wondered if her daddy once had had blue
eyes but lost them, somehow, and missed them and wished
he had them back instead of his gray ones. And when she
was a little older and romantic, she wondered if her daddy had
once had a blue-eyed sweetheart. It was only in recent years
she had understood it was merely a tune and a scattering of
words that had stuck with him for no particular reason and
that he was not thinking of blue eyes or anything at all.

But now it made her sad, nonetheless, because it reminded
her of her daddy, and her mama and home, and in an
exaggerated poignant way. She cried for the first time since
her first night in the house. The tears broke her mood and
she went cheerfully to the closet where, after a brief struggle
with her conscience over the propriety of the action, she
took the terry-cloth robe from its hook and draped it around
her thin body.

She felt immediately warmer but guilty. What if the lady
who owned the house came in and caught her? She looked
quickly at the bedroom door as if the owner might be

standing there, outraged. The relief she felt at not really being caught helped overcome her feeling of guilt and she put on her shoes and went to the kitchen humming a tune out of her own experience, something she had heard at a dance in the school gym.

Because it was raining and she could stay in the house another day with a clear conscience, she decided to celebrate with a special breakfast. She opened the box of biscuit mix, made dough, molded a dozen biscuits and put them in the oven. It was the best stove she had ever used.

Wouldn't Mama dearly love a stove like this? she thought, dancing dreamily to the tune she was whistling, with a glass door in the oven so she could look inside and see how things were doing. She wondered what her mama was doing right then and if she was worrying about her, knowing she was because it was the first time she had ever been away from home all night that her mama did not know where she was or what she was doing.

When the biscuits were done, she split three of them and spread them with jam, wishing she had butter to go with them. With a second cup of coffee she ate three more. She put the others away for later.

After she washed the biscuit pan, the mixing bowl and her coffee cup and put them away she explored for the first time the portion of the house she had not earlier found it absolutely necessary to use. There was a second bedroom, obviously occupied by a man, the evidence being a pipestand without pipes on the dresser and men's summer clothing in the closet. The closet smelled of fish, the odor coming from a crumpled pair of dirty duck trousers on the floor.

I bet his wife gives him what for when she comes back and finds out what he left in the closet, Marlene thought. Just like a man to go off and leave his dirty smelly fishing pants behind. The way they smelled, he should have taken them out in the yard and buried them.

The living room was full of comfortable summer furniture, rattan, with the cushions in slip covers for the winter. The floor was covered with a light brown woven grass rug of the sort in the woman's bedroom and strewn with bright throw rugs. In one corner was a narrow two-row bookshelf with a dozen or so volumes in it, which she did not inspect, and next to an easy chair was a brass scuttle full of magazines. In another corner was an expensive old-fashioned combination console radio and record player. Marlene opened the cabinet door and found volumes of 78 RPM records and a few long-playing albums, mostly Broadway shows and one Lawrence Welk.

In the dining room was a heavy oak table which was a relic of the owner's town home and out of place in a summer house, though Marlene did not know that and was impressed by it, and six matching chairs. Cut-glass tumblers, goblets and a cake dish were visible through the glass front of a china cabinet, and underneath, behind the cabinet doors, were chinaware, cutlery and several partially full liquor bottles. Marlene did not quite approve of either the fine tablewear going to waste or the presence of liquor. Though on very rare occasions her daddy had come home drunk they had never kept alcohol in the house. She had tasted whiskey— harsh and tawny in flat pint bottles the boys brought to dances and kept outside in their cars—and detested it, and also the way it made the boys act when they had had too much of it.

She unlocked the front door and went out on the front porch, which was screened and protected from the weather by wide, roll-down shades made of long green laths stitched together with heavy cord. It was cold and very damp on the porch and the rain beat heavily on the roof and sides. Marlene shivered and went back into the living room to rummage among the magazines. She found *Life*, the *Saturday Evening Post* and movie fan magazines, none dated later than the previous August. She had read little except what was required of her in school but she enjoyed photographs of actors and stories in movie magazines.

She took the movie magazines to the bedroom, where she propped herself up under the spread and leafed through them in the dim light while the rain beat incessantly on the roof. She felt a deep sense of privilege at being warm and comfortable with absolutely nothing to do while outside everything was being battered and drenched. She wondered if it was raining at home, and if it were, had her daddy ever fixed the leak in the roof over the stove. This was a good, tight house, and the water did not come in anywhere, even around the windows.

She looked at some of the magazine pictures for a very long time, almost as if in a trance, particularly those which showed starlets scarcely older than she relaxing glamorously in their own apartments or entertaining young actors as well groomed and beautiful as themselves at tables for two.

She envied the girls in a vague sort of way but would not have changed places with any of them unless by so doing she could also have changed her condition of pregnancy. Though she missed her mama, it was the only condition she would change at the moment if she had the chance.

She was somewhat attracted by the beautiful young men because she imagined they were attentive, thoughtful and above all gentlemen who would never get a girl in trouble but if they did would stick by her, though she was not sure she would like to keep company with one of them and certainly would not want to marry one. To be married to a boy prettier than yourself would create problems she preferred not to face.

Late in the morning she made herself a cup of coffee and brought it back to the bedroom and sipped it while she looked at some of the pictures a second time. Tiring of this at last, she made the bed, leaving the sheets on this time, and worked on her nails with a manicure set she found in the bureau drawer. As usual, she felt guilty about using something which was not hers but comforted herself with the thought she was not using anything up. It was growing increasingly easier for her to find such comfort.

There was nail polish in a bureau drawer and she took it to the kitchen where the light was better and painted her nails, rationalizing that although she was using something up the polish would probably be caked and useless by the time its owner came back. Feeling chilly, she lit the oven and moved her chair close to the open stove door. She waved her hands in the warm air from the oven to dry the polish, then spread her fingers and admired her nails.

It made her feel as if she were going to a dance because she only wore nail polish on special occasions. Her daddy had disapproved of nail polish on moral and economic grounds but not so strongly as to actually forbid it. When her nails were dry she took off her shoes and socks and propped her feet on the open oven door and let them toast. Then she painted her toenails. It was the first time she had ever done so and she felt glamorous and a little wicked, like the starlets in the movie magazines.

Marlene closed her eyes and leaned back in the kitchen chair. When she got her job as usher in the picture show, instead of meeting a tall fair-haired boy there would be these movie stars there for a public appearance and this big talent scout would be with them and he'd notice her when she showed him to his seat down front with her flashlight and carry her off to Hollywood for a screen test. A big producer would see it and give her acting lessons and send her to school where they taught beauty secrets and how to walk with a book on your head and in no time at all she would look just like the girls in the magazines and be an overnight star.

But what about the baby all that time?

She opened her eyes and stared at her flat belly as if it were a mortal enemy, her daydreams shattered for the moment but only for the moment. It was too good a daydream to relinquish so easily. Since even in a daydream she could not evade the reality of her pregnancy she decided that when she reached Hollywood she would confess her predicament to the talent scout, who was an old man of fifty and very understanding because he had seen so much of life, being from Hollywood, and he would take her to the doctor, who was also understanding, and he would do whatever they did to stop a baby and then the talent scout would take her to the big producer but would never tell anyone about the baby and neither would the doctor. And she wouldn't let her mama and daddy know anything about anything, which would be the hardest part of all, until they had this big premiere at the Chinese Theatre and she would send them tickets for the airplane, still without letting them know why, and she would walk up to them in her silver evening dress with this tall fair-haired actor, not one of the pretty ones, and say, "Daddy, I want you to meet my *husband*," because, oh, yes, while she was making the picture her costar would fall in love with her and as soon as it was finished they would get married and she would have this big diamond ring.

Marlene sighed and looked around the kitchen, listening to the drumming of the rain on the roof. It was not a discontented sigh. She really did not want to be a movie star with a diamond ring and an actor for a husband even though it was fun to think about and gave her a warm feeling in her stomach where the baby was. All she really wanted was not to have the baby there and be back home with her mama, only the house would be the one she was in now instead of the one she had left and it would, somehow, be hers instead of theirs but she would let them live there, in the other bedroom. Or, better still, she would live with them somewhere else and have this house to come to and be alone in whenever her daddy acted mean or any other time she wanted to, and have cousin Fay Marie or other girls come and spend the night and they would sit up until all hours in pajamas talking and looking at movie magazines and all the girls in high school would be just dying for an invitation to spend the night in Marlene Chambers' house and if a girl ever got in trouble the girl would come to her and tell her about it and she would let the girl stay in her house until everything was all right again.

How she wished she could do the same, just stay here until everything was all right again. But everything would never be all right again for her. Because no matter how long she stayed, all the time the baby would be growing inside her until it had to come out.

Despairing and no longer content to sit quietly dreaming and toasting her feet, she put on her socks and opened the ironing-board cupboard. There was an electric steam iron above the folding ironing board. She slipped on her shoes and, holding a big piepan over her head, ran outside to the fusebox and turned on the electricity. She felt guilty about that, knowing she had no right to turn the electricity on after the people who owned the house had turned it off, but she did not intend using much, only enough to iron her blouse and skirt and have a light on in the bedroom one last night.

She filled the iron with distilled water from a jug on the same shelf as the iron and plugged it in. After she ironed her skirt she held it to her face and felt the warmth and smell of home. Instead of making her homesick it cheered her up. It gave her the illusion that this was her home.

Instead of lunch, she made a batch of fudge from ingredients in the food cupboard and, over a period of hours, ate it all.

It grew dark earlier than usual because of the rain and she went to bed. She looked at magazines until she became sleepy and lay still for a while debating whether or not to turn off the light. The people who owned the house might not like it if she left a light on all night and, besides, she was no longer afraid of the darkness in the house. It was a friendly house. She got up and turned the light off and burrowed under the covers. She was almost asleep when she remembered she had not put the day's dollar under the cup in the kitchen. She was wide awake instantly. She slipped on her shoes and added a fourth dollar bill to the three in the kitchen. She fell asleep at once after she climbed back into bed.

4

It turned cold during the night and Marlene slept uneasily, curled into a ball. She was stiff in the morning and her nose ran. She slipped into the terry-cloth robe and some scuffs several sizes too large for her and went at once to the kitchen to light the oven. Outside the day was crisp and burnished. She opened the back door and took a deep breath, full of inexplicable well-being.

The air was freshly scrubbed and scented with moss, grass and the sea, and the trees were as sharp against the fathomless sky as if outlined in black. It was a day that pulsed with life.

Marlene ate, remembering to put a dollar under the cup, and dressed herself in a man's denim trousers and khaki shirt she found in the other bedroom. She held up the trousers by pulling two belt loops together with string. She rolled the pants legs to her ankles and let the shirttail hang down. It reached almost to her knees. Over all, she wore the terry-cloth robe, the warmest garment in the house.

It was too cold to wade in the Gulf but it was pleasant walking on the sand bathed in sunlight which suggested rather than delivered warmth. The cold was not penetrating, only invigorating, and Marlene walked and trotted until her lightly freckled face flushed and it was hard to breathe.

Everything had such a new look she felt new herself. Somehow, everything was going to be all right. Nothing could possibly be wrong on such a scrubbed, sparkling day. She had no thought of leaving on such a day; it was too precious to waste on aimless wandering. She decided with sudden daring to stay on until her money was gone. After that ... Well, after that she would just see what happened.

Having decided to stay nine more days, Marlene set about making herself as comfortable as possible. She put the spread from the man's bedroom on her own bed, there being no blankets in the house, and explored the rooms for heaters and gas outlets, finding none. The house was intended for summer use only and there were no arrangements for heating.

She could keep the kitchen warm with the oven, she thought, as long as there was gas. She went outside and checked the aluminum-painted butane tank on its wooden rack under a window. The gauge showed it almost full. They must have had it filled just before they left, she thought. They didn't care how they spent their money. She remembered how her daddy had complained about too much use of the stove because of the cost of butane. He was old-fashioned about stoves, anyhow, and was always talking about how good his mother had cooked on a wood range when he was a little boy.

But butane was really not that high. If she kept the oven on all day, the amount she used could not cost so very much. Still, it all added up. She was eating three meals a day and using the water, gas and electricity, besides using the bed and the robe. That was worth more than a dollar a day. A lot more.

But most people wouldn't even think about paying anything, she thought. Or taking good care of everything the way I do and not stealing. And they're rich so it won't matter to them if I eat up what's in the kitchen and use the stove and the lights. Except that won't they be surprised when they come back next summer and find the cupboard bare, well not bare, exactly, because they left so much, but lots of stuff gone, and fourteen dollar bills.

" 'Who's been sleepin' in my bed?' said the mama bear," Marlene said aloud, and giggled. She held the robe out from her body, thinking the lady who owned it was sure big enough to be a mama bear. She thought about the lady's husband, the papa bear, sitting in a big chair in the living room with a pipe in his bear's teeth reading *Life* magazine and she giggled again. Since there wasn't any sign of children, maybe she could be the baby bear herself. With that, the notion ceased being so amusing to her.

The idea of being a part of the family that owned this house, despite the sharp sense of disloyalty to her own mother and father it gave her, was appealing. If she really were the baby bear of the family, she would have the right to be in the house. And maybe if the man who owned the pipe rack was her daddy instead of her real daddy, he would not have called her bad names and thrown her out of the

house. And if he had, his wife would have had more to
give her than fourteen dollars and she would have had a
real suitcase all packed with nice things instead of a cardboard box. Or he would have known a doctor who could stop
the baby and had the money to pay the doctor to do it. It
took an awful lot of money for that, she had heard at school.

Maybe they were an old couple who didn't have any children but wished they did, and if she just stayed here and had
her baby all by herself and they found her when they came
back for the summer they would want her and the baby so
much they would adopt them both and take care of them.
But she was just fooling herself. She couldn't stay here
that long, not more than six months, and anyway she couldn't
have a baby all by herself without a doctor or anything.

But she could stay here nine more days. That was for sure.
And that was at least something.

Just thinking about it brought back the reckless high
spirits of the beach and she made a thorough inventory of
the food cupboard to see what she would have to eat during
her stay. She found, with keenest pleasure, a wealth of
things she liked best and some which she had always considered luxuries. Dozens of cans of pork and beans, Spam,
corned beef, okra, Vienna sausages, sardines, salmon, toma-
toes, whole kernel corn, peas, hominy, plums, pears, bottles
of ketchup, jars of peanut butter, jelly, dried lima beans in
a heavy paper sack, breakfast cereal, a sack of grits, biscuit
and cake mix, a box of brown sugar and a small can which
she thought must be a joke but which made her stomach
contract anyhow—chocolate-covered bees, the label said.

As happy as she was to find the kitchen so well stocked she
nevertheless felt a deep sense of disapproval that anyone
should leave so much food behind, some of it possibly to
spoil. Whenever her family moved, as it had so often, they
took everything with them. Of course, this was different, she
admitted to herself, because this family was coming back.
But at least they could have taken the things that might get
stale or moldy. She giggled. It wasn't going to get stale or
moldy. Because she was going to eat it up. She thought,
more seriously, that if she used as much of that sort of thing
as she could, the dollar a day might not be too little because
the food might spoil anyhow.

During the ensuing nine days Marlene's life settled into
a pattern which gave her a feeling of such permanency she
seldom thought of the time when she must leave at last and

almost never thought of the child she was carrying and
the problems thus facing her. Because she was completely
alone and comfortable, she lost all sense of time and the
inevitable consequence of time. It was as if, as she had so
often wished, time had stopped and she remained suspended
exactly as she was, the baby not developing and the hour of
its birth drawing no closer. She ate when she pleased, three
times a day usually but sparingly, played and walked on the
beach wrapped in the robe when it was cold, explored the
house over and over again, discovering things she missed in
earlier inspections, played records and danced to them—
the radio was broken—looked through all the magazines again
and again, read the book titles but not the books, washed
and ironed the dirty trousers in the man's closet and at no
time suffered from boredom.

She would have extended her explorations to the white
frame garage behind the house, which was connected with
the shell road by two strips of crushed shell a car-width apart,
but the double doors were padlocked. She found a metal ring
full of keys but did not try them in the lock. Though the
house was acceptable territory now, the garage was alien
and since she felt no real reason for looking inside she also
felt she had no right to do so.

Her sense of belonging became such that she felt no different in the house than she had living at home with her
parents, except that she had a greater sense of proprietorship
here, and at night when she was in bed she did not fear the
darkness except for brief periods when unfamiliar sounds in
the night breached her tranquillity.

And therefore the nine days ended abruptly, so abruptly
that when she removed the last dollar bill from her purse and
understood there were none left she felt cheated and betrayed.
Time, which had seemed to stand so still, had in reality been
cunningly and cruelly racing by at a headlong pace to catch
her unprepared. The time when she would once again
have to face the world and which nine days ago seemed so
distant was upon her.

And she could not face the world. She was even less prepared for it than the night she had stumbled blindly to the
highway clutching her cardboard box. Then she had been
numb with hurt and bewilderment. Now she was aware of
her predicament with all her senses, more vulnerable, and
felt that she had been offered a solution only to have it
snatched away.

I won't leave, she thought definantly. It's not fair and no-body can make me. She raked the kitchen with her eyes as if challenging objectors and, finding none, pressed her lips together in grim triumph.

"I won't leave," she said aloud. "Not till I'm good and ready."

She waited a moment, listening, as if not at all certain there would be no answer. When no challenge came, she felt that her decision had, somehow, won approval and that she was free to stay as long as she liked.

She celebrated by baking a cake with chocolate icing. It was not a good cake because the mix required eggs she did not have, but she ate an enormous piece for lunch and enjoyed every bite.

As if in confirmation of her decision, the day was warm and she lazed comfortably on the beach all afternoon. This was the life, she thought. No school, no household chores, no one to answer to. Almost perfect. But she did miss her mama and surprisingly, her daddy, but as he had been before that terrible night.

That night, after supper, she again missed her mama with a brief but intense yearning. After supper was when her mama had been closest to her. Other times she was too busy or had to do for her daddy, but right after supper, when Marlene had washed the dishes and put them away, they would often sit and talk.

And when she was in bed she thought unwillingly about the boy who had caused her to be here, not as he had been after she told him she was in trouble or even as he had been when he got her in trouble—despite a certain physical yearning she fiercely rejected thoughts of sex—but as he had been before, awkward, sweet, beseeching. If he would always be like that she might not mind having him here, or better still the tall fair-haired boy she was yet to meet. He would work and earn money and at night bring home little surprises, like a quart of hand-packed ice cream in a round carton or eggs for the cake mix. It would be like being married, only better, because he would provide for her but not make any demands on her.

Some of her old guilt at using the house returned because she was not paying, but as the days passed and she fell more and more into an easy, lulling routine, it vanished completely and she felt not only as if she belonged in the house but also as if, somehow, fate had ordained that she live there, that the house had been waiting for her arrival. The full tank of butane, the full food cabinet, even the terry-cloth robe she wore when it was cold seemed to have been left for a purpose. Her sense of proprietorship grew so strong that she seldom thought of the real owners of the house or that some day they would be coming back to reclaim their property.

And just as she seldom thought of that day so she seldom thought of the baby growing inside her. To ignore the baby was made less difficult by the fact that she ate sparingly and gained so little weight that her stomach remained almost flat and she showed little physical evidence of her pregnancy. When she studied her body, in those rare moments when she thought about the baby, usually in her bath, she could read the signs in her slightly distended belly and increasing fullness of her breasts, but she knew no one else could tell, not that she intended letting anyone see her naked. And she permitted herself to hope that she was only imagining these small changes in her body and that despite the other evidence of pregnancy she might be mistaken about it and all her suffering had been for nothing. Yet not for nothing, really, for because of it she had this house.

On the thirty-second night of her placid exile she was awakened by sounds of movement in the tall grass outside her window. She lay clutching the sheet to her mouth in mute terror while the sounds passed. She held her breath until she thought she must faint listening for more sounds, and thought she heard a fumbling at the back porch door. She lay trembling in bed, wondering if turning on the light would frighten away whoever or whatever was there, knowing it would only betray her presence and so not doing it, wondering if whatever it was was still outside her window, listening as she was listening, waiting to hear if there was someone inside as she was waiting to hear if there was someone outside.

But who would be in this lonely place so late at night? Nobody would come way out here, she thought. Unless it was that Mr. Treadwell from the store. Maybe he had seen her on the beach. But he couldn't have. You couldn't see anything from his store but just the very tops of the houses above the trees. But maybe he had guessed she stopped there. He'd acted like maybe he didn't believe she lived in New Orleans. But he'd have come looking a long time ago if he thought she was there, and in the daytime, not in the middle of the night.

There came an abrupt rending sound from the back porch

and then the complaint of rusty hinges. Oh, my God, she thought, it's pulled loose the latch. She trembled more heavily, her body encased in chill. She strained for more sounds but her own ragged breathing filled her ears. Each exhalation made a short, gasping noise, as if she had been hit in the stomach. The air came back into her lungs shallowly, to be forced back out immediately by her terror.

Above the clamor of her breathing she heard the kitchen window slide up, then a fall and cursing.

It was a man.

She pulled her knees up to her belly in an unconscious effort to make herself as small as possible, to squeeze herself into invisibility. She tried to hold her breath so she could hear but could do so only for seconds at a time.

A kitchen chair went over with a clatter and there was another curse and then, in an interval between her shallow breaths, she heard the click of the light switch.

He don't know I'm here, she thought with faintly mitigated terror. He wouldn't turn on the light or cuss if he knew anybody was here. It must be a robber.

And her terror mounted to its former level. For a robber would come in every room looking for things to steal and he would find her, all alone and helpless, and he would . . . She held her thighs together until they ached with strain, but it was not really the threat of violation that paralyzed her with dread but rather the thought of a strange presence before which she was utterly helpless, as she was helpless before life itself because of the life growing in her belly. To be raped or killed was terrifying, but to be so utterly helpless against the threat of something vaguely worse than either was even more terrifying, tinged with dark deep dread of the supernatural and hell and damnation and unspeakable indignities.

She could hear him walking around in the kitchen, opening cabinets and closing them. Yes, it was a robber, and soon he would be coming and he would find her.

She closed her eyes tightly as if to shield herself behind the fragile wall of lids. What she could not see could not see her, a fantasy of her childhood when, in moments of shame or fear, she would put her hands before her face and cry imploringly, hopefully, "Don't see me!"

And then she heard the rattle of a pan, the running of water and the clink of a cup, the familiar sound of a thousand mornings, and knew that he was making coffee.

Making coffee?

A robber would not do that. A robber would come in and steal things and leave as quick as he could. But if it was not a robber, who was it? And suddenly she was filled more with shame than terror.

It was the man who owned the house. She was caught. After he had his coffee he would go to his room and know someone had been in it and come looking through the house to see who and he would find her. And take her to the police and everybody would know she was a trespasser and a thief because she had used things that weren't hers.

But she paid for them, she thought imploringly. She had paid for them with every cent she had and they could not say she was a thief, just a trespasser, and she thought of the psalm that said forgive us our trespasses and of signs she had seen on fences, "Posted. Trespassers will be prosecuted." She was a trespasser and would not be forgiven. She would be prosecuted.

She knew only vaguely the meaning of prosecuted. She thought of criminals in the courtrooms of movies she had seen being tormented and humiliated by cold, cruel district attorneys, and stern judges sometimes in wigs condemning them to the penitentiary or death, and of heretics being burned alive and Christ nailed to the cross and crowds of people with faces masked with outrage and of her daddy's face when he drove her from the house and of his upraised fist and she wanted her mama.

Maybe he would just send her away, as her daddy had done, because she had paid for everything. She would show him where she had put the fourteen one-dollar bills and promise to pay him a dollar for every day she had stayed in his house without paying and he would not take her to the police and with a blinding flood of hope she remembered that she had washed and ironed his dirty fishing pants and she would show them to him and he would know she was a good girl who had not meant to do anything wrong and would not take her to the police.

And suddenly the pants were her salvation and deliverance, like her baptism in the cold water of the muddy creek when the preacher had ducked her under, head and all, or the excuse signed by her daddy when she had been sick and missed school.

Mindless with hope, she crawled from the refuge of the bed, took off her terry-cloth robe in which she slept, dressed, slipped on her shoes and crept noiselessly to the other bedroom, stealthily slipped open the dresser drawer where she had put the neatly folded pants, clutched them to her constricted chest and tiptoed to the kitchen door. She took a long, painful breath and opened the door.

He was sitting at the kitchen table, propped on his elbows, a cup held to his lips with both hands.

All her fear and strength gathered in a shriek which did not pass her lips though she thought she had screamed it aloud.

"Dear Lord in Heaven, it's a nigger!"

5

He turned his head with a jerk, having become aware of the opened door, gave a gasp of sheer terror and sprang to his feet. The chair in which he had been sitting fell over with a crash and he flung both arms out in a warding gesture which sent the cup in his hands flying across the kitchen to smash against the wall, coffee splashing out in a great brown rosette and running down to the floor.

His face was young-old and chocolatey brown, his hair kinky. More chocolate showed at the open neck of his white shirt and at the left shoulder, where it was torn. There was dark stains, like dried blood, on his shirtfront.

They stared at each other in mutual fright and immobility. Marlene was the first to shake free of the paralysis which gripped them. She turned to run. Her movement freed him, as well, and he leaped toward her and caught her after a few steps. He grabbed her by the wrist and began pulling her back into the light.

It was the first time in all her seventeen years that Marlene Chambers had been touched by a Negro, although she had lived among them her entire life. And now the painful grasp on her wrist brought enhanced fear, but also an overwhelming sense of outrage.

"Let go 'a me, you black nigger!" she cried.

He dropped her wrist at once and his face contorted into an expression of such hate, anger and humiliation that she shrank back against the wall and waited numbly for the blow that would destroy her. And as she waited she had the eerie feeling that this had happened before, and remembered when. It was when her daddy had driven her from the house.

But the black man's hand was not raised against her as her daddy's had been but clenched at his side rigid and trembling as if in a seizure. His bruised heavy lips were drawn back as if in pain from his glistening teeth, and his broad nose flared with every labored breath. One eye, she saw now with indifferent clarity, was half-closed and the brow above it swollen.

And suddenly the anger and humiliation left his face, leaving only the hate, the hand unclenched, the body relaxed and he stepped back and made a mocking, curiously formal little bow.

"Excuse me, White Lady," he said.

She gaped at him, stunned by the change in him, by his gesture and by the way he spoke. His voice sounded like that of a white man, an educated Northern white man. The realization he did not intend to harm her unlocked her rigid limbs and eased her tight chest. She closed her mouth, straightened slowly and moved away from the wall.

She was no longer the trepasser in this house. He was. For this was a white man's house and she had more right to be here than any black man. She tried to remember how a Negro should be talked to. Despite her years among them, her life had seldom been directly touched by Negroes. Her family had never, as had many white families, even poor ones, employed a Negro to do the washing or clean house, nor had she ever played with Negro children or sat next to a Negro or exchanged other than impersonal words with one. But her daddy knew how to handle niggers. When Daddy said frog, she recalled with pride, they hopped. What would he say in this case?

"What you doin' here, boy?" she demanded, the lady of the house.

He took the question as if it were a blow. Belligerence fought a battle with wariness in his bruised face.

"Don't call me boy," he said through clenched teeth.

Though some instinct told her she was in no immediate physical danger and she had the deep, untaught conviction that a Negro would not touch a white person unless insane or in mortal terror, his insolence was as unsettling as an act of violence. Niggers did not speak to white folks that way.

She had never in her life heard a Negro talk back to a white person except once, when a man had accidentally brushed a Negro woman and sent her stumbling off a street curb.

The Negro man with her had glared, and the man had said, "You think I done it on purpose, boy?"

"Then, apologize," the Negro man had said with nervous defiance.

The small crowd which had quickly gathered became tense, anticipating excitement, but the white man had only laughed and said, "Me? Apologize to a nigger?" and walked away, leaving the Negro man shaking with humiliation.

Marlene's father, who had witnessed the incident with her, had been indignant.

"I'd of half-killed that nigger if he talked back to me like that," he had said in a loud voice to the muttered agreement of those around him, and Marlene had realized with a tremor of fear and pride, that he would have.

But as the memory possessed her now she realized she could not half-kill this nigger. She was not physically able to nor despite his insolence had she any desire to do so. What she really wanted was to know why he was acting so ugly to her when she hadn't done a single thing to him and to make him understand how bad it made him look to talk back to her that way. A good nigger would never do a thing like that.

He did not understand her silence.

He sensed that she was no longer frightened and that she was bewildered and disapproving but he could not understand why she was disapproving rather than afraid.

These white Southern bitches thought every black man was crazy to jump into bed with them and it scared hell out of them. But this one wasn't frightened. Maybe this one was hoping he would. My God. The vanity of this skinny white bitch. If I ever got that horny, I'd cut it off before I'd . . .

He was giddy with fatigue and the unreality of the situation. He laughed aloud and she stared.

"What's so funny?" she demanded.

"What do you think I'm doing here?" he said warily, answering her original question.

"Huh? Oh. Stealin', that's what you're doin'. You got no business in this house and you know it."

But she had no business in this house, either, and with an outsider to call her attention to it she knew that, too. More business than he did, because he was just a black nigger, but she had stolen, too, even if she had paid for things while she had the money.

Her guilty knowledge gave her self-righteous accusation a tinge of uncertainty which did not escape his notice.

"I wasn't going to steal anything," he said indignantly, but even in his indignation puzzled by the falseness of her attitude as an aggrieved householder. Maybe it was to hide her fear of him, of his blackness, he thought. They were all afraid of blackness though they pretended to be otherwise. It was a kind of paranoia with them.

"I don't steal," he continued quietly.

"Then what are you doin' here where you don't belong?" she demanded, emboldened by his restraint though still aware of her hypocrisy.

"I was . . . I was cold," he said, strangely defensive.

He shivered as if in confirmation of his words, and Marlene saw that his dark arms were ashen and pebbled with goose-flesh. His molten brown eyes were haunted and she thought, Why, he's scareder than me. He was just putting on, acting so brassbold, trying to keep from showing how scared he really is of white folks.

"Why didn't you knock, then, boy?" she said.

"I am not a . . ."

He shrugged and broke off helplessly. It was a gesture she expected of a Negro and it reassured her and made her feel obliged to help him.

"I am twenty-eight years old," he went on carefully, "and it has been a long time since I was a boy." A look of ineffable sadness crossed his face and he half-whispered, "A very long time."

"I'd of let you in," Marlene said. "If you'd knocked like you should of."

He laughed without humor and shook his head.

"You'd have let me in? A strange *black* man in the middle of the night? And I didn't know anybody was here. It didn't look like anybody was in any of these houses."

"There isn't, this time of the year," she replied, smug in her knowledge of the way rich white people lived. "The people that own these houses, they only live here in the summer. The rest of the year they . . ."

Something about his expression stopped her. His look was knowing and confident.

"What . . . why you lookin' at me that way?"

"What way am I looking at you, White Lady?"

When she did not answer he said, "Am I looking at you askance?"

When he saw she did not understand the meaning either of his words or his attitude, he began enjoying his superiority.

"Am I looking at you myopically, or would you say I was looking at you . . ."

"Don't you start talkin' smart with me, you hear? Or I'll just . . ."

"You'll just what, White Lady?"

She began to grow afraid again. His arrogance was not a cloak for fear.

"That's all right what I'll do. You just stop talking so smart."

"Oh. I'm sorry it upsets you for me to talk smart. I'll talk dumb, so you can understand. You can understand dumb talk, can't you, White Lady? You look like you can understand dumb talk. In fact, you look like dumb talk is your natural language."

"Now, you lookie here . . ."

"Lookie here? Now White Lady's talking Chinese. You must be very educated to talk Chinese, White Lady."

Tiring of the game, he grew serious though no less scornful.

"What are *you* doing here?" he demanded.

"What am *I* doing here?" she repeated, trying to sound astonished and assured. "Why, I *live* here."

"All by yourself? A fifteen-sixteen-year-old kid?"

"Seventeen. And I live here with my mama and daddy."

"And your *daddy* sent his little girl to catch the big bad burglar instead of coming himself," he said ironically, pronouncing "daddy" exactly as she had.

It sounded strange and somehow embarrassing coming from his lips and she resented it, but she was more worried than resentful. He was trying to trick her in some way and she was not sure why. He knew she was alone, so that was not what he was trying to find out. But what?

"They went to town," she said. "To the picture show. And they're comin' back any minute and when they do you better watch out 'cause my daddy don't take no sass off of nig—"

She stopped herself; just in time, she thought.

"Niggers," he prompted.

"What?"

"Off of niggers," he said. "That's what you were going to say, wasn't it?"

"Yes," she said defiantly, tossing her hair and stamping her foot in a childish gesture. "That's exactly what I was goin' to say. And if you don't just get out of this house fast as you can, you'll be sorry."

"I wouldn't be here if I could help it. I wouldn't even be in this God-damned miserable state. I wish to Christ I'd never set foot . . ."

His fury mounted, and anguish with it, and he seemed on the verge of a dreadful revelation of some sort but the perplexity in her face helped him regain his self-control

"Somebody beat you up, didn't they?" she asked when she saw he was not going to continue.

"Yes," he said with grim pride. "And he'll never . . ." and he stopped himself again.

"Sassed somebody, didn't you?" she asked knowingly. "Well, served you right. You Northern nig . . . people come down here and think you can run all over folks the way you do up East. You're gonna get yourself in trouble one of these days if you keep on doin' that."

"Oh, yes," he said, his bruised lips smiling at some secret, desperate joke. "I'm going to get myself in trouble."

"Just 'cause somebody beat you up is no sign you have to come in here and act ugly to me. It wasn't me did it."

"It never is," he said wearily.

"Huh?"

"We're straying from the point."

"The point?"

"We were talking about what your daddy was going to do to me when he got back from the picture show."

"Yes, and if you know what's good for you you won't let him catch you here."

"Who do you think you're kidding?"

"Huh?"

"You don't live here with your mother and father. And they don't own this house."

He knew, she realized. But how? Bad as it was he knew, it was worse that he came right out and said so. A nigger was disputing her word, a white girl's word.

"You lookie here!" she cried.

"You're talking Chinese again," he said coldly. "You don't belong here any more than I do. I don't know what you're doing here but I do know that. It's obvious."

"I do, too. This house belongs to my daddy and he . . ."

"Do you think I'm as stupid as you are? I know damn well you don't belong here. When you talked about the people that own these houses. . . . Any fool could tell you're not one of them. I should have known just by looking at you."

Even in her embarrassment in having been caught in a lie and her resentment at it having been a Negro that caught her, she could not avoid being impressed and baffled by the precise, mannered way he spoke. Even her high-school teachers did not speak that way.

"Just by looking," he was saying. "Because you know what you look like to me? Poor white trash."

Nobody could call her that and get away with it. Without conscious effort she struck him, not a girlish slap but an awkward, closed-fist blow that sent a streamer of pain from her thumb to her elbow. The blow landed on his bruised eye. He gave a low moan of surprise and pain and reeled back clutching his eye.

"I'll kill . . ." he cried.

The threat choked in his throat and Marlene saw again the haunted look. Her rage had vanished the moment the blow landed, and he had gone from fury to this puzzling quiescence too quickly for her to become afraid.

"I shouldn't of done that," she said, the apology sticking in her throat and bringing back the memory of the man who had refused to apologize, and with the memory a feeling of having betrayed the man and her daddy and all white people. "But don't you dare say a thing like that."

"There are three kinds of white trash," he said, as if he were her teacher in high school. "There is poor white trash, rich white trash and the white trash in between. Which includes about everybody."

"Lookie . . . look here, boy, we don't stand for that kind of talk down here."

"Oh, shut up," he said wearily.

The way he said it made her angrier than if he had been deliberately insulting. He was brushing her off as if she were some pest, and him just a nigger and her white.

"Don't talk to me like . . ."

"Will you please stop acting so God-damned *white!*"

He put a hand to his head.

"Jesus Christ!" he muttered to himself. "How can a man think?"

The loose skin of his forehead gathered in deep folds and his face grew lost in utter concentration. Marlene felt as if she were watching his brain work and she wanted desperately to know what he was thinking about, sensing that whatever it might be it involved her.

"Look," he said at last, being polite with great effort. "I cant leave here just yet."

"You've got to. You can't stay here with . . ."

"I can't leave," he said flatly. "I'm beat. And I'm cold and I'm hungry. If I go out there they'll . . . I've got to stay here until I rest up."

"You can't! Where'll I . . ."

He couldn't stay. Because if he did, where would she go?

She was safe and comfortable here and she could not bear the thought of wandering aimlessly on the road again, vulnerable to every Mr. Doughface who drove by in his car, and having to find someplace else to stay and getting a job and growing bigger and bigger every day until everybody knew what was inside her. It was the first time she had thought about the baby in days and her hand went unconsciously to her stomach.

"You just can't," she wailed.

"I can't help it. Why the hell did you have to be here?"

Why the hell did you have to come here? she thought, her mind balking an instant at the word "hell" because she never used it except the way preachers did and then it conjured up an image of devils with forked tails and leaping flames and pitchforks and tormented sinners. Why the hell did you have to come here? And now her mind lingered on and relished the word and she could see him writhing blackly in the flames where he belonged. Why the hell did you have to come here and ruin everything, you black nigger? And she thought of Eve in the Garden of Eden—there was no Adam in her garden—and the snake who came along to spoil everything only it was not a snake but a black nigger and she wondered, when Eve was thrown out of the Garden of Eden the way her daddy had thrown her out of the house, did the snake stay on. It's not fair, it's not fair, it's not fair.

"I was here first," she said, despairing and rebellious at the unfairness of it, her voice a moan. "I found this house and it's mine."

He was taken aback by the intensity of her despair and looked at her almost with compassion. But his face hardened quickly.

"I dont get it," he said. "A kid like you all alone in this God-forsaken . . . Well, it's not my problem. I've got enough of my own."

"You just don't know," she began, wanting to make him see how important it was that she have this place exactly as it was, why he had to leave, but she could go no further. She could not tell her problems to a nigger. But maybe she could, easier than to a white man because she was above a nigger's criticism.

"Hell," he said disgustedly, "it is my problem. Because you being here is a problem."

He shook his head as if to throw off the fatigue enveloping him, and yawned.

"I've got to get some *sleep*," he said, pleading but not to her, to some invisible and relentless presence. "I'm beat."

"Here?" she cried.

"What do you mean?" he asked dully, his senses at last surrendering to exhaustion.

"You're not gonna sleep *here*?"

"Damn it," he said, impatience giving him a brief flaring of strength. "I told you I can't leave. Not right now."

I knew it was too good to last, she thought, resigned. I knew something would happen so I couldn't stay.

"All right," she said woodenly. "I'll get my things."

He came awake again.

"Your things?"

"I ain't goin' to leave 'em here. They're mine. You think I'd take anything that wasn't . . ."

"What do you think you're going to do?" he demanded, fully alert now, fighting off fatigue with the last of his resources.

"Why, I'm goin' to leave, that's what I'm gonna do. I can't stay here if you . . . Why did you have to come here and spoil everything anyway?"

"You can't."

"Can't what?"

"You can't leave."

"You think I'm gonna stay here with you in this house?"

"I know damn well you are."

"You got another know comin', boy."

She turned to leave the kitchen and he seized her by the wrist. His grip had lost strength and determination and she jerked loose.

"You can't leave," he said. "You'll tell . . ."

She waited for the rest of it but it did not come.

"Oh, I won't tell nobody you busted in, if that's what you're scared of. You just mind you don't steal nothin' when you go."

"We'll talk about it in the morning."

"The mornin'?"

She drew back, fear stirring in her again. He intended spending the night in the same house with her. He was just like all the rest of them after all, even if he did talk like a smart white man. All that talk was just a disguise so she wouldn't know what he really wanted to do. She thought about Mr. Doughface and the horror of his hand on her knee, but at least bad as it had been it was a white hand and the thought of this black hand on her filled her with revulsion and terror.

"You better not try!" she gasped, close to hysteria. "They'll catch you and there won't be enough left to feed the buzzards on."

He stared at her, dumb with fatigue and shock at her outburst.

"Try what?"

And then he understood and began laughing in near-delirium.

"You're too much, White Lady!" he gasped. "You're just too much!"

The laughter stopped and the hate she had seen when she first surprised him in the kitchen glared out at her.

"You don't have to worry about that," he said with deliberate cruelty. "Even if I wasn't about to drop in my tracks. Because have you ever looked in a mirror, White Lady? You've got to know it. You are *ugly*. U-g-l-y."

The insult made her feverish and giddy and she leaned in the doorway groping for the words which would smash him, let him know, really know for once and for all, that he was just a nigger and niggers did not talk that way to white ladies, not and stay healthy.

He took a deep, hate-filled breath.

"Now you get back to wherever you were and don't try to leave. Because if you do, I'll hear you."

"If my daddy was here . . ." she began.

"But he's not. There's nobody here but you and me."

Oh, Daddy, help me, she thought. If you were here he wouldn't dare talk to me like that.

She tried to think of her daddy rushing to protect her, smashing in the door to get at this horrible black man, but the only image of her daddy she could summon was a bleak, vengeful one with fist upraised, threatening not the black man but herself.

She turned and went meekly to her room, crying.

6

She did not sleep in what remained of the night but lay abject and wide-eyed, weighted with humiliation. Her refuge had been invaded and she had been abused and ordered around by a Negro. She listened as she lay in the comfortless warmth of her bed, wondering if he were sleeping and if he were cold, hoping that he was cold, burning with it, the cold hotter than any fire.

She did not try to escape not so much because she was afraid he would catch her as because she did not have the will to face the cold and darkness outside. Nor to blurt out the story of her humiliation to other white people. She could picture their faces as she told her story. First outrage and ferocious vengeance because a nigger had forgotten his place with a white girl. But behind the outrage and ferocity the unspoken speculation. She was in trouble and therefore no good. Why had she let the nigger talk to her that way? What was there about her that had made him think he could get away with it? What kind of white girl was it, anyhow, that would stand for a nigger talking to her the way he did without doing anything about it? And spending all that time in the same house with him.

Day came, and the sound of his movements in the kitchen. Then his quiet tread along the hall. She held herself rigid. He was coming for her. He was rested now and thinking about her, a helpless white girl all cozy and warm in bed, with nobody to stop him. All that talk about her being so ugly. She knew now he had just been saying that to lull her suspicions and make sure she wouldn't slip out and tell on him and just stay there like a fool until he was good and ready to do what he wanted to.

Because she knew she was not ugly. Maybe she wasn't pretty, and maybe once upon a time she had thought she was ugly, but that was before she knew she had something the boys wanted, wanted so bad they begged and shivered

57

and couldn't breathe. White boys. And if white boys did, a nigger wanted it even more. Just being white made her pretty to a nigger, a lot prettier than any white boy thought she was, and being white made her something a nigger was just crazy to have. They all did. That was the real reason they wanted to get into school with them and all. She had heard her daddy say exactly that, and other people, too.

Just let him try. She would show him. She would kick him where it hurt and then he'd find out who was ugly.

She was frightened by his stealthy approach down the hall but somehow vindicated and triumphant, too. For all his uppity ways he had the same thing on his mind as any other nigger. The doorknob turned slowly and she lay transfixed with terror, all triumph gone, and all confidence that she could stop him by kicking him where it hurt.

Oh, Mama, she pleaded silently. Oh, Mama, Mama, Mama.

The door opened noiselessly and she saw the gleam of a white pupil in a black face and the scream built in her chest and gathered excruciatingly in her throat. She closed her eyes as tightly as she could and prayed. And then there was the click of the door closing and the sound of his receding footsteps.

Oh, Mama, oh thank God, she thought. He was just making sure I was still here.

She felt a grudging gratitude to him for not taking advantage of her helplessness and at the same time a resurgence of confidence, and under it all a tinge of hurt vanity because perhaps he really did think she was ugly, not that it mattered what a nigger thought. And now that it was daylight she had less reason to fear him. He was just an uppity nigger and he would get what was coming to him. She got quietly out of bed and tiptoed to a shuttered window. She worked at the latch but was not strong enough to push the hook out of the eye-screw that held it. She thought of knocking it loose with the heel of a shoe but realized it would make too much noise.

With her shoes in one hand she eased open the bedroom door and stole down the hall and through the living room. She wondered what he would do to her if he caught her trying to get away. But he wasn't going to catch her. She was going to be so quiet he wouldn't even know she was gone. It was very important that he didn't know she was gone. Not until she came back with help. She wanted to see his face when she came back with the white men. She'd see how sassy he was with them. If he thought the other white man had beat him up, he'd find out what it was like to get really beat up.

And she thought, what if they were so mad they did more than just beat him up. Sometimes they killed uppity niggers. Not that it didn't serve them right but she didn't want them to kill this nigger. He had acted right ugly but he hadn't really hurt her, not even when she hit him in the eye. She would make that very clear to the men. He hadn't tried to do anything to her, either. He knew his place that much, at least.

She reached the front door and slowly turned the handle. The door opened noiselessly and she stole across the porch to the screen door. She remembered that the hinges squeaked and pushed against it very gently. It made a small sound, not loud enough to be heard back in the kitchen, she hoped. She found that by opening it very slowly and steadily the hinges hardly made any noise at all. She opened the door just enough to slip through, put on her shoes and scurried down the wooden steps and through the clammy grass to the shell road.

She was yards from the house before she realized she was cold. She had forgotten to put on the terry-cloth robe. Despite the cold she was not sorry she had forgotten. She would look funny going into Mr. Treadwell's store in it.

Because that was where she would go. To the store. It would be easier to tell Mr. Treadwell because he knew her, in a way, and was nice. She couldn't tell her story to just anybody who came along.

She began running. She would run until she got to the highway and then she would walk along it and maybe somebody would give her a ride. If they asked questions, she would just tell them she was going to the store. And when she got there she would tell Mr. Treadwell there was this uppity nigger back there in the house.

And he would go after him and teach that nigger not to get smart with a white girl. And then . . . What happened after that? Mr. Treadwell would want to know why she wasn't in New Orleans with her folks, and how come she had been in the house in the first place, and he would find out she had been living there all this time, using things that weren't hers, and maybe he would tell on her.

Maybe he even knew the people who owned the house and could call them up on the telephone and they would come and take her to the police. And maybe Mr. Treadwell would guess why she was hiding in the house and he would tell the people that, too, and everybody would know she had a baby inside her without being married.

And no matter what, she couldn't stay in the house any more.

She slowed to a walk but continued toward the highway, walking toward the end of her idyl in the Garden of Eden.

Oh, you dirty black nigger, why did you have to bust in and ruin everything? Why didn't you stay up North where you belong? I'll tell them you tried to rape me and you know what they'll do to you? They'll hit you with sticks and cut your thing off and hang you on a tree and shoot you full of holes and set you on fire with gasoline and it'll serve you right for busting in and ruining everything.

Tears of rage and frustration rolled down her cheeks as she walked blindly along the shell road and she did not hear the sound of running footsteps behind her or know she was being pursued until she felt a strong grip on her arm and a hand over her mouth. The hand sealed her scream inside her throat and for a panicky moment she thought he was trying to smother her. She bit his palm where the forefinger joined it and he flung her from him and slapped her with a single violent motion.

Marlene fell to the road in a heap, scratching her hands and knees on the shells, and crouched there, propped on her palms, looking up at him in mute dread. The familiar hate was in his face, and murder. He stood over her, his hands clenching and unclenching. She could see blood on one of them but did not know if it were her own or where she had bitten him. When, after an intolerable and deadly silence, he spoke, it was as if the words were strangling him.

"You . . . you . . . get up!"

She did not move. She could not.

He reached down and jerked her to her feet. She stood there, tottering.

"You're not hurt!" he cried angrily, guilt and shame peeping out from behind the anger.

Marlene felt no pain either from the slap or from the abrasions on her knees and hands. All feeling, even of fear, was blotted out by a monstrous reality.

A nigger hit me!

"Go on back," he commanded.

She began walking dumbly toward the house. Whatever happened now did not matter. Even if he raped her. Because he had hit her, a nigger had hit her, and the heavens had not poured down instant and terrible retribution.

"I want to tell you something," he said harshly, hating her more because he could not resist a compulsion to defend himself. "I never hit a woman before. In all my life."

She gave no sign that she had heard but continued to walk trancelike toward the house.

"Did you hear me?"

He seized her shoulder and shook it. Her head swayed loosely, mutely.

"God damn it, answer me!"

Her lips opened and the words came out cold and lifeless.

"You dirty nigger."

He shook with suppressed fury.

"Oh," he groaned. "Oh. I'm glad it was you. I'm glad it was a white bitch."

He shoved her toward the house and she walked on without looking back at him, her face expressionless. But her brain churned with such violent thoughts she felt as if it must burst out of her skull.

Kill you . . . Black nigger . . . Dirty black . . . Hit me . . . Hit a white . . . With a knife . . . Right in your black belly . . . Black throat . . . Black blood . . . You try to, I'll kick you there . . . Cut it off . . . Throw it on the table like a burned cornstick . . . Ma had this tin thing . . . To make them that shape . . . Split, with margarine oozing out . . . And cold milk . . . Stick it in your black throat and watch the black blood run out . . . Hit you over the head with the kitchen chair . . . Hit, hit, hit . . . Till your brains run out all over the floor . . . Think you're so smart . . . Show you who's smart . . . Black bastard . . . bastard . . . bastard . . .

"Bastard!"

She did not know she had said it aloud until he said, "It can talk."

They were at the porch now and she did not know how she had arrived there. She looked around her, as if emerging from a nightmare, saw his painful, hate-filled grin and knew the nightmare had not yet ended.

"You left something out," he said.

Talk all you want, smart nigger. You can't make me answer.

"The complete expression is black bastard. Aren't I good enough for the whole two words?"

Her reeling mind fastened on the "Aren't I." She had never heard anyone say that before. It sounded silly and prissy and

so bizarre it blocked all other thoughts. She walked ahead of
him toward the kitchen, not thinking of what he might intend
to do there when they reached it but instead considering and
exploring the "Aren't I." Her English teacher in high school
said, "Am I not?" and every time she did it half the class
giggled and the teacher would look puzzled and wonder what
she had said that was so funny.

Strong black hands pushed her down into a kitchen chair
and the bruised black face looked into hers.

"Are you all right?"

She heard sound but no words. Her senses were shut off
except for the ludicrous ticking of "Aren't I," "Aren't I,"
"Aren't I" in a remote corner of her mind. What a silly, stuck-
up way to talk.

"I didn't hit you that hard," he said angrily, then anxiously,
"Did I?"

When she did not answer he went to the sink and brought
back a glass of water. He put it to her lips and the contact
brought her back to reality. She turned her head away. She
was not taking anything from him, not even a drink of water.

"Leave me alone," she said dully.

He sighed with relief.

"It's alive," he said with heavy irony in an unsuccessful
attempt to hide his concern.

He dragged another chair to the other side of the table and
sat down. As soon as he did so she started to rise. She was
not going to sit down at the same table with a nigger, especially a mean, no-count one who would hit a white girl.

"Sit down," he said.

And she did, but not because of the command in his voice
but because her legs would not support her. The shock and
humiliation of being struck by a Negro had drained her.

"You ready to talk sense?" he asked almost politely.

Good, she thought. He's scared about what he did. He's
going to beg me not to tell on him. But I will. I don't care
what they do to him, it'll be too good for him.

She stared at him stonily.

"Don't answer me then," he said, losing patience. "I don't
give a damn whether you do or not. Just shake your stupid
head yes or no."

She looked past him at the drawer where the knives were.
There were lots of knives, a long slender one with a blunt
end for carving, a short one for peeling vegetables, a fat one
with a sharp point for . . . for killing niggers who slapped

white girls. She wondered if she could do it. Back there, on the road, when she was so mad, she could have. But how about now, when she was still mad but not crazy mad? Maybe not with a knife, but if she had a gun, her daddy's shotgun, she would have the nerve to shoot him. All you had to do with a shotgun was point it and pull on the trigger.

If I had a shotgun I could blow his black head off, and I would, too. But I don't have one, just a knife over there in that drawer and even if I was to get it he'd just take it away from me unless I could get it when he wasn't looking and then sneak up behind him and . . .

"Damn it, pay attention to me!" he snapped.

She looked at him, blinking, realizing he had been talking to her and wondering what about, and if he knew what she had been thinking. She looked away again, pointedly, and he hit the table with his hand.

"I said pay attention to me!"

I won't, she thought. That's what makes him the maddest.

"Are you still sulking because I . . . because I slapped you?" he demanded, annoyed and ashamed at having to acknowledge the blow.

Sulking, she thought. Sulking! Sulking's not what to do when a nigger hits you. He's going to find out what happens to niggers that do that.

"I'm sorry about that," he said with an effort. "Even if you did ask for it. Because I don't go around hitting women."

It hurt him to apologize. She could see it and was glad. But it wasn't going to help him any just because he apologized. If he thought so he had another think coming.

"Okay," he said. "Sit there and sulk. But get this straight. I'm not here because I want to be."

Then why you sitting there? Marlene thought. Why don't you just pick up and leave? Nobody's asking you to stay.

"But I am here and I've got to stay here a few days. Until things . . ."

"No!"

"You've got nothing to say about it. You've got no more right to be in this house than I have."

"Yes, I do!"

"Why?"

"Because I'm . . ."

He waited but she did not continue.

"Oh," he said. "Because you're white. And this is a white man's house."

She nodded eagerly, taking hope from his understanding of the situation.

"That's no reason. Not to me."

It is to me, she thought. And to whoever owns this here house. And whoever finds out a nigger broke in and slapped a white girl.

"If they catch you here . . ." she said viciously.

"If they catch me anywhere."

"It'll be a lots worse if they catch you here with me."

"Your solicitude touches me, White Lady."

You think you're so smart, always using fancy words, she thought.

"You're not still under the illusion I have designs on you . . . You're a lot safer in the same house with me than some white bastard."

He grinned cruelly at her expression of indignation.

"You'd be safe with anybody, the way you look."

That's what you think, nigger. Why do you think I'm here, anyhow. If you knew how he begged and almost cried and how grand and wonderful he said it was.

She felt a powerful urge to tell him and wipe the cruel, knowing smile from his face but she suppressed it. And was almost glad she had been wanted and had by a white boy all the other girls thought was cute but she was the one he had to have. Because she was the only one, he told her. He never had before, either. He swore he never had.

"What are we so smug about? Oh, oh. Maybe you did get yourself balled. I hope I never get that hard up."

"You don't have to talk ugly. And I never did. What you said. If you mean what I think."

She blushed, thinking about what he thought. And hated herself for answering him and for blushing over anything a nigger might think, a nigger who had hit her. It was just as bad for him to talk that way to her as it had been to hit her. She had never talked dirty like that with anybody before, except in hints with the other girls. Except that time that girl got in trouble in high school and got expelled. And a nigger had tricked her into talking like that.

"Look at you," he said. "You're red as an Indian. Did I touch a nerve?"

She sought refuge in silence again.

"Okay. We'll drop the distasteful subject. Just keep out of my hair and I'll keep out of yours."

He pushed back his chair, stood up, stretched and said,

"God, I'm hungry," as if everything had been settled.

She remained in her chair, wretchedly immobile, while he prepared the breakfast which had been interrupted when he realized she had fled the house. When he sat down across from her again with a bowl of cereal and a steaming cup of coffee, she rose silently and walked toward the door. The smell of the coffee reminded her that she, too, was hungry, but she was not going to eat with a nigger. Her hand was on the doorknob when the thought struck her that he was eating while she was going hungry, when she was white and he was black, when she belonged here and he did not. She was not going to let a nigger keep her from having breakfast.

She went back to the cupboard, prepared breakfast and took it out on the back steps in the sunny cold.

A mockingbird flew from the pecan tree and she watched it until it was a speck in the distance and then nothing.

I wish I was a bird, she thought. If I was a bird I would fly and fly. And never light.

7

After breakfast he washed and dried his dishes and put them away and noticed the fourteen one-dollar bills for the first time. Marlene had come back inside with her own dishes.

"What have we here?" he said, lifting the cup and taking the money. "Somebody's little nest egg?"

He counted the limp bills and said, "Fourteen dollars."

They're mine, Marlene thought. Least, they were. Now they belong to whoever owns this house. And you better not try to steal it.

She was on the verge of protesting when he put the money back under the cup. She was somehow disappointed. Niggers stole. Maybe he put it back just because she was watching.

"Funny place to leave money," he said.

"I reckon people are entitled to leave their money wherever they want to," she said.

He made a mocking bow.

"I beg your pardon, White Lady. Ah reckon yore right."

You can't even mock me, Marlene thought. I don't say yore.

"By people, I presume you mean your people," he continued. "Because my people generally don't have fourteen bucks to leave behind under a cup."

Whose fault is that? Marlene thought. You're all every one of you lazy and would rather steal than work. The niggers they'd farmed next to one time worked hard, but her daddy said they were different from most. Old-fashioned niggers, good niggers, the way they all used to be before the smart niggers and meddlers came down from up North. Some people said it was the Communists but her daddy said it wasn't them at all, just smart niggers and dumb whites from up East. One time when one of the nigger kids from the next farm got sick and the nigger's old truck was broken down, her daddy had driven the boy's daddy to town in his truck and let him sit right in the cab with him instead of making him stay

66

out in the bed the way some people would. Her daddy said there wasn't anybody better than a nigger that knew his place or worse than one that didn't.

I expect you're just about the worst there is, she thought, looking at him where he stood warming his black hands at the oven. 'Cause you sure don't know your place. But you just wait.

He caught her looking at him.

"I'm glad looks can't kill," he said. "White Lady, I can't stand you either, but I try not to let it eat me. Roll with it, don't fight it." He laughed harshly. "Why should I give you good advice? You're too stupid to take it."

She resisted an impulse to make a face at him and instead marched out of the kitchen, closing the door softly behind her to show him he couldn't make her mad again, no matter what. She went to her room and sat in a chair with a coverlet over her shoulders looking at movie magazines. She wished she had new ones but she was not too discontented with what she had.

She found it hard to concentrate. Did he really mean to stay in the house and keep her there? He didn't act like he really wanted to stay. Maybe he just told her that so he could wait until night and slip out while she was asleep so she wouldn't get a chance to tell on him. She might even wake up in the morning and find him gone. The thought lifted her spirits for a moment, then she sighed, thinking it was too good to be true.

She rearranged the coverlet on her shoulders. It was the one from the man's bedroom. She was glad she had taken it because if the nigger did stay it meant he wouldn't have one and would be cold that night. She wondered if he'd use the bed instead of staying in the kitchen the way he had the night before. Maybe even he wasn't uppity enough to sleep in a white man's bed. But either way, he'd be cold. Everybody knew niggers couldn't stand cold as good as white people, coming from Africa the way they did.

I wish he'd go back to Africa, she thought. Where he belongs. She could see him in the jungle with scars on his face and a bone in his nose the way she had seen them at the picture show, all painted, with a bracelet made out of teeth around the top of his arm and carrying a shield and a spear. And another native coming out of the trees and sticking him in the chest with a longer spear, or dragging him away and tying him to a post and building a fire around him. Or a big snake sneaking down from a tree and winding around him and squeezing him until there wasn't anything left but the bone in his nose.

But it was hard for her to picture him as an African native even if his skin was dark and his nose flat and his hair kinky.

Aren't I? she thought, and giggled despite her vexation. There he was with his face painted and a bone in his nose saying, "I'm an African, aren't I?"

And a whole tribe of natives beating on hollow logs and jumping around and shaking their spears and chanting, "Aren't I?"

And she was the white queen sitting on a throne made of gold and elephant tusks, with long blond hair—her hair had somehow got much lighter—and a leopard-skin dress that covered her modestly enough but could not hide her pretty shape and they dragged him in front of her and he fell on his face and knocked his forehead in the dirt begging her not to burn him up. She would pretend to be thinking it over and let him sweat and then she would smile to make him think she had decided to let him go and say, "Burn him up!"

She was dragged from this pleasant reverie by sounds from the next room. He was prowling around, opening dresser drawers. Looking for something warm, she thought, smiling because she knew there wasn't anything. Then she heard him in the closet rattling among the empty coat hangers. He went out after that and there was silence for a while, then noises from the front of the house.

What's the nigger up to now? she thought. She tiptoed down the hall and, finding the living room empty, crossed it and peeked out of a window facing the front porch. He was wiring the screen door latch with a piece of coat hanger.

Showed he was scared she might try to get away again, she thought. Well, it wouldn't do him any good to have the front door wired shut when he had that big knife sticking out of his chest.

And she knew she was fooling herself, she could not stick him with the knife except to save her life or virtue and she wondered if a girl who was pregnant and not married had any virtue to save, knowing, of course, that she did if it was a nigger she was saving it from but not so sure if it was somebody like Mr. Doughface.

He had put on the fishing pants she had washed. His own were underneath, she could tell from the way the pants bagged. The nerve of the nigger, she thought. She hadn't

washed and ironed those pants for a nigger to wear. And he
had a khaki shirt on over his own shirt, sizes too large for
him the way the woman's clothes were for her. The man
who owned the house must be big, she thought, a lot bigger
than the nigger. If he was to come around checking up on his
house and found the nigger there he could beat him up easy.
And she would help him. He would hold the nigger and she
would slap him the way the nigger had slapped her.

His face was sad and worried as he worked with the
stubborn wire. He did not look at all as he had when he was
belittling and threatening her.

Why, he's just another scared nigger, she thought. Got
himself into something he don't know how to get out of. Well,
if he thought she was going to forget the things he'd said
and done he had another think coming.

He looked around and saw her peeking out the window.
His expression grew truculent. She started to step away from
the window but caught herself. She had as much right there
as he did. More.

"What you think you're doing?" she demanded.

"Fixing the latch to keep the trash out," he said. "But a
little too late, far as you're concerned."

"You're 'fraid I'll run off again and tell on you, ain't
you?"

"You're damn right. I'll bet you'd love to see me strung up
by the . . ."

He did not finish.

"I know what you were goin' to say," she said, flushing.
"I don't 'preciate that kind of talk."

"Pardon *me*. I forgot myself."

He sucked on a finger he had bruised twisting the stiff
wire. The gesture made him look much younger and she
remembered one of the nigger boys from the next farm who
had shuffled his feet on the broken-down porch, scared to
death to be noticed by a white girl and afraid she might
catch him noticing her. It had made her feel important
and condescending. She felt a little that way now.

"Just don't talk like that any more," she said.

"No, ma'am," he said mockingly. "Ah shore won't."

He was puzzled by her new attitude.

You can't even talk like a nigger when you try, she
thought. You *are* a mess.

She tossed her hair contemptuously and went back to her
room, leaving him staring.

After a few minutes he opened her door and peered inside.

"Don't you knock before you open a lady's door?" she demanded, still in her regal mood.

"Always. If it's a lady."

"You think you're so smart."

"Only by comparison."

But he came only halfway into the room as if unwilling to enter where he was not welcome. He noted the coverlet on Marlene's shoulders and the one on the bed.

"Any blankets in here?" he asked.

"This is a *summer* house," she replied condescendingly. "Don't they have summer houses up East?"

"Not the crowd I run with," he said sarcastically. "Where's that thing you had on last night? That robe?"

"That's a lady's robe."

"Then what were you doing wearing it?"

When she did not answer he said, "Looked big enough to fit me."

"It's mine! I mean . . ."

She stopped guiltily. It wasn't hers, not really. It belonged to the people who owned the house. But she had found it first and she was white. And a lady, no matter what he said.

"Funny," he said. "You with two spreads and none in the other room."

"I was here first."

He shrugged.

"Just like the great big world outside," he said. "You with two. Me with none."

He studied her.

"I could take it away from you. I could take both of them away from you."

"You just try."

He was more amused than angered by her defiance.

"How'd you stop me?"

"I'd . . . I'd . . ."

She stopped in frustration. He smiled his cruel, superior smile.

"Don't worry, White Lady. I'm not going to. If you're too selfish to give me one willingly, to hell with you."

Oh, you black nigger, she thought, biting her lip in helpless fury. Always making it look like I'm the one in the wrong. Well, you could come in here crawling on your hands and knees before I'd give you one, and I wouldn't even do it then.

"I didn't ask you to come here and spoil everything," she snapped.

"Who asked *you* to come here?"

"None of your business."

"It puzzles me," he said. "It really does. Why you're holed up here. Why? What is a stupid kid like you doing here all by herself?"

None of your business, you black nigger. I won't tell you. Not if you killed me. So you could laugh at me and act biggity and call me poor white trash again. You wouldn't think it is any reason anyhow. It don't mean nothing when a nigger girl gets in trouble. They get in trouble all the time and nobody don't think anything about it. Because niggers haven't got any morals.

"So don't tell me," he said. "I couldn't care less."

He left and Marlene went to the door and listened to see if he was wiring up the back screen, too, but heard nothing to indicate that he was. Maybe he figured if there was only one door to watch he could still keep her from getting away if she tried again. She could not make up her mind whether she was going to or not. He'd caught her so easy the first time and, besides, he had said he'd only stay a little while. If she did manage to slip away and turn him in, she'd lose the house forever. Was it worth that much to get even with him? She remembered the slap and the insults and thought yes, and the loneliness of the highway and the nastiness of Mr. Doughface and thought no. She would just not have anything more to do with him than she had to until he left and after that, well, she would decide whether to tell on him or not.

She missed lunch because she did not want to be around him, but hunger sent her into the kitchen that night despite the fact he was in the room warming himself at the oven. He looked up at her when she came in but returned immediately to the contemplation of his warming hands.

Marlene checked the cupboard to see how much food he had eaten. With two in the house it would go fast. Maybe she should eat less until he left to make up for what he would be eating. She ate sparingly.

After she cleaned up she checked to see if the money was still under the cup. She was disappointed when she found the fourteen dollars still there.

She went back to her room intending to stay awake late so she could hear him if he slipped away in the night, but she was too weary from her sleepless previous night and could not keep her eyes open. Her last thought before she fell asleep, and a pleasant one, was that it was cold and if he did stay the night it would be a bad one for him because she had both coverlets.

When she awakened in the morning she sat upright in bed, listening, hoping she would hear nothing. She sighed when she heard the sound of his movements. He had stayed after all. Well, she thought, in her heart she knew he would. It was just her luck.

She waited until he was out of the kitchen before going for breakfast. The screen door was open and she thought briefly about slipping out and cutting through the trees behind the house, but decided against it when she remembered how quickly he had missed her the day before.

He came to the kitchen once to check on her and she was glad she had not taken the chance. He did not speak when he looked in, and she pretended he was not there.

After she went back to her room she heard him come to the door. She heard him stop there and waited for his knock. After a pause he merely opened the door and walked in.

"Didn't I tell you to knock!" she demanded. "What if I wasn't . . . wasn't dressed or something?"

"Well," he said thoughtfully, "if you apologized I suppose I'd overlook it. But try not to let it happen."

"You . . . What you want in here?"

Instead of answering her he walked across the room toward the closet.

"Where you think you're goin'?"

He opened the closet door and looked inside without answering. He took the terry-cloth robe from its hanger and put it on.

"That's better," he said to himself.

The robe fit him much better than it had her but he looked grotesque in it with his black face above the white terry cloth and a khaki sleeve showing where the coat was too short. Marlene giggled. His face seemed to grow darker.

If niggers can blush, he's blushing, she thought.

"I was cold," he said. "What's so God-damned funny?"

"You. If you could just see how you look."

"How do you think you look, White Lady? And you're wearing your own clothes."

Despite his pretense of indifference he cast a furtive look at the dresser mirror. A slow grin spread over his face. He turned and looked directly into the mirror.

"Why, hello, Charlie," he said to the mirror. "I had no idea you looked so sweet in drag."

Marlene watched, fascinated. He saw her in the mirror.

"Who's the lady, Charlie?" he asked. "Looks like she's been using skin bleach."

"Why, no," he answered himself. "She's a white lady."

"A white lady? She may be white but she doesn't look like a lady."

"Careful, boy. They don't like that kind of talk down here."

Marlene did not know whether to be angry or amused. Or frightened.

He turned to face her.

"How about it, White Lady?" he said. "Do you think I look sweet in drag?"

"Huh? What you mean, in drag?"

"In women's clothes."

"You ain't got on women's clothes," she said primly. "Just that old coat."

"Oh, hell," he said disgustedly.

"Who's Charlie?"

"Nobody," he said. His face lost its animation and he said again, softly, "Nobody."

"That's your name, ain't it? Charlie?"

"What difference does it make?"

"It don't make no difference to me. Your name could be mud for all I care."

"Dr. Mudd?"

"Huh?"

"Don't you know where they got that expression?"

"What expression?"

"Your name is mud, stupid."

"Don't call me names."

Curiosity got the better of her.

"What do you mean, Dr. Mudd?" she asked unwillingly.

"He's the doctor who treated John Wilkes Booth. Don't you know that?"

She shook her head.

"Don't you know anything? You know who John Wilkes Booth was, don't you?"

"He shot Abraham Lincoln," she said angrily. "Everybody knows that."

"If you do, everybody does."

"What about him?"

"Who?"

"Dr. Mudd."

"You've got a one-track mind. I'll say that for you. He set Booth's leg and they threw him in prison for it. When all he was doing was being a doctor." He shrugged. "I don't know why I should get upset about it. It was just white people rousting white people."

"How'd you know that? I mean about Dr. Mudd?"

"Learned it in school, naturally. Don't they teach you anything in separate-but-equal?"

He looked at her sharply.

"Hey," he said. "Why aren't you in school?"

She did not answer.

"It gets curiouser and curiouser," he said. "You being here. Are you in hiding?"

Though she did not answer, her expression told him.

"You are, aren't you? Isn't that a coincidence? How long have you been here?"

"None of your business."

"It's been days, hasn't it? Maybe weeks."

When she did not answer he went on.

"What did you do with yourself all that time? Nobody to talk to. Nothing decent to read."

"I had fun," she said angrily, unable to keep silent in the face of his casual familiarity when he had no right to be in her room or even to talk to her after the way he had behaved himself. "It was right nice. Until you had to come along and spoil everything."

Her anger rekindled his spite.

"Just what did I spoil?" he demanded. "Doesn't look like you were doing so good to me. Hiding out like a stray cat. You know something, White Lady? You *look* a lot like a stray cat. Fur all straggly. Dirty."

"I'm cleaner than you. I'd be cleaner than you if you took a million baths."

"Sure," he said with a harsh laugh. "Negroes smell bad. I guess it's me that stinks to high heaven and not your dirty hair."

Her hand went unconsciously to her hair. It felt thick and gummy. She hadn't washed it for weeks but it wasn't her fault. Washing your hair in cold weather was the best way to catch a cold. And she had brushed it every day. Well, almost every day.

"I'd rather have dirty hair than wool," she said.

His hand went unconsciously to his hair just as hers had, and an expression of fury transformed his face.

"For two cents . . ." he began.

Then he turned abruptly and strode out of the room, shutting the door behind him.

Slammed it, she thought vindictively. I made him good and mad. Least I didn't slam the door when he made me so mad. Shows the difference between white folks and niggers.

But she was almost sorry he had left, and was ashamed of herself for it. He did know some interesting things, like about Dr. Mudd. That was the trouble with niggers, though. The minute they got a little education they thought they were so smart. Smarter than anybody.

She tried to think of a quotation she had learned in high school. She closed her eyes and pressed her lips together, the way she always did when she was trying to think of the answer to a test question. She had the feeling that was what she was doing, trying to think of the answer to a test question.

"A little knowledge is a dangerous thing."

That's it, she thought. "A little knowledge is a dangerous thing."

She would have to remember that and if he got to acting like he thought he was so smart again she would tell him that. And then he would see who was stupid.

Her hand strayed to her hair. It felt dirty. But it didn't smell bad, no matter what he said. He was just saying that because he knew that niggers smelled bad and he was trying to cover up. He didn't fool her. Not one bit.

Thinking about her hair made her head itch. She scratched luxuriously with both hands. Maybe she would wash her hair. But then he would think it was because of what he said. Who cared what he thought? If she wanted to wash her hair, she'd just do it and none of his business. She wished he hadn't taken the robe. She could wear it while she washed her hair to keep from getting her blouse wet. But she could use a towel instead. There were plenty of towels in the hall closet.

When she went to get one she found the stack in disarray. He'd probably been poking around in there, she thought, looking for blankets. She was glad there hadn't been any. She selected a big beach towel and went to the bathroom.

When she turned the knob he yelled, "Hey! I'm in here!"

She blushed and jerked her hand back as if she had touched fire, then turned and fled to her room as if he were in pursuit.

Safely inside, she stood with her back planted against the door, breathing heavily. She felt as if she had just narrowly escaped catastrophe.

What if he hadn't yelled and she'd opened the door and he'd been in there, all black and naked?

She had seen many naked black backs running with sweat behind a plow or leaning over a shovel, and smelling to high heaven, but never the rest of a black body. But she had heard about the rest. All niggers had great big . . . Her mind recoiled from thinking the rest and she felt almost sick at her stomach. And that reminded her of what she was carrying inside her.

Marlene felt her stomach, then prodded and probed it. It was hard and tight but she could feel nothing inside it. Her stomach stuck out a little but not enough to notice. Maybe it wasn't growing. She'd missed three or four periods, she wasn't sure exactly which, but maybe something had happened to it and it wasn't alive in there.

Dear Jesus, she thought, let it not be alive. Let it just shrivel up and disappear and let me be like I was before. And let me get away from him and go back home to my mama. If I'm not going to have a baby, maybe Daddy will take me back and I can go back to school like nothing happened and I can tell everybody I've been away visiting my Aunt Donna at her place on the Gulf of Mexico.

And she thought about him in there taking a bath and how he had yelled like he was afraid she'd come in and see him naked, as if she cared about seeing a nigger naked any more than seeing a hog or a cow naked because that's what they were, niggers—animals—even if he did talk smart. And he was in there taking a bath because she had told him how bad he smelled. All that talk about her hair. He knew how he smelled. But he could scrub and scrub and he couldn't scrub away the stink. And he knew it. And he knew that she knew it.

Marlene smiled.

8

He would not permit her to leave the house nor did he leave it himself. He spent a good deal of time on the front porch looking out between the slats as if expecting someone he did not wish to see. He had not wired the back screen door because he wanted to have a quick way out if necessary.

Confinement was far more oppressive to him than it was to Marlene. Except for the fact that she resented his presence in the house and begrudged him the food he ate, she was content to eat, sleep, look at magazines or just sit, daydreaming. She missed the beach, but not enough to matter. Though she hated the Negro, she no longer feared him.

He was always restless and on edge. He drank coffee which he did not want, dipped into the few books in the front room but could not read for more than minutes at a time, prowled endlessly through all the rooms but Marlene's and paced up and down the hall as if measuring it. Marlene often heard him outside her room walking back and forth, relentlessly, monotonously. And when she awakened in the night she would hear him thrashing around restlessly. It was not from the cold, she knew, because he had taken all the extra towels and sheets for cover.

Sometimes he would open her door and look in, desperate for conversation, even with her, and despising himself for it. She refused to be drawn into conversations except when he said things that angered her until she realized it diverted him to make her angry and she stopped showing her anger unless provoked beyond endurance.

Because it annoyed her, he did not knock before opening her door until he surprised her with her blouse off, sewing on a button. He backed out awkwardly in great confusion and did not return all afternoon. Though she had on a slip belonging to the lady of the house she had been embarrassed, too, until she saw how much more embarrassed he was.

The next time he knocked before entering.

77

He sure learned his lesson, Marlene thought. I wish he could have seen his face in the mirror the last time. And, remembering it, she smiled to herself.

"What are you smiling about?" he demanded.

Instead of answering she smiled more broadly.

"Do you have to keep that idiotic grin on your face?"

Though her face was growing stiff from the effort, she kept the smile in place.

"If you knew how you looked . . ."

"Nobody asked you to look."

"Well, you're talking, that's something. I thought you were in a trance. That's the trouble with you. You're so stupid it's hard to tell if you're unconscious or not."

"I made all Bs except one C on my card," she said. "So there."

"Deliver me!" he said helplessly, looking up at the ceiling.

Could he really be calling on the Lord, she wondered. Because if he was . . .

"Are you a Christian?" she demanded.

"What kind of question is that?"

"Are you a *Christian?*"

"Of course I'm a Christian. What do you think I am, a Black Muslim?"

"I don't know what that is."

"Then why did you ask such a stupid question?"

She ignored the insult.

"Some people call themselves Christians but they're not," she said righteously, unaware that she was quoting a preacher of her childhood. "You're not a Christian unless you've been saved."

"Saved?"

"I thought you were the one who was supposed to be so smart. Everybody knows what saved means." Quoting again. "It means you've accepted Christ as your personal Saviour."

He looked at her incredulously.

"What's that got to do with anything?"

"When you said, 'Deliver me,' I knew you were a Christian," Marlene said eagerly. "And if you're a Christian and I'm a Christian . . ."

"So that's it. Don't try the religious bit with me, White Lady. You ever see a black face in your church?"

He rushed on before she could answer.

"Hell no! And your preacher. I'll bet he stands up there and looks at all your mealy white faces and talks about how all men are brothers. All white men, that is." Though angry, he was enjoying his anger and the opportunity to express himself to a white audience. "Let me tell you something. I don't want a white man for a brother any more than he wants me. I need a white man for a brother like Abel needed Cain."

She waited impatiently for him to end his tirade, wanting to show him how wrong he was, and when he paused for breath she spoke quickly and earnestly and, she thought, with most Christian patience.

"You've got your own churches," she said.

"And you burn them down."

"I don't know anything about that."

"You wouldn't. You only know what you want to know. There's no point in discussing it."

He left the room feeling dissatisfied and angry.

They ate at different times. He ate when he pleased and if Marlene came into the kitchen and found him there she would go back to her room and wait until she heard him in the front part of the house. When, as it sometimes happened, he found her in the kitchen he would deliberately sit down across from her at the table and stare at her with a sardonic smile when she rose and took her plate back to the back steps or, if it were night, to her room.

The first time it happened he said, "Just pretend you're in a dining car, White Lady."

"Huh?" she said, unable to resist answering.

"I think it's self-explanatory."

"I never been in a dining car," she said, walking toward the porch. "And anyway, this ain't no dining car."

Marlene kept careful watch on the contents of the food cupboard and after every meal knew exactly what he had eaten unless it was cereal from one of the big boxes. She was surprised and relieved to find he did not eat much. She had always thought that Negroes ate a lot, much more than white people. She had heard it was not uncommon for them to eat a whole chicken at a sitting, and one of her classmates in high school had told her how the family's washwoman had once baked a cake in their oven and then sat down and eaten the whole thing herself.

"An' she wasn't no fatter'n you, Marlene," the girl had said. "I don't know where they put it."

"Maybe she was just *hungry*," another girl had said, flushing when everyone stared at her.

Despite his slender appetite, the food was melting away as

he delayed his departure. How long was he going to stay, Marlene wondered. He had said only a few days and now it was over a week. She wanted to ask him but she was afraid that would just make him stay longer out of spite. The longer he stayed, the faster the food went. Maybe she shouldn't eat so much herself, she thought, so it would last longer.

And leave it for the nigger? Not for anything in the world, she thought. The next meal she ate more than she really wanted, forcing down the last few mouthfuls. Anything she ate was something he wouldn't get.

But what if he stayed until everything was gone? He would have to leave then. He couldn't stay on if there was nothing to eat. And then she could go to Mr. Teadwell's and buy groceries with the fourteen dollars. It would be like stealing because the money belonged to whoever owned the house, but she had already used so much more than her money's worth it wouldn't make any difference and, anyhow, she hadn't eaten it all herself and if they knew a nigger had been in their house they wouldn't care half as much about what she had done. And she could tell Mr. Treadwell that her folks had moved back to the state from New Orleans so he wouldn't wonder what she was doing around there.

Every morning Marlene felt her stomach and, when she was sure he was in the kitchen eating, pulled down her skirt and looked at it in the mirror. It did not look much bigger to her. It just stuck out a little, but not nearly as much as her mother's and lots of other women's, or even as much as some of the girls at high school, and they couldn't all be pregnant. Only that one who got expelled. Marlene wondered what really happened to her. If she hadn't had the baby stopped, it would be born by now and maybe given away.

She had been big enough to tell when she got expelled. Marlene wished she had known the girl better, and had known all about it so she could know how long the girl had been carrying the baby before it really showed. Because if it hadn't been any longer than she had been carrying herself, maybe it really had stopped growing. And if it had stopped growing, all she really had to worry about was the nigger. And he couldn't stay there forever.

Though Marlene was his prisoner she gained, in some ways, an advantage over him. To him the house was a cage. To her it was a refuge. While he roamed and fidgeted, sometimes angrily and always restlessly, slept badly and picked at his food, she sat in her room in seeming content, slept heavily at night and ate with relish at mealtime. He grew increasingly resentful of her placidity.

One morning he came out to the back steps where she was basking in the sun, the morning being unusually warm for that time of year, and followed her gaze. Seeing nothing but the bare limbs of the pecan tree, he demanded, "What are you looking at?"

"Nothin'," she said, surprised by the question.

"What do you mean, nothing?"

"I ain't looking at nothin'," she said with far more patience than she thought he deserved.

"Then what are you thinking about?" he demanded, ruffled by her calm.

"Nothin'."

"You expect me to believe that? You're sitting there thinking how you're going to turn me over to the Klan, or whoever is in charge of taking care of Negroes who act like men down here."

"I hope they do catch you. But I ain't thinkin' about it. Not now. Sometimes I think about it, but not now."

"How can you just sit here not doing anything and not even thinking? How the hell can you *keep* from thinking?"

"I don't keep from thinkin'. I just don't think. How can you think when there ain't nothin' to think about?"

"Nothing to think about? Oh, my God! White Lady says there's nothing to think about. Don't you care what's going on?"

"Going on? Where at?"

"Oh, my God!" he said again. "Listen to the girl! Where at, she says."

He calmed himself with visible effort.

"Look, even if you don't care what's going on in the great big world, you must have something to think about. Books you've read. Things you've . . ."

"I don't read books," she interrupted.

"Well, hell. Your problems, then. Or maybe you don't have any problems. Maybe it's not a problem to you to be penned up like an animal in this damned house."

"I like it in this house. Least I did till you . . ."

"Well, think about that then. Think about how nice it was before I got here and how nice it'll be after I leave."

"It mortifies you 'cause I like it here, don't it?" she asked with unexpected shrewdness.

"You're damn right it does!" he cried, turning and stamping

across the back porch to the kitchen and through the kitchen toward the front of the house.

Goody, Marlene thought. Goody, goody, gander. I'll just sit here and not think till you turn blue in the face.

Then she giggled, thinking about a nigger turning blue in the face. Because how could a nigger do that when he was already black in the face? And then she realized with a pang of regret she had failed to deliver the telling retort she had been saving for just such an occasion. 'A little knowledge is a dangerous thing." But she had mortified him enough without that. She could still use it some other time.

That night when she was washing up her supper dishes he came into the kitchen and watched her without speaking. She ignored him and, just to show him how little his presence bothered her, began humming tunelessly. She watched him covertly and saw his face grow angrier and angrier. At last he could endure it no longer.

"Will you for God's sake stop that noise."

"Don't you like music?" she asked innocently. "I thought all nig . . . all you people liked music."

"Music my . . . Look. I want to talk to you."

"Well, I don't want to talk to you."

"Sit down."

When she did not comply, he took a half-step toward her and repeated coldly, "I said sit down!"

Intimidated, she scuttled to the table and sat down, looking at her hands. He sat down across from her.

"I want to leave here," he said quietly.

Her chest hurt with the sudden joy of it and she leaned forward attentively.

"But I can't if you're going to run right out and say I was here."

"I won't!" she cried eagerly. "Oh, I won't!"

"How do I know that?"

"I cross my heart and hope to die!"

She touched her right forefinger to her tongue and then traced a cross on her chest. He smiled fleetingly and was grimly serious again.

"You hate me," he said. "As much as I hate you. You'll start thinking about how I . . . how I slapped you. And insulted you."

"No, I won't! I swear I won't."

"On the Bible?"

"Yes. Yes. On the Bible."

"You know if you swear on the Bible and then go back on your word you'll burn in hell?"

" 'Course I know that. I'm a Christian."

Again the fleeting smile.

"All right," he said. "I'll get it."

He rose and went after the Bible which was among the books in the front room. While he was gone Marlene got up and twirled around the kitchen, too elated to sit still.

He's goin'. Oh, dear Jesus, he's really goin'!

When he returned with the Bible he found her sitting primly at the table smoothing her skirt over her knees. He put the Bible on the table in front of her.

"Put your left hand on the Bible and your right hand over your heart."

She did so eagerly.

"Now repeat after me."

She nodded.

"I swear on the Holy Bible . . ."

"I swear on the Holy Bible."

"I will not tell anyone at any time . . ."

"I will not tell anyone at any time."

"That Charles Roberts was . . ."

"Charles Roberts?" she interrupted, taking her hand off the Bible. "Is that your name?"

"Put your hand back on the Bible."

"It is Charles Roberts," she said, putting her hand back. "You said Charlie that time you talked to yourself in the mirror."

"You don't forget anything, do you? But you better forget I was here. Where was . . . Oh, yes. That Charles Roberts was here."

"That Charles Roberts was here."

"Nor will I try to communicate . . ."

"Nor will I try to communicate," she repeated, thinking, He talks just like he's reading out of a book. He really is smart, for a nigger. But Daddy always said that was the worst kind, the smart ones.

"With anyone concerning him."

"With anyone concerning him."

She looked at him a moment, her hand still on the Bible, and added of her own volition, "I swear and hope to die."

He studied her.

"Do you believe your word is sacred?"

" 'Course I do."

"Even when it's given to a . . . a Negro?"

"It don't matter who it's given to. I wouldn't give my word to a nigra or anybody less I expect to keep it."

It was the first time she had extended the courtesy of "nigra," and the fact was not lost on Roberts. He wondered why. Was she just setting him up so she could run out and get the sheriff as soon as he was out of sight? Or was it because she was so glad to get rid of him? Or was there just the dim chance that it finally had gotten through to her he was a human being? He doubted the last. These people weren't just stupid. They were blind with ignorance. She wasn't smart enough to try and trick him.

"I believe you," he said.

"I should think so," she answered stiffly, thinking, Just who does he think he is, acting like he's doing me a favor to believe me and him a nigger.

Her reaction convinced him she would say nothing. He got up and put the coffee water on to heat. She remained at the table, fidgeting.

"When you leavin'?" she asked at last.

"Tonight."

"Tonight? Oh, goody!"

She put her hand over her mouth as if to call back the happy words, feeling, somehow, that she should have kept her delight to herself, that it might make him change his mind because he was so hateful he might stay just to spite her. But he only laughed.

"Don't apologize, White Lady," he said. "I feel the same way about you. Don't think for a minute it's the pleasure of your company that's kept me here."

He looked at her speculatively.

"There's not but one thing about you interests me," he continued. "What you're doing here."

He shrugged.

"Hell. What difference does it make?"

Again he gave her a speculative look.

"Don't you ever wonder what I'm doing here?"

It was her turn to shrug.

"You're in some kind of bad trouble," she said indifferently.

"Don't you ever wonder what kind of bad trouble it is?"

"No. 'Cept it serves you right."

"How can you say that without knowing the facts? That it serves me right?"

" 'Cause you're just a smart nig . . ."

She stopped herself. It wouldn't do to make him mad all over again when he had decided to leave.

"I don't know," she said. "I just think it does."

He made himself a cup of instant coffee.

It's the last time, thank goodness, Marlene thought. There was lots of coffee in the pantry but the way he drank it it would be gone in no time.

"Want a cup?" he asked unexpectedly.

She shook her head.

"Didn't your mother ever teach you about 'No, thank you'?" he demanded.

"No, thank you," she said grudgingly, and then only because she was getting rid of him at last.

"There," he said, as if addressing a backward child. "Didn't hurt a bit, did it? And didn't it make you feel all good inside?"

"No," she said sullenly. "Coffee keeps me awake," she added artlessly.

He looked at her almost with admiration.

"You are the end, White Lady. You are the absolute end."

Her expression showed she had no idea what had amused him or what he meant, and he chuckled.

"You know something?" he said. "I hate to admit this, but when I get back among normal people again I'm going to miss you."

"Huh?"

"Laughs aren't that easy to come by, and I'll say this for you, you're good for a lot of laughs."

"Well, you ain't."

He finished his coffee in silence and left the kitchen. Marlene remained at the table wondering when he was going to leave and hoping it would be soon. After a while he came back wearing the fishing pants and khaki shirt over his own clothes. They exchanged a brief look as he walked through the kitchen toward the back porch. He paused at the door, looked back at her, raised his shirt collar to cover the back of his neck and vanished abruptly into the darkness. It was so quick and easy it seemed almost impossible he had ever been there and had caused her so much anguish.

She leaped to her feet and ran to the door to make sure he had really gone. There was nothing outside but chilly darkness.

He's gone! The nigger's gone!

She was filled with almost unbearable relief and joy. It

was as if the gates of Heaven had opened and she had walked inside.

Marlene latched the screen door, locked the back door and looked around the kitchen with her hands on her hips. It looked completely different than it had only a few moments earlier.

Her kitchen. Her kitchen again. Her house. And she would never leave. Not ever. Reality thrust itself at her but she fought it back. She refused to consider what must happen when the baby came. She made herself a cup of hot chocolate, half evaporated milk, wishing for nothing beyond a marshmallow to float, melting, on top of the creamy brown surface, and drank it carefully, concentrating her senses on the warmth and rich taste of it in her mouth and inside her throat when she swallowed. She wondered, Does your throat taste or just your mouth? When she finished the hot chocolate she washed the cup and went to her room to snuggle cozily into her bed and fall quickly into deep and serene slumber.

9

It seemed to Marlene she had scarcely closed her eyes when she was awakened by a rapping on the shutters outside her window.

"Hey!" a voice was calling low and urgently. "Open the back door."

Her eyes flew open and she sat up and stared through impenetrable darkness toward the source of the words.

"Who . . ." she gasped.

"It's me. Roberts. Open the back door." Pause. "Hurry up. It's cold out here."

She scrambled out of bed and across the cold grass carpet to the window.

"Go 'way!" she cried hysterically. "You promised!"

"Stop that yelling and let me in."

"I won't! You said you were goin' off."

"Something happened. I couldn't help it. Are you going to open the door or do I have to tear it off? It's cold as hell out here."

She stumbled back to the kitchen, desolate, and opened the kitchen and porch doors with unwilling hands. He hurried inside, blowing into his cupped fingers, and turned on the light. He was wearing a sheepskin coat and a red hunter's cap with earflaps. He did not look at her at first and when he did, and saw the reproach in her face, he looked down at the floor.

"I couldn't help it," he said belligerently. "I needed something warm." He gestured at the coat. "And damn near got caught."

"You said I could have my house back," she said in an anguished, accusing voice.

"God damn it, do you think I'd have come back here if I could help it?"

"After I swore on the Bible and everything."

"You know what they'd do to me if they caught me?"

87

"I wish they had! I wish they'd caught you and . . . and . . ."

"I'll say it again," he said more quietly. "I can't help it. I'm in serious trouble. Maybe you are too, or you wouldn't be here, but it can't be as bad as mine. I wouldn't tell you this cxccpt damn it I did tell you I wasn't coming back. I owe you that much, I suppose."

Her implacable expression did not change and he struck his palm with his clenched fist.

"The hell I do!" he cried. "The hell I owe you anything. Or any white sons of a bitch. Whose fault do you think it is I'm in trouble? Some white son of a bitch. I'll tell you something, White Lady, he'll never cause trouble for any . . ."

He had said too much and knew it. He stripped off the coat and flung it on a chair. Despite the cold, there were dark sweat splotches at his armpits and Marlene thought dully, Niggers sweat. When she thought of him as just a nigger he did not seem quite so frightening or hateful to her. She felt something close to reluctant sympathy for him.

"What was it you did tonight?" she asked. "That's got you in such bad trouble?"

He stared at her, surprised by both her words and tone.

"It wasn't tonight. It was when . . ."

He caught himself again.

"What was it happened tonight?"

"It was up the highway. Some two-bit little store all by itself. I was cold so I pushed in the door. I found that coat and was looking for some gloves when a man come busting out of the back. He must have a room in back of the store."

"Mr. Treadwell," Marlene said.

"What?"

"Mr. Treadwell. He owns the store."

"How did you know?" His brow furrowed in thought. "Does he know you're living here?" he asked, worriedly.

"No. Nobody knows. 'Cept you."

He sighed heavily.

"That's a relief."

"He's nice. That Mr. Treadwell."

"I see. You weren't thinking about paying him a little visit when it got light enough, were you? To tell him about me?"

"No," she said indignantly. "I swore on the Bible."

"Sorry," he said, genuinely contrite.

"Anyhow," she said, "he thinks I went to New Orleans. If he knew I was stayin' here, he'd . . ."

And now she knew it was she who had said too much.

"He'd what? Throw you out? Is this his house?"

"Mr. Treadwell? He ain't near rich enough to own a nice summer place like this."

"But you don't want him to know you're here?"

She shook her head.

"I don't want nobody to know I'm here," she said hopelessly.

"That makes two of us."

He thrust his hands in his pockets and looked dejectedly around the kitchen. And sighed. Marlene echoed the sigh and they looked at each other silently.

Suddenly there was a bond between them, reluctant, tenuous and fleeting, but still a bond. He stretched and the sweat stains under his arm resembled two gaping holes in the khaki shirt.

"I've got to have something warm," he said. "Is there cocoa?"

Marlene nodded.

"Want some?" he asked.

She nodded again.

He made the cocoa and poured it. Then he sat down and waited for Marlene to join him. Instead she stirred in sugar and took her cup over to the drainboard. He smiled at her without malice.

"Well," he said, "at least some things haven't changed."

Marlene felt somehow embarrassed, as if she had done something impolite. But he's a nigger, she assured herself. She stared into her cup and said nothing.

The bond did not survive the night. Morning found them as alienated as before. To Marlene, it seemed that she was reliving the early and most unpleasant part of Roberts' invasion of her privacy. It was, if anything, worse now because she had expected to be rid of him. It was as if his first invasion of her little world had been a bad dream and his return a translation of the dream into reality.

It was also worse for Roberts, who again took up his vigil on the front porch. His narrow escape from Treadwell affected him deeply after the days of isolation in the house and the false sense of security they had given him. He was a fool to have come back here, he thought. He was stuck here with the girl again and despite their moment of rapport in the kitchen she was stupid, probably treacherous and, worst of all, white. And some thick-necked Southern sheriff might get the idea of checking all the unoccupied houses in the area when the storekeeper reported a burglary. But it had been the only place he knew to hide, the only place with food and warmth, the only place of safety he had known since he had fled from the protest march and the ensuing violence.

Yet it was not a safe place at all. It was a trap. The house was isolated on a peninsula and there was no way he could escape if they came looking for him. If they came he hoped he would have enough warning to slip out the back door and through the trees to the inlet dividing it from the mainland. He'd have to swim for it. Even if he made it to the other side, what chance would he have in open country, cold and wet?

If only the storekeeper had not blundered in and surprised him. He could be out of the state by now. But the storekeeper had blundered in and the whole area was probably all stirred up. Some sheriff might be smart enough to relate it to what had happened miles away and days ago. Even if that happened, the house was still the least risky place for him to be. He was not going to panic and run again.

When several uneventful days passed he began thinking the local sheriff must be too stupid to take the elementary step of checking unoccupied houses in the area of a reported burglary. Or perhaps the storekeeper had not reported it at all. They had peculiar notions about law and order in the South. He knew it only too well.

He was even almost grateful for the presence of the white girl. There had been no recurrence of the brief rapport of his return, and he was not sure he would welcome it should it develop, but any company was better than no company at all. Though her ignorance and bigotry could infuriate him, it amused him to play on it. The only drawback was, he thought, she was so stupid she seldom realized he was deliberately goading her.

And she gave him something to think about other than his own plight. What was she doing here all alone? She said she was seventeen, although she did not look even that old. What was a seventeen-year-old white girl doing all alone in a house where she admittedly did not belong? At first he had thought perhaps some man had her hidden away from his wife, even though she was hardly the type to make a man want to do a thing like that, but if it were so he would have come to see her once in a while. She did not seem to have anyone, not even a past, though she had mentioned her daddy several times at the beginning. Could she have committed a crime? If she had, and was hiding out, she did not show it. She seemed to have no fear of the law turning up.

And yet she had not really tried too hard to run for help except the one time at first when she slipped out and he had caught her. And slapped her. The memory of that was still shameful. He could not deny the fierce satisfaction he had felt momentarily at lashing out physically against a white person, though it could not match the savage joy of his fight with the white man and its total victory, but the fact that he had hit a woman disturbed him.

He had spoken the truth when he told her he had never hit a woman before. Still, if he had to hit a woman he was glad it was a white woman and a particularly bigoted one. The stupid bigots incensed him more than the intelligent ones, though he had never really been able to reconcile intelligence with bigotry except when, in moments of greatest honesty, he faced his own prejudice against white people.

The blind, bland assumption of superiority by his obvious inferiors infuriated Roberts. The intelligent bigot, however misguided or paranoid in his attitude toward the Negro, at least could lay claim to some achievement or standing on which to base an attitude of superiority and, perhaps, would feel almost the same sort of superiority to the white girl as to himself. Yet, clean this girl up, do her hair and put her in decent clothes and she could go anywhere and, if she kept her mouth shut, be accepted as an equal by people who looked down on him.

Why hadn't she tried harder to get away? Was he wrong about her not being in trouble with the law and was she more afraid of the law than of him? If she were a Negro girl, he could understand a fear of Southern lawmen so great as to overcome all other fears because to a Negro in this state white law was a horror—not that white law was anything a Negro could rely on in any state. But she was not a Negro girl. And thank God for that, he thought, because he would be ashamed for a Negro girl to be so stupid. But why should he be ashamed of a Negro girl's stupidity merely because he was a Negro?

What was she doing here and why did she cling so desperately to this house?

It irritated him that this should concern him. Nothing about her should matter to him except that she did not betray him to the law. She was not worth his thoughts. And yet it gave him something to occupy his time in this boring, God-forsaken place.

Bite your tongue, he thought. Better here than where you'd be if they caught you.

He began, to a degree unwillingly, to study her closely at every opportunity, searching for some clue to her voluntary isolation in her words or expression. His curiosity grew so obvious it made her uneasy.

"See somethin' green?" she demanded one morning when he stood in the door of her room watching her brush her long and, she thought triumphantly, clean hair.

"What's that, White Lady?" he replied, puzzled.

"How come you keep starin' and starin' if I'm so ugly like you said?"

"You're not ugly like I said. You're ugly period."

"Then why do you have to keep lookin' at me like that if I'm so ugly?"

"Because you puzzle me. You really do."

I wonder if he knows, she thought. I wonder if that's why he keeps staring at me, to see if I'm getting bigger.

Her hand went unconsciously to her stomach and she looked at him guiltily to see if he had noticed. She could not tell.

Most of them, you can tell what they're thinking, she thought. They can't hide their feelings. They laugh and show their blue gums when they're happy and when they're sulking they stick out their fat bottom lip. They ain't smart enough not to. But not him. You can't tell what he's thinking, except that it's something mean. You say I'm ugly, she thought. You're the one's ugly. You and your nigger lips and nigger hair and your nigger nose.

After that, whenever she found him staring at her, her hand would drop to her stomach as if to reassure herself that she did not show. Each time it happened she promised herself it would not happen again, but she was unable to keep the promise.

And then, one day when they happened to be eating at the same time, him at the table and her leaning against the back door, he stared at her and asked unsympathetically, "Your stomach hurt?"

He derived a deep, rich comfort from the fact that her prejudice against Negroes forced her into a position where it was a Negro who sat and she who stood.

Marlene snatched her hand away from her stomach.

"Yes," she said after a moment of hesitation. " 'Cause I've got a belly full of you."

"Touché."

"Huh?"

"Touché. Don't tell me you don't know what that means."

" 'Course I do."

"Then tell me."

"Tell you what?"

"What *touché* means!" he cried, exasperated.

As always, it infuriated him when, through sheer ignorance, she managed to upset him and, even more so, that he continued reacting as he did.

"It means . . . it means . . . If you don't know, I ain't goin' to tell you."

As she spoke, her hand stole to her stomach again and, realizing what she had done, she pulled it back. The gesture had a calming effect on him.

"You've sure got a belly full of something," he said thoughtfully.

He leaned forward and stared brutally at her stomach. Marlene tried to suck it in, feeling as if his eyes were two prying hands inside her twisting and tying everything into hard knots, and her stomach suddenly seemed grotesquely, damningly, large.

"Well, I'll be damned!" he said in a low, exultant voice.

Don't you say nothing smart, you dirty nigger, she thought wildly. If you do, I'll kill you. I'll take a knife and I'll stick it in you and then you'll see who's got a belly full of what.

He shook his head in a mock wonder.

"And I thought you were such an innocent little white girl," he said. "Dumb, but innocent."

I am innocent, something within her cried. If I wasn't innocent, how you think I got in trouble? Why do you think I'm here, you horrible black nigger?

He sat back, grinning.

"Got ourselves knocked up, didn't we?" he said.

"Don't talk dirty to me!"

"Why, that's not talking dirty, White Lady. That's just the facts of life. You know about the facts of life, don't you? Don't answer that one. Your fat little belly already did it." He shook his head. "And to think it took me all this time . . . I apologize, White Lady."

"Apologize?" she asked, a note of hope in her voice.

"I really do. For saying you were too ugly for anybody to look at. Because somebody didn't think you were too ugly."

"He was sweet and big and smarter than you!" she cried, fighting back defiant tears. "And if he was here he'd teach you to talk like that."

"But he's not here, is he? And that raises an interesting question. Why? Could it be he didn't want anything more to do with you after he knocked you up?"

The tears were very close and if she had a knife in her hand now she could use it. She knew she could. A nigger sitting there and saying ugly things to her, all the uglier because they were true.

"Why didn't that daddy you talk about go after him with a shotgun and make him marry you?" he went on relentlessly. "Isn't that the way you do things down here? I heard it takes six things down here to make a marriage official. A preacher, two witnesses, a bride and a groom. And a shotgun."

"I hate you," she said in a low agonized voice.

She had said it often before, and in many ways, but never so powerfully, so deeply felt and, he realized with a wrench, with such justification.

Jesus Christ, he thought, what kind of a son of a bitch am I? A man doesn't talk that way to a woman, even a dumb little white nothing like this one.

Tears began running down her pale cheeks and she turned and pressed her face against the back door, one hand covering her eyes and the other clutching the rim of her dish, from which food spilled unnoticed to the floor. Her shoulders shook convulsively but she made no sound. He rose quietly and went to her, stopping awkwardly a step away. He put out his hand as if to touch her on the shoulder, then drew it back without making contact.

"I'm sorry," he said. "I really am."

Christ, he thought, why am I acting so upset? It happens every day to better girls than her. She probably balled every boy she could drag into the cotton patch with her or wherever it was country kids went to do it. And what about the Negro girls down South that got raped by some white bastard and nobody gave a damn about? And, he thought wryly, what the hell do I know about white bastards raping Negro girls except the stories I've heard second hand, just like this poor dumb white brat thinks the only reason Negroes want to go to school with her is to get in her pants. And hell, what difference does it make what happens to other girls? This is her.

How could he get her attention without touching her? He knew if he touched her it would make matters worse. If he could only call her by name.

"I don't even know your name," he said, for the first time thinking it remarkable that he should live here with her so long and not know. "Isn't that something?" And gently, "What is it?"

And when she did not answer, again gently, "What's your name?"

Her shoulders gradually stopped shaking and after a few moments she turned around, her hand still covering her eyes, her back against the door. She dropped her hand at last and looked at him, her hate overwhelmed by humiliation and despair.

"What do you care?" she said dully.

"Well, hell," he said. "I just happened to realize I didn't even know your name after all this time."

Why should he think it so strange? They never know our names, except sometimes the first name. Why learn a name when it's easier to say "Boy" to every black face? She'd called him Boy. Why not call her Girl?

"You know mine," he said coaxingly. "Don't you?"

She nodded and said, "Charlie," as if in a stupor.

"That's right."

He was pleased, almost flattered, that she remembered, and he was angry with himself for feeling flattered. Why should he care if this worthless white girl remembered his name or not? He was ashamed of himself for having behaved so unfeelingly but he resented being trapped into caring. Yet he did owe her an apology and he was determined she accept it, just to balance the ledger.

"What's my last name?" he asked, his patient tone now calculated.

"Your last name?" she answered vaguely, still baffled by his sudden change from brutality to concern.

"Yes. My last name."

"I . . . I don't know."

"I told you. Don't you remember?"

"You did? All I remember is . . . is Charlie."

"That figures," he said, trying to keep the resentment out of his voice. "It's Roberts. Charles Roberts."

"Oh, yes. That's right."

"So what's yours? Or do I just keep calling you White Lady?"

"I don't like it when you call me that," she said with a glimmer of spirit.

Good, he thought. She's coming out of it.

"What else can I call you if I don't know your name?"

She considered what he had said.

"Marlene," she said. "Marlene Chambers."

He had a feeling of achievement.

"Marlene," he repeated. Then, to get her attention, "Marlene" again. When he had it, he said, "I'm sorry I made fun of . . . of your condition. I apologize. Okay?"

That's the first time a nigger ever called me by my first name, she thought. But he wasn't acting smart. Just the opposite. And when somebody knew they were wrong and admitted it, and apologized, you had to accept the apology, even from a nigger.

She nodded.

"Good," he said, feeling that he had discharged a debt. "Now let's forget all about it."

Marlene did not answer.

Maybe you will, she thought. But I won't.

10

Though they avoided each other for the rest of the afternoon, now that Marlene's secret was out there was a lessening of tension for both of them. Roberts knew at last why she was in the house and, for her part, Marlene could stop worrying that he might find out. Things had been as bad as she expected they would be when he found out, but he had been sorry for the things he said, which she had not expected.

That night, when they chanced to be in the kitchen at the same time—they both had come to regard the kitchen as neutral territory—he felt an urge to talk, whether from a lingering vestige of guilt or merely out of boredom he was not certain.

"Marlene's an uncommon name for down here, isn't it?" he asked. "I thought you went in more for Emmy Lou and like that. How'd they happen to name you Marlene?"

"They just did," she snapped.

Was he getting smart again, she wondered. Just because she'd accepted his apology didn't mean she intended to listen to a lot of smart talk.

"Did they name you after Marlene Dietrich?"

"Marlene who?"

And you can't even pronounce it right, she thought. Marlane. It's Marlene.

"Dietrich. Marlene Dietrich."

"Who's that?"

"You're putting me on. Don't tell me you don't know who Marlene Dietrich is."

She shook her head.

"Good God! What do you get out of all those movie magazines? Don't tell me you can't even read."

"I can so. She's not in my magazines."

"She should be. She's a movie star."

"She is?"

Marlene looked thoughtful.

"Oh, *her*," she said, with growing interest. "I *have* heard

97

of her. But I never saw one of her shows. Wait a minute."
Now she was quite animated. "Yes, I did. I did, too. It was
on the television. She had on this long white dress, see, and they
were out in the desert, her and this man. He was foreign."

Jesus Christ, he thought. A few hours ago she was all broke
up and angry enough to cut my throat and now she's all fired
up over an old movie.

". . . and it was kind of sweet," she was rattling on. "And
his name was let me see, it was . . . it was Charles, too," she
said triumphantly, "just like yours. Charles . . . Charles . . ."

Roberts sighed.

"Boyer," he said.

"That's right!" she said in excited agreement. "Charles
Boyer."

She pronounced the "er" but Roberts did not bother to
correct her.

The Garden of Allah," he said.

"That was the name," she said. *"The Garden of Allah."*

She looked at him and, it seemed to Roberts, for the first
time was not seeing color between them like an opaque
screen.

"Did you see it, too?" she asked.

"Yes, I saw it, too."

He had seen many old films on television and in art houses
and was fond of them. Why, he could not understand, because
the world of the old films was a white world in which Negroes
did not exist except rarely, and then only as comic servants.
Many times he had come away from a motion picture feeling
like a traitor because he had liked it and, while it was running, had become totally involved except for occasional excruciating moments when the realization pierced him that
he was a fool to be caught up in the affairs of the people on the
screen when he would not be welcome in any of their houses
and that it was not the hero he should be identifying with
but with the waiter who came shuffling in with a tray.

". . . real good, wasn't it?" she was saying.

"Junk," he said. "Real sentimental junk."

She stared at him as if he had defiled something beautiful
and in so doing tricked her.

"They all are," he said. "They're all false, most of them,
anyway. They never show how things really are in the world."

And how were things, really, and why was he here talking
about a crummy old motion picture with some poor, stupid,

knocked-up little white girl and in such deep trouble, trouble that had been forced on him.

"What do you mean?" she said.

What do I mean? he thought. I mean the way things are in the real world have nothing to do with hearts and flowers and all that crap. The way things are in the world is that it's a white man's world and they've got all the power.

"You wouldn't understand," he said, suddenly wretched.

"I know I'm not smart," she said matter-of-factly. "But I can't help that. How come you keep making fun of me?"

And why do you keep acting as if I were dirt because I'm black, he thought. I can't help that, either. But I don't want to help it. I don't want to be any other color. And that's what really burns me. Because you think I want to be white like you. All of you do.

"Do you think I wish I was white?" he blurted.

The question startled her. She hesitated, wondering what sort of answer he expected and groping for the one least likely to provoke him to further insults. She was not devious enough to cope with the problem.

"You do, don't you?" she said at last.

"Like hell I do! That's what you all think."

"Well," she said lamely, "why don't you? 'Cause if you were, you wouldn't . . ."

She did not know where the words might be leading her and stopped when she found herself unable to express her thoughts.

But he knew what she intended to say.

"If I were white I wouldn't be such garbage," he said, deliberately choosing a crueler word than she might have used. "That's what you mean, isn't it?"

Before she could answer he motioned toward the kitchen table.

"Sit down," he said.

He was always trying to make her sit down at the table with him, she thought. That proved he wished he was white.

But there was something in his tone that brooked no refusal, nor did the thought of refusing occur to her. She had grown interested in the conversation. She sat down and he sat down across from her as he had done when he made her swear on the Bible.

"You think I think if I were white I'd be a better man?" he demanded.

She nodded.

"All right. Now, do *you* think if I were white . . . if I were white, you wouldn't feel uncomfortable sitting at the same table with me?"

"But you're not," she said. "White."

"Damn it! Don't you think I know that? I'm asking, if I were."

He continued with deliberate emphasis, "If I were, would you feel uncomfortable sitting at the same table with me? Yes or no."

"No," she said thoughtfully. "Not if you were white."

He sprang to his feet and leaned over the table.

"You see!" he said triumphantly. "That proves it."

"Proves what?"

"That your thinking's all wrong. That you don't even know why you think the way you do."

"I don't know what you mean."

"Of course you don't. But I'll explain."

He sat down again and spoke very carefully.

"Look. You think that Negroes are different from white people. In every way. Not as good. Not as . . . not as, damn it, *equal*. Right?" He did not wait for an answer. "But in spite of that, if I were white and otherwise no different from the way I am right now, just that I was white instead of black, you wouldn't mind sitting down with me? That's what you said, wasn't it?"

"If you'd been talking ugly the way you do sometimes I would."

Marlene felt strange and, in a way, not herself. It was almost the feeling she had had, without the attendant remorse and consternation, after she had lost her virginity and realized she had done something which went against everything she had been taught was right and which could not be undone.

Here I am, she thought, sitting at the same table with a nigger and talking to him just like he was anybody. I sat down with him before, but that was just to get him out of the house. I'm glad Daddy can't see me now.

And yet it was not like losing her virginity because when she got up from the table she would be the same girl who had sat down at it, not someone who had been pure and was no longer and would never be again.

"I accept that stipulation," he said. "Assuming you weren't mad at me for anything specific I had done, and I was white and that was the only difference. You wouldn't mind?"

She listened carefully, more carefully than she had ever listened to her teachers in school unless it was something she thought would be asked on the examination, trying to understand his every word. For he sounded to her like a school-teacher with the major difference that what he was saying was interesting.

"No," she said. "I wouldn't mind."

"But you think Negroes are different from you," he said relentlessly, jabbing his finger at the space between them. "Not as good. So if the only difference was I was white instead of black, I'd still be all the things you think make me inferior?"

She shook her head, trying desperately to follow him but not, quite, being able to.

"Do you mean no, or you don't know?" he demanded.

Marlene shook her head again.

"Sometimes I get a strange feeling I'm talking to myself," he said. "What I'm trying to get across to you is that if it's only the skin color, the skin color alone, that makes the difference, you're all wrong about other things. About Negroes not being as industrious, or moral, or equal. Just turning white wouldn't change those things."

"But you're not white," she said, as if refuting everything he had said, "You're a . . . you're black."

"Jesus, Jesus, Jesus!" he cried, and Marlene thought, You're always taking the Lord's name in vain and I thought niggers were supposed to be so religious.

"You ever read *Huckleberry Finn?*" he demanded.

"Huh?" she said, taken aback. "No, I never. It's a *boy's* book. Why'd you ask me a crazy thing like that, anyway?"

"A boy's book, she says! Miss Marlene, you're talking about the great American novel. Or close to it."

She shrugged, uninterested.

"I still don't see what that's got to do with anything," she said. "You weren't talkin' about readin'. You were talkin' about bein' white."

"Damn it," he cried, "I know I wasn't talking about reading. I just wanted to make a point."

He threw up his hands and stared at the ceiling.

"How can you make a point to a . . . to a . . ."

He trailed off helplessly and lowered his hands and voice.

"In Huckleberry Finn, Huck is trying to explain something to Jim. He's a runaway slave, see, and uneducated. The way you think we all are. And they were, in those days, not

that it was their fault, and that's the basis for all your . . .
Hell, that's not the point. The point is, Huck got so mad when
he couldn't get through to Jim all he could say was, 'You can't
argue with a nigger.' "

His use of the word confused her.

"But what *is* the point?" she asked helplessly.

"The point is, Miss Marlene, that Huck was wrong. You
can't argue with a white."

"You sure been doin' it," she retorted belligerently.

He looked at her in unwilling admiration.

"Miss Marlene," he said, "you are something else. You
really are."

That ended the conversation and they rose and went
separately to their rooms without saying good night.

The strange feeling Marlene had sitting at the table with
Roberts persisted after she went to bed. She had been wrong
about thinking she would be the same girl after she got up
from the table, for she felt changed, not changed herself,
exactly, but naggingly aware that *something* had changed.
It was as if she had once had a clear sharp view of a world
with everything in its rightful place and now some of the
things had been moved around. She had not understood everything Roberts said, and those things she had understood she
did not agree with, but the fact that he had said them and said
them so articulately impressed her more than she was willing
to admit.

She was ashamed of herself for having listened to such talk
and for having sat down with a nigger, and more so for having
almost enjoyed it, and puzzled that it had not been a disgusting
experience, especially after he had said such terrible things
about her being in trouble. Still, she was glad it had been a
nigger who said them because what a nigger said, even a
smart nigger like Charlie—with a shock she realized she had
thought of him by name—didn't count, at least among people
she knew and cared about.

What would Mama and Daddy say if they knew I'd sat
down right at the same table with a nigger? she thought. Daddy
wouldn't believe it, not ever. But if he did, he'd whip me good
the way he did when I was little, only worse. And Mama.
Lordy. Mama never said a whole lot but this time I bet she
sure would. And cry and say she didn't raise me to sit down
with no nigger.

But all I did was *sit* there, she protested, as if her mama
were actually in the room.

And her mama would say, Marlene Harkins Chambers—she would call her that, not Sugar Baby—you mean you don't see nothing wrong about sitting down with a *nigger*, and she would have to admit she didn't, not if all she did was just sit, because she had sat down with one and nothing had happened, except that things had been moved around a little.

But she would never, never tell her mother about some of the things she had listened to from a nigger. She thought about the terrible things he had said to her about her condition.

They hadn't been any worse than her daddy had said, and Charlie had at least been sorry afterward he said them. She wondered if her daddy was sorry about the ugly things he had said to her and if she went home now would he take her back. But she knew he wouldn't. Her daddy never changed his mind about anything, even when he was wrong, and she was not sure he was wrong in this case. Maybe it wouldn't hurt to try, though. She could go home and all he could do was slam the door in her face.

But Charlie wouldn't let her. He was afraid she would tell on him. But after he'd talked so nice and all, maybe he'd believe her now if she promised not to tell. She would swear on the Bible again if he wanted her to.

She thought about being out on the highway again, hitching a ride home because she didn't have any money for the bus, and everybody and his brother seeing her stomach sticking out and knowing she was pregnant and noticing she didn't have a wedding ring on.

No, there was just no use thinking about going home. When she left, whenever that was, she would just have to have the baby whether she wanted to or not. But what would she do with the baby? Maybe give it away if anybody would take it and find a job. Or go back to school.

Because that was what she wanted to do, she realized with a jolt. If she got her diploma everybody wouldn't think she was dumb, and somehow, however grudgingly, "everybody" meant an ugly black Negro face and a cutting tongue. She would show him who was dumb. And she was provoked with herself for not remembering to tell him a little knowledge is a dangerous thing.

Roberts, as well, was not untouched by the events of the day. That's all I need, he thought bitterly. To be locked in with a pregnant little white bitch too stupid to understand how really stupid she is. And yet he did not feel truly justified or even comfortable thinking of her as a white bitch now. For she was a pitiable little thing in her trouble and ignorance.

He was angry with himself for wasting his pity on a white person with all the pitiable Negroes there were, and pitiable because of what whites had done to them. You've got to be hard, he thought, like the white man is hard. Think of them as animals the way they think of us and it's easier to be hard. And most of them were animals, in this state, anyhow.

He thought of the contorted, insane white faces that had surrounded him, and of the vile, incoherent epithets, and the rocks and ballbats, and one enraged, demented white face in particular, and hitting it again and again and seeing fear transform it into something more human but no less hateful.

And Roberts felt a surge of some primordial blood pride for what he had done and then went cold and knew that what had happened had altered his life more than that silly little girl's life had been altered by her encounter in the cotton patch or wherever it happened. It was ridiculous to attach such importance to the shredding of that fragile membrane. What did it matter, really? It was going to happen to her some day, anyhow, unless she grew up to be an old maid and, judging from her looks, it was even money that she would, although it was true even the ugliest, most unlikely people seemed somehow to find mates.

All those ugly, screaming harpies who came out from under rocks when Negro children went to white schools had found husbands and maybe this one would, too, and grow up to be just like them. He shuddered. How could anyone grow up to be like that? It angered you but it frightened you, too, to realize that human beings could be like that. The Muslims said they were devils, the whites, not human, but he could not buy that even though he agreed with much of what they said. They couldn't convince him you could fight the white man by staying away from the white man. You had to meet him on his own ground and show him you were better.

He groaned aloud. But how can you meet the bastards on their own ground when they've got all the power? You've got to get your foot on a ladder before you can climb it, and there's always a white foot to stamp on your hand when you reach for a rung. There was one white foot that would never do that again. But what was one white man more or less when there were thousands just like him.

And this pregnant little idiot next door. Was she carrying another future paranoic in her belly, who would grow up and throw curses and rocks and defend his noble Southern heritage, which went exactly as far back as a quick roll in the bushes and a father who wouldn't claim him and whom he'd never know?

And Roberts thought of all the pregnant white bitches all over the country, some of them getting pregnant right that minute, and of all the seeds of evil and blind hate even now growing toward the day when they could spew their venom and ignorance, and he had a fleeting, irrational urge to go in and kick her belly until whatever was in it was mashed into harmless jelly.

He tried to picture Marlene in carnal embrace with some rednecked white boy but could not, not that scrawny, vacuous child. He knew that if the image did come it would be disgusting, not erotic, for he did not find any white woman sexually attractive and this one was even less than that to him, she was sexless. He could not imagine her conceiving despite the evidence that she had done so. And when he first arrived she had been afraid he was going to rape her. He laughed bitterly.

Roberts had led a chaste life, as chaste as a man of twenty-eight could without being abnormally so, and he had sometimes wondered if it was because he did not naturally have as strong a sexual urge as his fellows appeared to or if it were purely psychological, that he was proving to a white world that Negroes were not oversexed. And wondered, too, if that was the reason he never got drunk as young men often did, both white and black young men, and why he studied so hard in school and cultivated such a wide range of interests and seldom used slang and always pronounced his *r*'s and *g*'s.

Such thoughts could drive Roberts close to desperation, for he could not bear to accept the possibility that it was the white man forcing him into morality and excellence and not the natural, normal drives within himself. He was certain of his own powers, yet, in a white world, how could he be sure he would have become what he was without white pressure no matter how often and how vehemently he told himself he had become what he was despite that pressure, not because of it, and that without it he would have achieved even more?

And he could not bear to think he was influenced by what

the white world thought of Negroes because he was not Negroes but a Negro, and not a Negro but a man.

And that was what the whole thing was about, he thought now, the need to be a man, just a man, to be accepted and judged as just a man and not a nigger by ignorant crackers, nor as proof a Negro was as good as a white by sympathetic liberals, nor as an example to other Negroes of what a Negro might achieve in the white world if he was bright enough and tried hard enough.

He wished he had told her that when he told her he did not want to be white, told her he did not want to be a white man or a black man but only a man and be judged as a man. Even when, in rage, he had hit her, and that had been wrong to do and he knew it, he had wanted her to hate the *man* who did it, not the *Negro*.

But why should it matter to him that he had not told her? She was not that important and would not have understood anyhow. And yet he felt that if only he could have made this semiliterate child understand, he would have accomplished something important. But why? Why should he feel so frustrated at being unable to do so?

His whole life was one long frustration, of battering at insensate walls which did not even know they were being battered. Until at last he had made one great and irrevocable impression on one white man and what had it done for Charles Roberts after that first savage, cathartic moment of triumph except to send him running to earth like a harried animal?

He stared through the darkness toward the wall which separated his room from the girl's and thought, You did it to me because you are one of them, yet at the same time knowing she, too, had been badly used by the white world.

But not because she was black. That was the big difference.

And yet he could no longer hate her as he did her world, because he had seen beyond the color of her skin when she turned her face to the kitchen door and wept without sound. The poor, miserable little white . . .

11

In the morning Marlene had second thoughts about the wisdom of having sat willingly at the table with Roberts. No telling what kind of ideas it might have given him about what she thought of him. He was still just a nigger, no matter what.

She slept late and he beat her to the kitchen for breakfast so she waited for him to finish. When he dawdled she became ravenously hungry, so after washing her face and combing her hair she went in to breakfast, thinking, Why should I let him keep me out of my kitchen and not even aware of the substitution of "him" for "that nigger."

Roberts had also had second thoughts and when she came in looked at her briefly, his face unsmiling, and looked away. He felt he had revealed too much of himself to her the day before.

Marlene had mingled feelings of relief and disappointment at his attitude. At least he isn't trying to act friendly just because I sat down at the table with him and argued with him the same as if he was white, she thought. But he wasn't near as mean last night as he was most of the time. And now he looked like he might be getting mean again.

Why did I have to turn so soft? he was thinking. What do I care if she's in trouble? If it was a white man in this house with a pregnant little Negro girl, she'd be out on her rear so fast it would make her head swim. Or worse. If she thought everything was going to be cozy now merely because he had got down to her level out of pity she was badly mistaken. He had apologized, she had accepted the apology and they were even.

Marlene was looking in the food cupboard.

"Well," she said, her hands on her hips, "looks to me like somebody's been gobblin' like a hog."

"Just what I've been thinking," he said coldly. "But don't apologize. After all, you're eating for two."

She whirled and faced him, eyes ablaze, thinking, I should

of known it, all that talk about being sorry for talking mean and apologizing and everything. Here you are talking about it again.

"I *paid* for my share," she cried. "Least I did long's I had any money. An' that's a lot more than *some* people can say."

"You paid?"

She marched to the tableware cabinet, flung open the door and seized the fourteen one-dollar bills. She turned and waved them at him.

"You're so smart, where you think this came from?" she demanded.

"Why, I don't know. I thought . . . You mean that's *your* money?"

"Yes. Least it was. It's theirs, now. Whoever owns this here house. Every day I put in a dollar. Till I didn't have no more. An' that's a whole lot more'n you did."

He looked at her with new but grudging respect which was not lost on Marlene. She prepared her breakfast jauntily, humming a little song that once had so angered him with its tunelessness.

While she was eating, Roberts went to the food cabinet for his own appraisal. He had noticed the supply was dwindling but under the pressure of his other problems had not worried about it particularly. Food, the acquisition of it, had not previously been a problem with him, and when he had thought about the food supply at all had not considered the possibility that Marlene had found the cupboard stocked when she discovered the house but had assumed she had brought the food from somewhere and could get more from the same source.

There were only a dozen or so cans and packages remaining, and of the instant coffee he had been using so prodigally less than half a jar.

"Old Mother Hubbard," he muttered.

"Huh?" said Marlene, who had been watching and enjoying his obvious discomfiture.

"Now don't tell me you don't even know about Old Mother Hubbard?" he demanded.

" 'Course I do. Everybody knows that one. 'Old Mother Hubbard, she went to the cupboard, to get her poor dog a bone. When she got there, the . . .' "

He clapped his hands in mock applause, interrupting her. It made her angry. She wanted to finish. She enjoyed reciting and she wanted to show him she knew it all.

"Very good, Marlene," he said.

The sound of her unadorned first name on his lips was strange to her, and unwelcome. Yet it was better than White Lady, or even Miss Marlene, the way he said it. "Miss," as he said it, was an insult. She decided not to object to his use of her first name, realizing with developing shrewdness that if he knew she did not like it she would hear it all the more.

"You know somethin'?" she said. "You really do think you're smart."

"Are you still using that tired old defense?"

She shook her head, no longer angry but quite serious.

"I don't mean for a . . . You're just a smart aleck. Like you say yourself all the time. It ain't got nothing to do with color."

"Well," he said lightly. "The girl is learning. Who knows where it might lead?"

But she had touched something sensitive. He was aware he baited her because he despised her and the white world she represented, but her words made him face another reason, and one which he found unflattering. He also baited her to flaunt his superiority. He was proud of his intelligence, his quick mind, his ready tongue. And stupid as she was, she understood that now. She was gaining on him and he did not like it. He was prompted to say *"Touché,"* but he did not feel that good a loser.

"That doesn't fill the cupboard," he said. "Am I to understand that all that food was here when you . . . took over?"

"Where'd you think it came from? You think I could carry all that stuff on my back?"

"I never really thought about it one way or the other."

"Well, if you intend to stay here much longer, you better start thinkin' about it one way or the other."

He shrugged helplessly.

"You got any ideas?"

"Mr. Treadwell's?" she said doubtfully, turning from the glow of her small victory to more practical matters.

"Are you out of your mind? That's all I need, to get caught in there again."

"I didn't mean *steal,*" Marlene said disapprovingly. "I meant buy stuff."

"You mean just walk in the front door and step up to the counter."

Marlene nodded.

"No thanks, young lady."

There was irony in the "no thanks" but not in the "young lady." He had said it unconsciously, his mind on the rashness of such an action, not on the person who proposed it.

"How come? Mr. Treadwell, he'll wait on nig . . . He's even got this . . . this place in back just for them to use."

"He has, has he? A real enlightened red-neck, isn't he? And I'll bet he's got a nice new rope to put around my neck, too."

"Why'd Mr. Treadwell want to do that?"

"Maybe he wouldn't," Roberts said evasively. "But he might get in touch with people who would."

"Why would anybody want to?"

"Just take my word for it."

"I guess it don't really matter. We ain't got any money, anyhow."

The "we," coming so naturally and unconsciously, was not lost on Roberts. He resented the moment of well-being it gave him. He did not think this was something they were in together and he did not want her thinking that. But it did have an advantage. He might not have to worry about the possibility of her trying to turn him in, or at any rate going out of her way to do it. She did not seem to care about what he might have done before he came into her life. The only thing that she considered was his presence in the house and now she seemed to be accepting that, or at any rate taking it for granted.

"We've got fourteen dollars," he said, using the "we" deliberately to test her.

"I told you. It belongs to the people who own this house."

"We need it worse than they do."

"That don't make no difference. It's theirs. You think I'm an Indian giver?"

"Is there anything to eat in the other houses?"

"I don't know."

"You don't know? As long as you've been here, you didn't even investigate?"

"I had plenty to last me right here. Until a certain party had to come along."

"If there's one thing you are, it's a gracious hostess."

"I ain't your hostess. If it was up to me . . ."

"Fortunately, it's not. Let's go see what we can find."

"You expect me to go with you?"

Could he have been wrong about her being unwilling to

give up her refuge even to get back at him, he wondered. Had she refused merely because she did not want to be near him any more than necessary or was there something more significant behind it? Would she go running off for help as soon as he was out of sight?

"I not only expect it," he said, deciding not to take a chance, however remote the possibility, "I insist on it. You think I'm going to give you a chance to run to Treadwell?"

"I wasn't studyin' anything like that," she said, affronted.

"I'll bet you weren't," he said, knowing even as he said it that he had misjudged her.

When she looked at him there was accusation and a knowingness in her face.

"You want me to swear on the Bible?" she asked quietly.

And he remembered with shame how he had sworn her to secrecy and how it had been he, not she, who had gone back on a promise.

"Damn it!" he said. "I couldn't help that. I had to come back. There wasn't any choice."

"Well," she said calmly, "If you're goin' to bust in those other houses, I can't stop you. But I don't have to go with you while you do it."

When he hesitated she said, "If you're goin', just go on. I think I'll just take me a nice bath while I got the house to myself for a change."

Roberts felt he was being dismissed and he did not like it. But there was no getting out of it. It had been his own idea.

The house next door had a back porch similar to the one he had left. He pulled on the screen door until the latch tore loose and, finding the kitchen door and window locked, broke the glass in a kitchen window to gain entry. He felt like a thief, though not so strongly as Marlene had, but after the first uncomfortable moments overcame the feeling by reminding himself that it was a white man's house and that a white man was responsible for his present circumstances.

There were several cans of food and an unopened can of coffee in the cupboard and on the floor an almost full ten-pound burlap sack of potatoes. Though some of them had sprouted, they were firm to the touch. He put the food on the kitchen table and went looking through the house to see what else he could find that might be useful. The house was barer than the one he had left but on a shelf in a closet he found a folded roach-eaten olive drab blanket and a small electric heater.

He piled the food and the heater in the middle of the blanket, wound the four ends of the blanket around his wrist and hand, and carried his finds back to the house. He hesitated an instant at the back door. He felt as if he should knock. Marlene had said she intended taking a bath.

"Hey, in there," he called.

There was no answer.

He felt a tingle of panic in his belly. He flung open the door and charged into the house, the blanket and its contents forgotten in his hand.

"Marlene!" he yelled

Her door opened and she came out wearing a bedspread as a robe and a towel, which she was kneading vigorously with both hands, wound around her head.

"You don't have to scream," she said. "I ain't deaf."

"Oh," he said, embarrassed. "I thought . . ."

Damn it, he thought, the little moron saw me panic. But just let her try to rub it in.

She looked at the bundle in his hand, still toweling her hair.

"What'd you get?" she asked, apparently unaware of the scare she had given him.

"Not much," he said diffidently. "Some canned goods and a sack of potatoes."

"Potatoes?" she said, wetting her upper lip greedily. "Sweet or white?"

"What did you say?"

"Sweet potatoes or white potatoes?" she said patiently. "Don't you know anything?"

"How the hell do you expect me to know what you're talking about?" he demanded angrily.

She looked at him calmly.

"You don't like it when somebody talks to you the way you talk to them, do you?" she said.

"Damn it!" he cried. "Irish potatoes," he said, forcing himself to speak calmly.

"Shoot. I sure wish they were sweet potatoes instead. I sure would like some candied sweet potatoes. Or mashed up with pecans and then baked with marshmallows on top. My Mama . . ."

She sighed.

"Is that all you think about?" he demanded, still smarting. "Your stomach?"

Her glance dropped to her body, its outlines hidden in the spread, and her face grew forlorn and she sighed again, this

time with infinite sadness. Roberts knew what she was thinking about. Not food for her stomach, but what was developing
inside her. Something cruel hovered on his lips but remained
unsaid. He did not intend letting her know how she had
stung him by turning his own words against him a moment
earlier.

"Don't you ever think about anything but food?" he said,
hoping by rephrasing the question to divert her thoughts.

"Yes," she said miserably. "I think about a lot of other
things."

"Look what else I found," he said, anxious to change the
subject.

He put the blanket on the floor and held up the electric
heater.

"Oh," she said, interested. "A heater. A real nice one, too."
She reached out to touch it, then her face went critical.

"You shouldn't of," she said.

"Shouldn't have what?"

"Stole it."

"Stolen it! Damn it, why . . . All right, if that's the way
you feel I'll take it back, and the potatoes, too."

"That's different."

"How is it different? What's the difference between a heater
and potatoes?"

"Everybody knows the difference between a 'lectric heater
and a sack of potatoes."

He looked at her sharply, resolved not to be blinded by rage
again. Was she putting him on? But she seemed quite serious.

"You know what I mean," he said. "If it's stealing to take
the heater, it must be stealing to take the potatoes."

"No, it ain't. We *need* the potatoes."

"Don't you think I need the heater, too? You think I don't
freeze my . . . I don't get cold at night?"

"Oh," she said awkwardly.

Her response puzzled him. She seemed disappointed and a
little embarrassed. Then he understood.

"You thought . . ." he began incredulously. "You thought
I intended to give it to *you?*"

She looked down at the floor and said in a faltering voice,
'Whatever . . . whatever gave you that idea? I wouldn't take
it if you . . ." she lifted her head and looked directly at him
". . . if you came crawling in begging me to."

"Don't hold your breath waiting for me to do that little
thing."

"Anyhow," she said, determined this time to have the last word, "you stole it."

"Didn't you know?" he demanded. "Niggers steal."

He gathered everything together in the blanket and took it to the kitchen without a backward glance.

Marlene went back inside her room to finish drying her hair. She felt humiliated that he had understood she thought he took the heater for her. She should have known better than to think that. He was so mean and selfish. And anyhow, it was stealing to take the heater. They didn't need it to live like they needed the potatoes. And the potatoes would rot just sitting there in an empty house. She toweled her hair so hard it hurt her scalp.

You can't get it really dry with just a towel in this damp air, she thought. If I just had that old heater for awhile I could dry it real good. She giggled, thinking about the time cousin Fay Marie came to school with a scarf wound around her head like a turban because she'd got too close to the gas heater drying her hair and singed the living fool out of it.

But I wouldn't ask him for it, she thought, no longer giggling. Not if my hair was to freeze into solid ice and crack off at the roots and leave my head as naked as a jaybird.

She heard the bed creak in his room and knew he had gone in there to sit up in bed and read, and was probably warming his feet at the heater he stole. She hoped he got his feet too close and burned them off. It would serve him right. He was plain selfish. Not like most niggers. Whatever else you could say about niggers, you couldn't say they were selfish. No good niggers.

But the comparison no longer rang completely true with her. She could not really judge Roberts in relationship with the other Negroes she had seen and with whom she had had small, impersonal contacts.

None of them talked ugly to her the way he did, or looked her in the face when they talked to her in any way. And they weren't educated like he was, and clever. As much as she still despised him, she had to admit he was clever.

She wound a dry towel around her head and went to the kitchen to see exactly what he had brought, taking pains to be quiet. She did not want him to know she cared about it one way or the other.

Except for the potatoes she was disappointed in his find. No Vienna sausage, no lunch meat. Just cans of peas, kidney beans and spaghetti, and one can of salmon. There was can of fruit salad and she wondered if he had noticed it among the others. If he had not, she could take it to her room and eat it all by herself.

She put the cans in the cupboard, leaving the fruit salad until the last. Then, reluctantly, she put that in the cupboard, too, fearful that he might know he had brought it with the other cans and would miss it.

12

Late that afternoon when Marlene was trying to make up her mind how she wanted her potatoes, Roberts came into the kitchen with the blanket draped around his shoulders. He stretched luxuriously and yawned, his mouth so wide open she could see the glint of a silver filling far in the back. Most niggers got gold fillings if they could afford them, she thought, especially in front. She remembered the time the dentist had told her mama that her mama needed a gold crown and her daddy had got mad and said the dentist was trying to make her teeth look like a nigger's and he wasn't going to pay good money for anything like that and her mama had lost the tooth.

"You know anything to do with potatoes?" Roberts asked. "Other than boil them?"

" 'Course," Marlene replied; then, aware of what he was getting at, "You weren't countin' on *me* cookin' for you, were you?"

"If you want some, you will."

"What you mean by that?"

"You know what I mean. I'm the one who found them, remember?"

"You mean after you been here eatin' me out of house and home you expect to hog all of 'em for your own self?" she demanded indignantly.

"In the first place, it's not your house or your home, or your groceries. And in the second place, I didn't say you couldn't have any. I said if you want potatoes you'll have to cook them. My share, too."

"I don't cook for no . . ."

He wagged a finger at her.

"Careful," he said. "And remember, no cookie, no eatie."

He picked a potato from those she had placed on the table and hefted it appreciatively.

"Look at it," he said. "So round and firm and fully packed

116

During the potato famine there's many an Irishman would've killed for a beauty like this."

"The potato famine?"

He did not feel like exploiting her ignorance at the moment. He had other thoughts.

"You know how I'd like to have this gorgeous potato?" he said. "Baked. With butter and sour cream and chopped chives. And well scrubbed so I could eat it skin and all."

Marlene made a face.

"What's the matter?" he asked. "Don't you eat the skins?"

"Sour cream," she said with a shiver. "Ugh."

"What have you got against sour cream?"

"When our cream clabbers, we throw it to the pigs."

"Which only proves that in this fair state the pigs eat better than the people. Which I happen to find appropriate."

"I never heard of puttin' all that stuff on potatoes, anyhow."

"What do *you* eat on baked potatoes?"

"Salt and pepper. And margarine, like everybody else."

"Margarine. Oleomargarine?"

She stared at him as if he were stupid, a mannerism which she had learned from him.

"You think we're rich?" she demanded.

Taken aback, he shook his head.

"No," he said, "I don't think that. I hardly think that."

He could not recall ever having eaten oleomargarine at home and he was not aware that anyone might think it a symbol of affluence to have butter on the table. He wondered if this white girl would think his family rich. What a switch that would be.

"Anyway," she said, "we ain't got any sour cream. Or butter or margarine neither. Just salt and pepper."

"Baked is out, then," he said regretfully. "Have you any suggestions?"

She put a hand to her chin reflectively.

"You need margarine for mashed potatoes, too, or they're not much good," she said.

She thought about how she always put a big lump of margarine in the center of her mashed potatoes at home and then smoothed the potatoes over it in a mound and ate around the edges until she came to the margarine-drenched core. Her father bawled her out for it whenever he caught her because he said it was a waste of margarine and she was not even getting any of it on most of her potatoes, only the middle part. Or gravy, she thought. Gravy was good, too, and you did it almost the same way. You made a hole in the middle of the potatoes and ate around the edges ever so careful not to punch through and let the gravy run out. And then you pushed in the sides all around and if the walls were exactly the right thickness there was just enough to soak up the gravy and not get any on the greens or whatever else was on the plate.

"So mashed is out, too," he said impatiently. "What else is there?"

"French fried."

His eyes glistened.

"Are you telling me you can make French fried potatoes?"

"You're droolin'," she said, adding pointedly, "Don't you never think about nothin' 'cept your stomach?"

Touché, he thought, but saying aloud, "Damn it, Marlene, I'm hungry."

"An' you ain't used to it, are you?"

"Certainly not. Why should I be?"

"Well, I am. Used to it."

She was not being completely truthful. She had never literally gone hungry. There had been periods when her family had been unable to afford things they liked, but they had never missed a meal. Her parents had, during the Depression, when they were her age. She had heard about that many times when she complained about the food on her plate, but they had never gone without food in her memory.

Yet in a deeper sense Marlene had been telling the truth. There was more to hunger than an empty belly. You could have all the rice and lima beans and even pork you wanted, she thought, but if that was all you had for days on end, with no roast beef or store jelly or peanut butter or pies, then you felt hungry. And Marlene had known that sort of hunger.

She's lying, Roberts thought, not wanting to believe she had gone hungry when he had not. Things did not work out that way in the white world. But if she were not lying, it was her own fault, or at any rate her father's, for being a lousy provider. He could understand and sympathize if she were Negro. If you were Negro, the bastards wouldn't let you make a decent living. But if you were a white man and couldn't make a living, it had to be your own fault.

His father had done well in spite of the bastards, but only because he was more intelligent than they were and willing to work harder. They couldn't hold his old man down, even though they only let him call on the Negro market. But he'd still won sales contests and bonuses. And if he'd been white or, what was more to the point, had the same opportunities they had, he would have gone twice as far. Twice, hell. Ten times. And he still had not done badly. Not badly at all. He had done well enough to own his own home and have weekly household help—strange how many of their succession of once-a-week maids had resented working for other Negroes and would quit when they got a day with a white family—and send his son to college. He'd like to stack his father up against hers. And if his father were to run into her father on a street in this state, her father would call his "boy."

". . . have to peel 'em," she was saying.

"What was that?" he snapped, still burning with the injustice of it.

"When was the last time you cleaned the wax outta your ears? I said all right, I'd cook 'em if you'd peel 'em."

"Me?"

"I don't see nobody else 'ceptin' you, do you?"

"I suppose that's fair enough," he said grudgingly.

She banged around in the cupboards and found a can of shortening, a deep aluminum pot and a strainer. She began spooning shortening into the pot and saw him still sitting idly.

"I thought you was s'posed to peel," she said. "When'd you count on doin' it?"

He shrugged.

"Where's . . . where's the thing I'm suppose to do it with?"

She put her hands on her hips and studied him scornfully.

"Well. If you ain't the most helpless . . ."

She got a basin, filled it with water and put it in front of him, then brought a bowl and a paring knife.

"Hold your hands out," she ordered, very much in charge now there was kitchen work to be done. "No. Palms up."

She slammed the potato he had admired into one hand, the knife into the other. He sat there looking at them.

"Now I s'pose you want me to work your hands for you, like you were one of them puppets?"

"Oh, no," he said with a start.

He began awkwardly peeling thick slabs from the sides of the potato. Marlene, back at her cooking pot, saw what he was doing.

"Can't you do nothin' right?" she demanded, coming back to him and holding up a quarter-inch slab of peel.

"What's the matter with that?" he said defensively. "I'm peeling it, aren't I?"

She giggled. There it was again. Aren't I. How prissy he did talk.

"What the hell are you laughing at?"

"You're throwin' away more'n you keepin', that's what's the matter," she said, no longer amused. "I swear, it looks like you never peeled a potato before in your whole life."

"I haven't," he said defiantly, feeling somehow ashamed at the admission.

"If that don't beat everything! Not in your whole life?"

"Why the hell should I have? I'm not a God-damn cook."

"No need to take the Lord's name in vain," Marlene said primly. "Lookie, you do like this."

She peeled a potato deftly in one long, unbroken spiral, an accomplishment of which she had always been proud, dipped the potato into the basin of water and swiftly cut it into frying-size pieces. Roberts watched, fascinated. It was the first time since his childhood he had paid such close attention to a kitchen chore. He was impressed by Marlene's dexterity. Her practiced movements reminded him a little of his mother's, though Marlene's were less deliberate. The comparison annoyed him almost as much as her mastery of a useful function at which he was so inadequate.

"See how?" Marlene said.

"Peeling potatoes is women's work," he said sullenly.

"If you want fried potatoes tonight, you better start learnin' women's work, then. 'Less you're not smart enough to."

"It's not a matter of brains," he said, but to no effect because she had already returned to her own work.

He began sullenly and painstakingly to peel potatoes. From time to time Marlene sent a sly look his way and once caught him trying unsuccessfully to make a spiral as she had done.

He sure looks just plain nigger right now, she thought. Even got his bottom lip pushed out. She wondered if she should say that aloud and decided against it. No use getting him any madder than he was. He might start in making fun of her again and she would lose her advantage.

He had not peeled nearly enough potatoes by the time the shortening was hot, so she took the paring knife from his willing fingers and finished the job for him.

When she finished frying the potatoes and draining them on paper towels from the cupboard, she divided them scrupulously and took her plate to the drainboard, as usual.

"Why don't you sit down at the table like a civilized human being?" Roberts asked. "Even if you're not."

"I'm fine right here."

Just because I sat down with you talking don't mean I'm going to sit down and eat with you, she thought.

"Look, Marlene," Roberts said with a trace of a smile. "If it's because you don't feel you're good enough to eat with me . . ."

She flushed angrily.

"You think you're so smart!"

He was silent a few seconds, then asked with disarming courtesy, "Will you do me a favor?"

"What kind 'a favor?" she demanded suspiciously.

"Eat a piece of potato for me."

"Eat a . . . Why?"

"I want to try a scientific experiment. Don't you like scientific experiments?"

"Not 'specially."

She shrugged and picked up a piece of fried potato. She dipped it in the pool of ketchup she had poured on her plate and ate it self-consciously under his intense scrutiny.

"Didn't you ever see nobody eat fried potatoes before?" she demanded.

"Not scientifically. Now, sit down over there."

He pointed across the table to the chair she had sat in before. Marlene hesitated.

"It's a scientific experiment," he coaxed. "Don't you want to help the cause of science?"

Mystified and curious, she brought her plate to the table and sat down, her back unnaturally straight and her arms tense.

"Now, Dr. Chambers," he said with mock solemnity, "select a potato of approximately the same proportions and degree of crispness as the specimen previously consumed."

"Huh?"

"This is a very scientific experiment. We must do it scientifically."

Again he watched intently as she dipped a piece of potato in ketchup and munched it.

"Now," he said gravely, "for the most important part of the experiment. How did the first potato taste?"

"Real good."

"How did the second potato taste?"

"It was good, too."

"Real good?"

"Yes, real good."

"I see. Would it be correct to say, then, that if the first potato tasted real good and the second potato tasted real good, one might conclude there was no difference in taste between them?"

"Huh?"

"In simpler terms, did they taste exactly alike?"

"'Course they did. They were cooked the same."

"Q.E.D."

He waited expectantly for her to ask him to explain.

Instead she said, "I know what that means. Q.E.D. We learned it in geometry."

"What does it mean?" he asked, disappointed.

"It means that proves it," she said proudly.

"Close enough."

"Proves what?" she said. "I mean what did the experiment prove."

"It proves a French fried potato tastes the same whether eaten standing or sitting."

"Anybody knows that."

"I haven't finished. Even if the eater happens to be sitting across from a Negro."

Marlene stared at her plate. She was aware that she had been tricked and made a fool of again, yet she was more confused than chagrined. She felt tricked not only by Roberts but by everyone who had contributed to her certainty that it was wrong, even indecent, to eat at the same table with a Negro. She had been so certain it was wrong that she had never even considered what the consequences of such an act might be because she had never dreamed she would have to face the consequences. And now she had done it and there were no consequences. Nothing. She was just sitting there, and he was just sitting there, and that was all.

It wasn't fair, she thought. It was like going to a Fourth of July picnic to see the fireworks and then, when it got dark and the time came, being told there weren't any.

"Anybody knows that doesn't change the taste," she said weakly.

"There must be a good reason why it's so dangerous to eat with a Negro," Roberts persisted. "If it's not that it makes the food taste bad, it must be something else. Maybe it has to do with digestion. How do you feel?"

"I feel fine," Marlene said peevishly.

"No heartburn, nausea, flatulence?"

"I told you, I feel fine," she said, wondering what flatulence meant.

"Maybe later, then. When it reaches the intestinal tract. That's when the trouble may start."

Marlene looked at him coldly.

"You purely do love to hear yourself talk, don't you?" she said.

"I am merely trying to enlighten you," he said stiffly, knowing she was right and resenting it.

"The potatoes are gettin' cold," she said matter-of-factly, bending over her plate.

They ate in silence, Marlene completely absorbed in her food as always. Roberts did not enjoy the meal as much as he had anticipated. It rankled deeply that Marlene seemed to have already forgotten what a travesty he had made of her prejudice and that she had, in the end, scored off him.

Marlene finished the last of her potatoes with a sigh, her contentment slightly flawed by the fact she had not made the potatoes and the ketchup come out even. There was still a dab of ketchup left on her plate. She picked the plate up in both hands to lick it off. With her tongue out and ready to wipe the plate clean, she saw him watching her and put the plate down with the ketchup untouched. Then she stretched contentedly.

"That sure was good," she said.

He envied and resented the simplicity of her needs. He wanted to say something that would hurt her, destroy her complacency, but before he could do so she rose to her feet and said, "We got dessert, too."

"Dessert?"

"Unh-huh. That fruit salad you found. I hope it ain't mostly apples. Sometimes it is."

"I didn't notice any fruit salad."

Shoot, she thought. He didn't know after all. I could of taken it to my room and had it all myself. Oh, well, wouldn't have been right anyhow. He did find it.

She opened the can and divided the contents equally between two saucers. She could not bring herself to wait on him so she put his saucer on the end of the table, where he had to reach for it, and went to the cupboard for evaporated milk. There were only two cans left counting one already opened. There wouldn't have been any if he used it in his coffee like she did, she thought. That was one thing to be thankful for, he didn't use cream in his coffee. But it didn't make a whole lot of difference if he did or not because even with the jar of instant he'd found, they would be running out of coffee one of these days and have to start drinking tea. There was still plenty of sugar, that was one good thing. And he didn't use that, either.

Marlene stood indecisively with the milk can in her hand, wondering whether to use evaporated milk on her fruit salad or save it for coffee. Before long she was going to have to start drinking her coffee black, as he did. So she might as well use some on her fruit salad, she thought.

He watched, bemused, when she poured evaporated milk over her fruit salad and cringed inwardly when she raised a spoonful to her lips.

"You put evaporated milk on fruit salad?" he asked incredulously.

"Didn't you ever see anybody do that before?"

"No. I've seen it served with mayonnaise. And that's bad enough, God knows. But evaporated milk."

"It's good," she said, instantly regretting her words because it might make him want to try some.

"I'll take mine straight, thank you," he said, to her relief.

After a while she said, "This sure is good fruit salad. Lots of peaches and grapes. What do you like best?"

"Watermelon," he said perversely.

"Watermelon? They don't put watermelon in fruit salad."

"I know. Terrible, isn't it? When we all like watermelon better than anything."

He pretended to grow excited.

"Hey, I've got a great idea! Watermelon fruit salad. I'll corner the Negro market."

He watched her closely to see if she realized he was being ironic. As usual, she did not and he felt defeated.

"You can't," she said. "Put watermelon in canned fruit salad. It's too, you know, watery-like."

"You're probably right," he said helplessly.

"I know I'm right."

He reached over and toyed with the milk can. Marlene watched anxiously, pretending unconcern. He poured a few drops on his fruit salad and took a tentative taste. Her interest quickened.

"Not bad," he said. "Not bad at all."

He poured more into his saucer.

Shoot, she thought. He used enough for two nice cups of coffee.

When he finished eating he pushed back his chair and sat with his legs thrust out.

"I wish there was something to do around here," he said.

"Nobody said you got to stay."

He swiveled to face her, putting his hands palm down on the table.

"When I think it's time to leave, I'll leave. And it can't be too soon to suit me. But now is not the time."

" 'Cause you're scared to, that's why. You're 'fraid they'll get you for whatever it was you done. I don't see why. It's been so long since you done it. Whatever it was."

"It's something they're not likely to forget in a hurry. The longer I stay . . . What about you? You can't stay here forever. You'll need a doctor eventually."

"I don't know," she said vaguely, not liking to think about it. "I just don't rightly know. 'Cept stay right here until . . . until . . . I don't know."

"Well, you've still got a little time to make up your alleged mind. I think you're a fool for staying here as long as you have."

"Where else could I go?" she demanded.

"You're asking me? This is your territory, baby, not mine. Where I live, they have places for girls like you."

"If they got 'em where you're from we got 'em here," she said defiantly. "Only better."

"Sure you have. Well, hell, we may both have to pull out before we want to. That cupboard's still pretty bare."

"If it was just me, it would've lasted."

"Don't start on that again. I'll break in the other houses tomorrow."

"Break in?"

"How do you think I got in this morning? I broke a window."

"Broke a window!" she exclaimed disapprovingly.

"Of course I broke a window. How'd you expect me to get in? Say the magic word?"

"But that's hurtin' somebody else's property. And it storms down here sometimes. The wind and rain and everything'll get in and just ruin everything."

"Good."

"Huh?"

"What do I care what happens to it? It belongs to some

redneck. I wish the whole house would get blown to hell. I'd like to see a storm come up big enough to blow away this whole damn state."

"If it did, we'd get blowed away, too," Marlene said earnestly. "This house and us."

She was speaking literally, he knew, yet there was something in her words that struck far deeper than she had intended.

"Yes," he said quietly, "we'd get blowed away, too."

13

One of the houses had a well-stocked cupboard—canned meats, evaporated milk, coffee, vegetables and an open sack of sugar crawling with ants. Shrinking with distaste, Roberts scraped the ants from the sufrace with a spoon and threw them and the top layer of sugar into the sink. The other house had no food of any sort and Roberts was irrationally angry with the owners for having cleaned out the cupboard. Anyone who could afford a summer house should not be so cheap. In a bedroom he found a portable radio and some old magazines which he brought back with him. He gave the magazines to Marlene but took the radio to his room.

Roberts and Marlene began eating together regularly, Marlene having accepted the fact it was more practical than eating separately. Eating alone meant restricting each meal to one thing and neither of them were satisfied with a meal of canned green beans or other vegetables. By eating together they could have two things at a sitting without being prodigal.

Marlene took charge of the kitchen without anything having to be said. Roberts, completely helpless at domestic chores, welcomed her assumption of authority. She selected and prepared the food and joined him at the table but balked at serving him. She always placed his plate at the end of the table where he had to reach for it. This both amused and irritated him.

They washed their own dishes until one night Marlene chanced to take for herself a dish that Roberts had used. She had always been extremely careful to use one particular plate every meal but somehow she got his instead.

"Ugh," she said, halfway through the meal. "This is your plate."

She looked as if she were going to be ill and it made Roberts furious.

"So what?" he snapped. "Do you think it'll poison you to eat from my plate?"

"Look," she said, pointing. "It's dirty."

There was a fleck of food stuck like glue to the edge of the plate. He had not washed it well.

"Hell," he said uncomfortably, "it won't hurt you."

"How would you like to eat off somebody's dirty plate?"

"So I'm a lousy dishwasher," he said, feeling more at fault than he was willing to admit.

"You sure are. And I'll thank you to keep your dirty dishes separate from mine."

"You're the one who got it mixed up with yours, not me."

Damn it, he thought, I'm arguing with her as if I'm as much a child as she is. I should just tell her to go to hell and leave it at that.

"I guess I did," she said contritely. "I'm sorry I talked ugly about it."

Roberts was completely disarmed by this unexpected concession.

"I'll try to do a better job of washing my dishes from now on," he said.

But he could not permit her total victory.

"Tell me something, Marlene. Tell me the truth. If that had been a white man's dirty plate, would it have bothered you as much?"

"Huh?"

She realized to her considerable surprise that she had not even thought about it being a Negro's plate, only a dirty one, and for the moment had not thought of Roberts as a Negro but simply as a messy man who put a dirty plate back in the cupboard.

"You heard me," Roberts said.

Marlene's brow wrinkled. An elusive truth had just been born and she was trying with all her powers to grasp it.

"You know somethin'?" she said with dawning comprehension. "You're just usin' that as an excuse."

"Using what for an excuse?"

"If I'd of thought about it, I'd of died 'fore I'd of ate off a nigra's plate," she said, talking not to him but to herself. "But I didn't think about it," she continued, looking directly at him now. "I almost got sick to my stomach 'cause it was dirty. Maybe I get sick to my stomach easy now 'cause . . . you know. Anyhow, you were the one. You were the one said it about a white man's plate."

He stared at her.

"An' you did it 'cause you didn't want to own up to not washin' it good," she went on.

Roberts was dumbfounded. She was actually trying to think. She was wrong, of course, but that paralyzed little mind of hers was actually functioning. And she was being absolutely honest. She had admitted she would not eat off a Negro's plate if she had thought about it and had made, for her, an even greater admission, that she had not thought about it.

"No," he said. "You're wrong. I wasn't making excuses. I really thought you were upset because it was a Negro's plate. And to tell the truth, I'm surprised that wasn't the reason."

"Well, it wasn't. So there."

Should have been the reason, she thought. And I wish it had of been. Because if it didn't bother me none to eat off a nigger's plate, there must be something wrong with me. Nigger-lover, they'd call her. That was almost the worst word you could call anybody. She remembered how her daddy's face would get when he called somebody a nigger-lover. Almost as mean as it had when he threw her out of the house. What would make him madder, she thought, her losing her virtue or being a nigger-lover? But she wasn't a nigger-lover. She couldn't help being with Charlie Roberts. It was really her daddy's fault if it was anybody's. His and that sorry boy that got her in trouble. Just because she put up with Charlie Roberts, and she only did it because she had to, didn't mean she would put up with just any nigger.

Why did she feel guilty when she thought "nigger" meaning Charlie Roberts? He *was* a nigger, and he was mean to her and he made fun of her for being white. But he was smart, smarter than her, and sometimes he did act right nice. When he wasn't making fun of her for being white or dumb, or wasn't mad at her for something she'd said or done, he acted a lot nicer than plenty of white people. Politer. Like he had manners when he cared about using them. She wondered where he had learned his manners. Probably working for rich white people. Maybe they had sent him to school and everything and that's why he was so smart.

What kind of work had he done for the white people? It couldn't have been in the kitchen. He was too dumb about kitchen work. That was about the only thing he was really dumb about, except some things about white people. Maybe he was a butler, like she had seen in the moving pictures. Or maybe a chauffeur. She had never seen a real butler but she had seen real chauffeurs, two or three. They had been old. She had heard a story about a young one one time, though. Him and the white lady he worked for. She had overheard her daddy tell her mama about it. Her daddy had said in the old days they'd have strung him up and run her out of town instead of just whipping him good and throwing him on a freight and throwing a rock with a note on it through her window, and he didn't know what the country was coming to.

She wondered if Charlie Roberts had been a chauffeur would he have tried to fool around with the white lady, knowing he wouldn't. He hated white people too much and he wasn't like other niggers, anyhow. But how could he have worked for white people if he hated them that much? Probably pretended he didn't. He could be the politest thing when he put his mind to it and you couldn't tell what he was really thinking the way you could with most of them.

Wouldn't that be something, if they had put him through school and all, and all the time he'd really hated them? She'd heard about niggers who had been put through school and everything by rich white folks, even set up in business in niggertown, but they had always turned out to be good niggers who appreciated it. That was because folks in the South could tell a good nigger from a bad one and the folks in the North thought they were all good and it served them right to make a mistake.

Roberts was thinking, too. Could she have been right? *Had* he used his color as an excuse? No. What the hell did he care if he'd missed a spot on a lousy dish? He had thought it made her sick at her stomach to eat from a plate he had used and that had made him sick at his stomach. Sick with resentment. And then he had felt guilty because he was wrong, had misjudged her. Nevertheless, her accusation disturbed him.

There had been other times when he wondered if he were using his blackness as an alibi. He remembered one occasion particularly, and he still felt shame when he thought about it. There was a fraternity he wanted in at college, not because he wanted to be among white boys but because there were certain advantages to being in that particular fraternity, and he had not made it. And he had complained bitterly about it to a Negro classmate, ticking off the ways in which some of

the white boys who had been pledged were less deserving than
he and thereby proving it was his color that kept him out,
only to learn that his friend had been pledged by that
same fraternity. Even now, nine years later, he could not
completely accept the possibility that it had been something
about him other than his color which kept him out of the
fraternity. There could have been a secret quota of Negroes,
or perhaps it was because his friend was an athlete and he
was not. But the fraternity was known to go after scholars,
not muscle men, and his grades had been a shade better than
his friend's.

That was one of the problems of being a Negro that even
the most well-meaning whites usually did not understand. The
problem of trying to face up to yourself honestly when you
had failed in some way and know with certainty whether it
was a personal failure or one forced upon you by the white
world. Just as it was a problem to know with certainty if
your achievements were forced upon you by the white world.

"Do you work?" Marlene asked.

"What? What sort of question is that? Of course I work."

"What kind of work?"

"What the hell brought that up?"

"How come you say hell and damn so much some times
and some times you don't say them at all?"

"God damn it to hell, woman! Sometimes you are the most
exasperating . . . I don't usually say hell and damn unless I'm
provoked, and the reason I say hell and damn so much some
times is because, damn it, you provoke the hell out of me."

"All I did was ask you what kind of work you did," she
said, aggrieved. "I don't see nothing wrong with that. Less'n
it's not honest. Your work, I mean."

Something loosened within him and he shook his head
helplessly, disarmed by her naïveté.

"Maybe it ain't honest," she went on. "Maybe that's why
you have to hide. Is that why?"

"Marlene, you are something else."

"What does that mean, something else? You say that all
the time."

"It means you're really something. Just when I'm certain
you can't stick to a subject you develop a one-track mind.
And to think I always believed a woman had to have a brain
to be interesting."

"It ain't honest, is it? Or you'd say 'stead of beatin' around
the bush."

Roberts laughed.

"I'm an attorney," he said.

Why did I say attorney instead of lawyer? he thought. Am I trying to impress her?

"A lawyer," he amended quickly.

"A lawyer?" she said, visibly impressed. "A real lawyer?"

"What do you mean, *real* lawyer?" he demanded, nettled. "You think a man has to be white folks to be a real lawyer?"

"I didn't mean it like that," she protested, genuinely contrite. "I know there's nigra lawyers. They're some of the ones causin' most of the . . . you know."

"No, I don't know. Suppose you tell me."

"Shoot, you do know, too. You know what I mean."

"I'm trying to find out if *you* know what you mean."

Her expression showed she was trying very hard to follow him, and he waited patiently for her to find words. He was no longer nettled. Perhaps he would find out from her how these people reasoned. Perhaps this simple child could explain the, to him, inexplicable.

She looked surer of herself, as if she had found an explanation for him, and he felt keen anticipation.

"Well," she said, "if you ain't smart enough to figure it out for yourself, I sure can't explain it to you."

"God damn it!" he cried, baffled.

"I wish I hadn't even said nothin' about that old plate. You're carryin' on so."

"Who said anything about the God-damned plate!"

He leaped to his feet and pounded his fist on the table. She jerked upright, her eyes filled with fear.

He let out a huge gust of air and sat down aagin. She giggled.

"What in God's name are you laughing at?"

"You sure do get mad. I wish I had a picture of you when you jumped up and beat on the table."

His anger flared, then flickered out.

"I'm glad you haven't. What is it you think Negro lawyers cause down here?"

"You know, trouble. If it wasn't for them an' some of the others from up North comin' down here to stir up our nig . . . the nigras, we wouldn't have all this trouble."

"You really believe that, don't you?"

" 'Course I do. That's why you came down here, ain't it? To stir up trouble?"

"No."

"Then why did you?"

That's a good question, he thought. Why *did* I come down here?

He had been asking himself that since the night of fear and violence. Had he come out of simple curiosity, to see how things really were down South, if the Southern Negroes were really as brave and dedicated as they represented themselves to be, or had it been from a more admirable motive, to be, for once, on the front line with his fellows, to make common cause with them, to place himself in physical jeopardy—if he had known how much jeopardy would he still have come—and make a personal protest? He had felt guilty not doing anything to help except work on committees and donate legal counsel and money in the safety of his Northern city.

He had come down here expecting to observe, to march with the demonstrators and then get back on the plane for home enlightened and, he admitted to himself, ennobled. But it had not worked out that way. In the end he had committed himself far beyond anything he had anticipated, far beyond any of the other marchers, and committed himself irrevocably.

How many times since that night had he cursed himself for having come South, whatever his motive, petty or profound, and, having come, failing to obey the discipline of the march? If only he had stayed home and worked from there. And yet he was proud, too, for having come and for making the ultimate commitment, for having fought back, for once, with more than briefs and slogans and carefully organized protests.

"I wanted to see for myself," he said at last.

"See what?"

"I don't want to talk about it."

Because he would not be able to make her understand, not even if he revealed more of himself than was wise.

"I'm gonna mark that down with a red crayola," Marlene said. "First time you ever didn't want to talk about somethin'."

They finished eating in silence. Marlene took all the dishes to the sink and washed them.

"It ain't man's work to wash dishes anyhow," she said. "My daddy never washed a single dish that I know of. 'Cept in the army. He said he washed enough then to last him. Were you in?"

"In?"

"You know, the army."

"No," he said.

He had been too young for Korea and later being a student had kept him out of the draft. He often wondered how he would have felt if he had been old enough to go to Korea and fight. Would he have been proud to serve his country or would he have felt bitter about being good enough to shed his blood for democracy without being good enough to enjoy its privileges? He had heard both sides from Negroes who had served. It was confusing. No wonder Negroes had been some of the best and some of the worst soldiers.

"There was this nigra boy who worked in town, Shorty," Marlene said, drying dishes. "He was drafted for Korea. An' he got this, you know, Silver Star Medal? My daddy saw it with his own eyes. He showed it to him, Shorty did. When he got home from the war. My daddy said he was the biggest hero that little town ever had."

I don't understand this, Roberts thought. Can she be talking about a Negro? She actually sounds proud of him.

"Why tell me?" he said.

"Well, you know," she said uncomfortably. "Him bein' a nigra, too, and all."

"What's that got to do with it?" he demanded. "I don't know him and he doesn't know me and I didn't have a damn thing to do with anything he did."

And yet he could not suppress a feeling of pride that a Negro had managed to distinguish himself in such a way that even Southern whites had been compelled to acknowledge it. And yet, damn it, she didn't sound as if she begrudged the admiration. She really sounded genuinely proud of him, as if he were one of her own.

"Was he what you call a good nigger down here?" he asked with deliberate unconcern.

Marlene nodded. It no longer affected her to hear him say nigger.

"My daddy said he wished they were all like Shorty. Then people wouldn't be actin' so crazy like they been doin'. You know, that's the first time I thought about Shorty in the longest. Must of been account of thinkin' about my daddy and the army and all."

Her face grew pensive. Roberts knew she was thinking about home. He felt sorry for her but more than that he felt a helplessness. He could not fathom this ambivalence she shared with other Southern whites or understand how she could reconcile so unquestioningly two opposing views about the Negro. Yet he knew they are not opposing views in her mind. Only in his.

14

Roberts listened to the radio late that night and when at last he turned it off had difficulty falling asleep. And when he fell asleep he had a nightmare, a familiar one, full of terror, pursuit and violence and, in the end, ecstatic frenzy and dread. He cried out in his sleep and Marlene heard him. She was frightened at first, then as his incoherent cries and restless thrashing continued, she felt compassion and the desire to wake him and stop his torment. But she did not do it. She was unwilling to go into his room.

The morning was bright and unseasonably warm. Marlene went to the kitchen and prepared breakfast for two, noting with a sigh how little there was remaining to eat. The cereal and biscuits were long since gone, as well as the canned fruit, and this morning they would eat the last carefully hoarded can of Vienna sausage.

If he hadn't come along I'd still have plenty to eat, she thought with more resignation than bitterness, even if he did bring things from the other houses. I could have done it myself if I had to. I could even have gone to Mr. Treadwell and bought groceries and candy bars and Dr. Pepper.

But she knew she would not have gone to the store even if she were alone because she did not want Mr. Treadwell to know she was living in the house, and anyhow the money she needed to buy food was no longer hers.

Roberts came in yawning, his face haggard.

"You sure were carryin' on last night," Marlene said. "You have a bad dream or somethin'?"

He grew apprehensive, then guarded.

"I don't remember."

"Funny, ain't it? I've done that, too. Had a dream and forgot it all the next mornin'."

Roberts sat down and stared into the coffee she had poured for him. It was in front of his usual place instead of at the end of the table.

"Did I say anything?" he asked casually.

"Huh?"

"When I had this . . . this bad dream?"

"Oh, that. You kind of, you know, yelled somethin'? But it didn't make no sense. Just, you know, kind of a yell. Like somethin' was after you."

"No wonder I feel so bushed. It must have been chasing me all night."

Marlene laughed, then grew serious.

"I purely hate to leave," she said.

Roberts sat up straight.

"What do you mean, leave?"

"We're 'bout out of groceries, that's what."

"Out of groceries? But you can't go. You'll . . ."

"You still worryin' 'bout that? I ain't gonna tell on you. I promised. Shoot, I don't know what you done and I don't care. You didn't do nothin' to me. 'Cept just that one time. And you 'pologized for that."

Roberts believed her and was ashamed of himself for doubting her. He knew that if she wanted to go he would not try to stop her. But he did not want her to go. He realized with a shock of disbelief that he would miss her. She was company and she did not seem nearly so hateful nor as stupid as she once had.

"Anyhow," she continued, "you're gonna have to leave, too. 'Less you can live on air."

Air was no less nourishing than what he had lived on all his life, he thought. Pride and hate. Yet he had grown strong on them. Strong and hard and self-sufficient. Who am I kidding? Strong and hard and self-sufficient. I'm hiding out here like a scared rabbit with an uneducated white girl for company and not making a move to help myself.

Maybe it's what I need. To have to leave. But where to go? Easy for her to talk about leaving. Even if she can't go home. There are places that will take her in and take care of her. But let me show my face in the wrong place at the wrong time . . . If I have to leave here the best I can hope for is another place to hide. But there must be better places to hide than this. Places with things to do and my kind of people. My kind of people. That's a laugh. I did too hell of a good job of cutting myself off from my kind of people. I'm not even my kind of people myself any longer. Not since . . . If I could go to a big city and lose myself there. Find something to do and lead a normal life. Compared with this almost anything would be a normal life. And I've got to leave eventually. I can't stay here forever. It seems as if I already have. And yet, strange, it seems almost like home now. Not home, exactly. The womb. Back to the womb. See nothing, hear nothing, do nothing. Safe, silent and warm. Well, hell, maybe not so warm. And not so silent, when Marlene starts chirping her native woodnotes. But it beats running and looking back over my shoulder. What was it Satchel Paige said about don't never look back?

"I said what was you countin' on doin'?" Marlene was saying.

"What? Oh. I don't know," said Roberts. "What will you do? Go back home?"

Marlene sighed.

"I can't. My daddy . . . Maybe my Aunt Donna."

"Your Aunt Donna?"

"Unh-huh. My mama told me to go there. But I just couldn't." She grew contrite.

"I bet it just worried the fool out of my mama when she didn't hear nothin'."

"Don't you worry about it, Marlene? About your mother not knowing what's become of you?"

"Some. But . . ."

She raised her shoulders helplessly.

"I just can't help it."

"Couldn't you phone her? Or write?"

"You see any phone around here? Or mailboxes? Anyhow, what would I say?"

"Isn't there some relative or friend?"

"I told you. My Aunt Donna. But I just can't go there."

"Why?"

Marlene looked down at her stomach.

"I just can't, that's all."

"Oh, good Lord, Marlene. It's happened to other girls."

"Not to me it ain't. And if Joe Tom and Fay Marie was to find out . . . I'd just die."

"Joe Tom and Fay Marie?"

"My first cousins. And she thinks she's so smart, Fay Marie, livin' in town and drivin' a car and everything."

Oh, Fay Marie, she thought. I remember the good times we used to have when my daddy let me spend the night and we played with our dolls under the covers when everybody thought we were asleep, and the time you came out to the farm and the calf chased you and you cried and I chased him off with a stick. And I'm never, never gonna let you see me with my stomach sticking way out this way and know what I did, or let anybody else see.

"You know what I'd do?" Roberts said.

She looked at him hopefully.

"I'd go to the juvenile authorities. You're a juvenile. Your father has to take care of you. Whether he wants to or not."

Jesus, he thought. I'm sitting here telling her to go to Southern law. I never thought I'd live to see that day. But it must be different for whites.

Her face fell in disappointment.

"You don't know my daddy," she said simply.

Don't I, though, he thought. I know him, all right. I've seen him a hundred times with his foot in somebody's face or standing on the sidewalk jeering. I've run from him and seen him at the end of my fist. Oh, I know him all right. The memory of the white man and his latest nightmare sent a shudder through him.

"You cold? It's so nice and warm today for a change. You oughta not be cold."

He shook his head.

"I'm not cold."

"Somebody walked over your grave, then," said Marlene. "What?"

"When you shiver like that for no reason at all it means somebody walked over your grave. Didn't you know that?"

It's not as foolish as it sounds, he thought. Because I've been the same as dead and buried since . . . And this house is my tomb. But not really. I'm alive and functioning. And while there's life there's hope. That's a white man's cliché. His mind seized on the conceit. While there's life there's rope. That's what there is for Charlie Roberts. His mind seized on the conceit. While there's life there's rope. He who hesitates is lost. Unless it's Charlie Roberts. Then it's he who acts is lost. He had acted and he was lost. He wouldn't stand for it. They couldn't make him be lost. He'd go back home and get a good lawyer. He knew good lawyers. He was one himself. But why kid himself? If he did, they'd bring him back here. And then the best lawyer in the world couldn't help him. He was a responsible citizen. A professional man with a reputation. But it wouldn't make any difference to a redneck jury. They saw no difference between him and any ignorant cotton picker.

"You sure are quiet," said Marlene.

"What? Oh, I was thinking."

His case appeared hopeless, but what about her? The world was wide open for her if she only had sense enough to realize it.

"Look," he said. "You're going to have to go somewhere. You can't stay here and slowly starve to death. You already look as if you haven't got two red corpuscles to rub together. You need good food and plenty of it. You and your . . ."

Some unanticipated delicacy of feeling kept him from finishing the thought. And his firm tone caused her to look at him expectantly.

"Where can I go?" she asked, not challengingly but as if awaiting counsel.

"Well," he replied, feeling awkward and unwillingly familial. "If you're sure you aren't welcome at home and won't go to your Aunt Whatshername . . ."

"Donna. My Aunt Donna."

"And there isn't anyone else? Another aunt or uncle? A married brother or sister?"

"I'm the only baby my mama had. That lived. Before I was born she had this little boy. If he'd of lived he'd be . . . No, there ain't nobody."

"There must be places would help you. Even down here."

"I don't know of none."

"They're not hard to find."

"How?"

"Go to a social agency."

"I wouldn't go to no place like that."

"An agency could send you where you'd be taken care of. They wouldn't care if you weren't married. Look, those places take care of hundreds of other girls just like you. They know what to do."

"They'd make me have the baby."

"What do you mean, make you have the baby? You're going to have it whether you go somewhere or not."

"Maybe not."

"What do you mean, maybe not?" he demanded, beginning to grow angry.

"Well, maybe if I just stay here and don't do nothin' to help it'll . . . you know, just stop growin' or somethin'."

"It's going to keep growing whether you help it or not. That's nature. Unless you do something to yourself. Would you rather die than have a baby?"

"Die? Shoot no. Who said anything 'bout dyin'?"

"It's a purely academic question anyway. You'll have to leave whether you want to or not."

"What does that mean? A academic question?"

He started to give a curt, facetious answer but, realizing she was truly interested in knowing, curbed his temper.

"It means this discussion is theoretical, not practical." When he saw she still did not understand, he continued. "It means I'm really only talking to hear myself talk. The fact is you can't stay here when the food is gone even if there isn't anywhere else to go."

And that applies to me, too, he thought ruefully. Here I am trying to advise her and I haven't the remotest idea what I'll do myself when the food is gone.

"We still got three or four more days' groceries," Marlene said. "Maybe we'll think of somethin' before then."

She seemed to take comfort from that, somehow, and Roberts envied her complacency and was determined to shake it. She had to face facts sooner or later.

"Such as?" he demanded.

She went to the back door and looked out.

"Somethin'," she said, stretching. "It sure is pretty today. Less us go for a walk on the beach."

Roberts shook his head and laughed helplessly.

"Less us go for a walk on the beach," he said unbelievingly. "That will solve everything."

She turned to face him.

"It's better than just sittin' here feelin' sorry for ourselves, ain't it?" she said calmly.

Was that what he had been doing? he wondered. Feeling sorry for himself? He had said nothing to give her that impression, had he? He had only been talking to her about her problem, trying to help her. Why should he? Try to help her? When she didn't seem to want help, or even realize she needed help? There was no one trying to help him, and God knew he was in a worse jam than she was.

"Why not?" he said, getting to his feet.

They walked across the shell road and into the strip of woods separating it from the beach, Marlene leading the way. Being out of doors gave Roberts a sense of release which he knew to be false but which nonetheless raised his spirits. Marlene had not been so illogical in wanting to go for a walk after all, he thought.

A cottontail rabbit exploded from a clump of dry weeds at Marlene's feet and disappeared in a frantic zigzag of

brown and white. Roberts fell back in near-terror at the
sudden sound and movement and Marlene gave a small cry.
Then she giggled.

"You see that?" she said. "You ever see anything run so
fast?"

"Where did it come from?" Roberts asked a little breathlessly.

Marlene caught the significance of his tone and said, "Sure
scared the fool outta you, didn't he? Me, too, at first. The way
they don't run till you practically step on 'em."

"It was a rabbit, wasn't it?" Roberts said, breathing more
normally.

She looked at him in disbelief of such ignorance.

"What'd you think it was, a grizzly bear? 'Course it was a
rabbit."

"I'm a city boy," Roberts said defensively, hardly aware he
had called himself boy to a white person.

"You sure are."

She resumed her dilatory walk toward the beach, reaching
out to pluck red berries from a glistening green yaupon tree
and then to pull at a dangling tuft of moss. Roberts tried to
match his pace to hers and found it insufferably slow. She
moved so aimlessly he was obliged several times to stop
abruptly to keep from running into her. He did not like to
dawdle.

"I had me a rabbit once," she said, looking back over her
shoulder. "A white one. My daddy bought him for me one
Easter. Bunny Boy. That was his name."

Her face softened with sweet nostalgia.

"He sure was cute."

"They're good to eat, aren't they?" Roberts said. "Rabbits?"

Her face grew stricken.

"Why'd you say that?"

"I'm hungry. Why?"

"I was thinkin' about Bunny Boy."

It had been very small when her daddy bought it and he
had kept it hidden behind the barn in a chicken-wire cage
for her to find at Easter when she went looking for the Easter
Bunny nest he made out of moss and which her mother had
filled with dyed eggs and jelly beans. He had not expected
it to live, but Marlene had tended it so devotedly that it
not only had survived but had grown so enormously her
daddy began making jokes about it being eating size.

She had not understood he was only joking and was terrified. She was so upset she scarcely had been able to eat or sleep. Her mama thought she was sick and dosed her with home remedies that only made her more miserable. Marlene had been afraid to tell her mama what was troubling her because she thought her mama would be on her daddy's side and she managed to keep it a secret until one night she crept out before dawn to make sure Bunny Boy was safe and her mama had caught her.

Later in the morning her daddy assured her he was only joking but she had not believed him. This angered him so that he said if she did not believe her own daddy he was really going to eat Bunny Boy just to punish her, and she had been as near to hysterics as she ever was before or since, counting the time she was baptized and felt the Holy Spirit entering into her. In the midst of the uproar—her daddy was yelling and she was wailing—her mama went quietly out of the house and let the rabbit out of its cage. It was the first time Marlene's mama had ever done anything to oppose her daddy.

For days afterward Bunny Boy would come back and hop around the house and then it stopped returning and eventually Marlene had forgotten him, until now. And she wondered, would her daddy really have eaten it.

"Guilty conscience?" Roberts asked.

"Huh?"

"You're so quiet. Did you eat Bunny Boy?"

"I should say not!" Marlene cried indignantly. "I kept him till . . . till he just grew old and died. And then I buried him in this little grave. An' . . . an' my daddy made me this little tombstone for him out of a cedar shingle and took his knife and cut 'Here Lies Bunny Boy' on it just as nice."

Oh, Daddy, she thought, why'd you have to go and say you were going to eat him and scare me so and throw me out of the house with no place to go and oh, Mama, why couldn't you help me like you did Bunny Boy?

"You certainly must have been attached to that rabbit," Roberts said. "You've got tears in your eyes."

"I have?" she said, surprised, wiping her eyes with the back of her hand. "I wish I had me a rabbit again. Maybe we can catch one. There's this kind of trap you can make out of wood. An' you put in carrots and lettuce and when he gets in you pull the string and it comes down on top of him."

"If we had any carrots and lettuce, I wouldn't waste it on

a rabbit. But that's not a bad idea about a trap. You know how to make one?"

Marlene shook her head.

They were at the beach now. It lay broad and tawny as peanut butter and hemmed in white froth where the waves dropped their crests as they came purling in from the inexhaustible green of the Gulf of Mexico.

"Great," said Roberts. "Just great."

He looked around apprehensively.

"Can anybody see us?" he demanded.

"Unh-unh. Not unless we were to go all the way to the end up there."

Marlene knelt impulsively and let a double handful of sand dribble through her fingers.

"Sand feels so funny," she said. "Like dry water. An' it's nice and warm. Feel."

Roberts squatted self-consciously and dug his hands into the sand.

"It is warm," he said, delighted. "And it's almost December already. You'd think people would want . . . Marlene, maybe they'll be coming back."

She knew he meant the people who owned the houses.

"Unh-unh," she said confidently. "He said they didn't come back till summer."

"Who said?"

"Mr. Dough . . . a man that gave me a ride in his car one time."

She wanted to tell him how funny Mr. Doughface had looked, but the memory of the way the man had acted still embarrassed her and she did not.

She took off her shoes and socks and worked her feet into the sand. She giggled.

"It feels so funny," she said breathlessly. "Sand squishing between your toes. Why don't you take you shoes off, too?"

"I'm a grown man," Roberts said uncomfortably. "I don't play in the sand."

"Aw, come on," she coaxed. "Try it. It feels good."

He looked around doubtfully, as if there might be witnesses to his folly, then sat down and took off his shoes. His long brown toes stuck out of the ends of his socks. Marlene giggled again.

"That's why you didn't want to take your shoes off," she teased. "You got holes in your socks."

"I can't help that," Roberts said belligerently. "I've been wearing the same pair every day for . . ."

Then he began to laugh, too, and wriggle his toes.

"I'd darn 'em for you if I had some yarn," Marlene said. "Mama does it with a real egg."

"Darn socks with an egg?"

"You put the sock over it, silly," she said, laughing. "An' use a darning needle."

"The shape these are in, you'd have to weave me a new pair."

He took off his socks and dug his feet into the sand.

"Don't it feel funny?" Marlene asked.

"Great."

"I know what. Less us build a castle."

"You build it," Roberts said, leaning back on his elbows. "I'll watch."

She began digging, piling and shaping and after a while forgot his presence in her total concentration on the project. Her tongue protruded slightly and from time to time she would push back her hair with the back of a sandy hand.

How like a child, Roberts thought, watching her paternally. Pregnant, almost out of food, nowhere to go and no one to go to, and she was building a sand castle as if it were the most important thing in the world. He envied her.

She looked up and saw him watching and for an instant was drawn out of her preoccupation.

"How you like it so far?" she asked hopefully.

"Fine. How soon can I move in?" He could not resist adding, "Or is it segregated?" and was sorry when he had done so.

But Marlene only shook her head in mild reproof and said, "Silly," and returned to work.

Having an audience prompted her to the most ambitious structure she had ever attempted. The castle rose almost a yard square, with oddly shaped turrets and battlements. Only her head and shoulders appeared above her creation as she crouched behind it, patting and molding. Behind her the waves came bounding in to deposit their crowns of froth on the tawny sand.

Roberts, lulled by the warmth and the sounds, felt his eyes closing and only with an effort kept them half-opened. If he lay back now he knew he would fall asleep and he was considering doing that when a gasp from Marlene brought him fully awake. Her mouth was open, as if with pain, and there was a bereft look in her eyes.

"What's the matter?" Roberts cried, scrambling to his feet. "You hurt yourself?"

"It moved," Marlene said in a trembling voice.

"What moved?"

He came around the sand castle and stood looking down at her. Both her hands were pressed against her distended stomach.

"It's alive," she said, as if she had been betrayed. "It's really alive."

"Oh," said Roberts, dropping to his knees beside her.

"It kicked," Marlene said dully. "I felt it just as plain."

"Is that all? I thought it was something awful."

"It was somethin' awful. Can't you see? It's alive. It really is."

"Of course it is. You knew that. Why did you think you were getting bigger?"

"I don't know," she said distractedly. "I just don't know. An' I thought maybe . . . Oh, I don't know what I thought."

But she had thought somehow it would never happen, that something would save her. But even that false comfort was gone now.

There's a little live baby inside me, she thought. There really and truly is and it's trying to get out.

She pressed her hands against the place where she had felt the kick but it was not repeated. Maybe she had only imagined it. But it had been too real. There was a baby in there, really and truly. Playing possum now, she thought, or resting. She thought about a baby, fully formed like the dolls she had played with, with its tiny hands clenched into little fists. And it was in there inside her. And some day it was going to get out. There was no escaping it and she didn't have a husband or anything.

Roberts helped her gently to her feet.

"Don't be so upset," he said soothingly. "It's only natural for a baby to kick. You'll be all right."

She shook her head.

"You can say that," she said bitterly. "You're a man."

In the midst of his concern he was suffused with a sudden and to him, unflattering, elation. For the moment, at least, she saw him not as a Negro but as a man. It was an achievement of sorts but he had let it affect him as if it were the most remarkable thing in the world. Was he that desperate for white approval that he should be so affected? But he didn't give a damn for white approval. He knew that. It was on thing he did know. He had nourished himself too long on white disapproval, so much so that at times he was displeased that he should care enough one way or the other even to welcome disapproval. The ideal was not to give a damn one way or the other, to be equally unaffected by approval or disapproval. Could he let Marlene change that, something he had clung to and lived by?

"Am I?" he said. "I thought I was a nigger."

And he was immediately sorry for having said it. Now was not the time.

Marlene gave him a disconcerted, hurt look, her eyes filling with tears.

"How can you talk to me like that?" she said, plaintively. "When everything's so . . ."

She could not finish.

"I'm sorry, Marlene. I really am. I said it because . . . because I was mad at myself."

"Mad at yourself?"

In her perplexity she no longer seemed quite so forlorn.

"It's very complicated," Roberts said. "Why don't we just forget it. Go on and finish your castle."

Marlene sighed.

"It ain't fun no more," she said. "Less go back."

15

Marlene and Roberts put on their shoes in silence and started back. Marlene was nervous and preoccupied and walked more quickly than was her habit. In the woods, she reached out and plucked a tuft of moss from a drooping branch. Roberts watched curiously while she shaped it absently into a mustache and beard. Though she obviously was not fully aware of what she was doing, she nevertheless shaped the moss with care.

"What's that you're doing?" Roberts asked.

She turned and gave him a wan smile, then held the moss to her face.

"Santa Claus," she said. "Don't I look like Santa Claus?"

Good God, Roberts thought. At a time like this.

"You look more like the bearded lady in a carnival side-show," he said.

"I do?" she said, laughing, pleased with herself. "I was to the fair. My daddy took me. But he wouldn't let me see the freaks."

She pouted a little at the memory of the old injustice and then, with returning awareness of her present predicament, grew sad and silent.

Back in the house, she sat with her hands folded over her round stomach as if awaiting an unwelcome indication of life. Roberts paced the length of the kitchen table kneading his scalp with his fingertips in heavy concentration. Even in his preoccupation he was aware that his hair was long and matted, the longest it had ever been since his early childhood and thought irrelevantly of how his mother had cried when his father took him to the barber for the first time. Or at any rate, how he had been told she had cried, for he had been too young to remember at the time.

"Look," he said, stopping in front of Marlene. "You can't stay here any longer. You know that, don't you?"

"Why not? If we could just get us some groceries . . ."

"We can't. But that's not the principal reason."

She looked at him expectantly.

"You need special food and special care. Or it'll be dangerous for you and the baby, too."

"I don't care about the baby. I wish it . . ."

"Don't say it," Roberts said quickly, irked with himself at what he knew to be a concession to superstition. "Some day you may be sorry you did."

"But I can't have a baby," she wailed. "I just can't!"

He squatted in front of her, steadying himself with a hand on the leg of the chair.

"You're going to have to, Marlene. Whether you want it or not. It's out of your hands. You've got to face it."

"What can I do?" she asked hopelessly.

"What I told you this morning. There are agencies in any large city that will help you."

"How'd I get to a city?"

"The same way you got here. Hitch a ride. Catch a bus."

"I couldn't. I just couldn't."

"Why couldn't you?"

"I don't want folks to see me this way. They'll . . ."

"They won't do anything. They won't know you're not married unless you tell them. And you don't have to tell anyone until you get where they'll help you. And they won't care. They're accustomed to this sort of thing."

"I ain't."

"I know that, Marlene. But it won't be as bad as you think. I promise you."

"That's easy for you to say," she said with a burst of spirit. "I don't see you breakin' down the door to leave here."

"It's different with me."

"It sure is. You ain't the one goin' to have a baby."

"Damn it, won't you understand! Can't you realize I'm in worse trouble than you are?"

Marlene bit her lip, trying to hold back tears.

"Don't talk mean to me," she said. "Not just now, with the baby an' . . . an' everything."

"Sorry," he said more quietly. "I'm not talking mean. I'm just talking sense. Plain, common sense."

"Don't make me leave," she implored. "Not like my daddy did. Please."

He was touched.

"I'm not *making* you leave," he said gently. "It's for your own good. You think I want to be here all alone?"

The words were out before he could stop them, even before

he knew he was going to say them. He had not intended to stay in any case despite the dangers which might await him. Then why had he said them? But he knew why. He did not want to be alone and, more than that, he had become accustomed to Marlene's inconsistencies, her childish delight in simple things, her naïveté and even her ignorance to the point where he actually enjoyed them. She was so artless he could no longer resent the fact she was white and the most bigoted kind of white, and yet she had a sort of instinctive shrewdness and wit, too, the source of which she understood no better than he.

And despite her deeply rooted prejudices against Negroes she had learned to accept him as a man. And that, he knew, was the true reason he hated to see her go, that and the fact that when she left he would leave, too, to face a perilous future. He had been putting off reality as much as she had, he knew, and perhaps as mindlessly.

The realization he had grown attached to her largely because she accepted him as a human being disturbed him. He told himself again, as he had done so often in recent days, that he should not care what she thought of him. And again he asked himself if he was impressed because a white person had accepted him for what he was or simply because another human being had accepted him as a human being with whatever faults and virtues he might have. She was still more a white than simply a human being to him. Was he still more a Negro than simply another human being to her? He wanted very much to know that. He stared into her face for an answer, conscious that his legs and thighs were cramped from remaining so long in a squatting position.

But he did not find his answer. She was smiling, her eyes still tear-filled but no longer forlorn.

"You mean I can stay if I want to?" she said.

Roberts sighed and rose groaning to his feet, and pressed his palms against the aching small of his back.

"Give you an inch and you take a mile," he complained. "Marlene, how can you stay? There's no food, nothing. And eventually you'll need a doctor. You should have begun seeing a doctor long ago."

"Not for four, five months," she argued. "And maybe by then . . ."

"Four or five months? You can't possibly stay here that much longer. Even if we had food and clothing and soap and . . ." he wanted to say toilet paper but that seemed both ludicrous and indelicate ". . . and all the other things we need."

"Why not? I already been here about three."

You only see what you want to see, he thought, frustrated. But are you so wrong?

He looked at her. Why not try to work it out? The longer he stayed out of sight, the better chance he had of getting away when he left. In another few months the whole thing might be ancient history. There could be other incidents to push it into the background.

Interpreting his silence as assent, Marlene rushed on.

"And maybe we could catch fish or something and find some vacant houses like these ones where people left stuff."

"I thought you were against breaking into other people's houses," he said, weakening.

"Well, I am, but we can't help ourselves."

"I've made a convert to expediency, haven't I?"

"Expediency?"

"Doing anything to get what you want, whether it's right or wrong."

"You sure do know lots of words," she said admiringly.

"Marlene, I've said it before and I say it again. You are something else."

"How come?"

"Don't question it. Just believe it."

"Unh-huh," she said impatiently. "But can I stay?"

"Yes," he said, sighing, "you can stay. If we find a way to keep ourselves fed."

"Like I said," Marlene said eagerly. "Fish, and stuff from other houses."

"We can't catch fish with our bare hands. And even if I could find empty houses with food in the cupboard, it wouldn't necessarily be what you need. Not in your condition."

"I wish you wouldn't talk about my condition," she said disapprovingly.

"Damn it," he began, and then laughed helplessly. "We can't ignore it," he continued in a less vehement tone. "If it weren't for your condition, you wouldn't be in the spot you are. But I won't nag you about it. Okay?"

"Okay."

He began pacing again. Food was the most immediate necessity. There was only a few days' supply and even that was not suitable for a vigorously pregnant girl. He had not realized until now how undernourished Marlene looked, all eyes and distended belly. There must be farms where he could get milk and eggs and other fresh foods. That's what she needed. And nourishing staples. But how to get them? They had no money except for the fourteen dollars under the cup and he could not blandly walk up to a farmhouse and bargain. The farmer might start wondering about a strange Negro in the area. He could steal, but that was dangerous. He knew that only too well from his experience at the store. But the store was there, and they had some money.

"Marlene," he said abruptly. "You're going shopping."

"Huh?"

"At that store up the highway. What was his name? Treadwell? With our fourteen dollars."

"I can't do that," she said, appalled.

"You worried about the money not being yours? Forget it. Expediency's the word, remember?"

"It ain't the money, it's Mr. Treadwell."

"I thought he was a friendly type. To whites, anyway."

"Well, he is. But I told you. I'm s'posed to be in New Orleans. Anyway," she continued desperately, looking down at her stomach, "he'd see me this way."

"Maybe he wouldn't remember you. It was weeks ago, you said."

"Oh, he'd 'member me, all right. Way he talked, he don't get too many people in there."

"What if he does? You can tell him you got married and moved back here or something."

She shook her head.

"He might suspicion something. Like where do I live and how come he don't know my husband if it's around here."

"I doubt that. But you'll have to take the chance."

She shook her head again and it angered him.

"Have you a better suggestion?" he demanded.

"Unh-huh."

He waited.

"You go," she said hesitantly.

"Me? Are you out of your mind?"

"He wouldn't think nothin' of a nigra comin' in. There's lots of 'em around here I bet he don't know. I bet he'd be glad. He said they don't trade with him much."

"No wonder. Last time I was in his store he wanted to shoot my head off."

"You was stealin', that's why. Did he see who you were?"

"It was too dark."

"Well, then, he wouldn't know you from Adam," she said complacently, then giggled.

"What in the hell are you laughing at?"

Marlene hunched up her shoulders in childlike glee.

"Mr. Treadwell not knowin' you from Adam. Adam was white."

"Who says?"

"The Bible."

"Where?"

"I don't know. The preacher said so. But shoot, you go to his store, he won't suspicion nothin'."

"Suspect," Roberts said absently.

"Huh?"

"The word is suspect. Not **suspicion**. Suspicion is a noun. Suspect is a verb."

"I know that. It's just the way I . . . the way I talk, is all. You know somethin'?" she continued bashfully.

"I think I do, until I start talking to you."

"No, I mean it. I kind of like it when you tell me words. It's like at high school, you know?"

"I'm flattered, Miss Chambers. But that's not putting any food on the table."

"Like I said," Marlene said firmly, as if proving her point. "You got to go to the store."

"And like I said, I can't."

"I thought you was the one so worried about my condition."

He was startled, amused and a little admiring.

"I thought we weren't talking about your condition."

"You got to go to the store," she said stubbornly.

"I still think it's too dangerous," he said, but with lessening conviction.

"Shoot, I told you he's not goin' to suspicion . . . suspect a nigra." She paused, her eyes narrowing in thought. "Not 'less you cause him to."

"Don't you think I've got enough sense not to make a slip?" Roberts demanded, bristling.

"That ain't it, exactly."

"Then what is it, exactly?"

"You just don't act like a nigra."

"I don't know if that's a compliment or an insult. But I'll give you the benefit of the doubt."

She shook her head.

"Neither one. It's just if you go actin' like you do, he'll

know you're from up North and then he *will* suspicion something's funny."

"So I don't go to the store after all. Is that what you're trying to tell me?"

"You are the . . ." she began, exasperated. " 'Course you have to go to the store. But you got to know how to act."

"I tell you, I know how to act."

"Show me." `

"Show you?"

"Unh-huh. Act like I was Mr. Treadwell."

"That's the most ridiculous thing I ever heard of."

"No it ain't, neither. Go 'head."

Roberts sighed.

"All right,' he said. "You're supposed to humor a pregnant . . . Sorry."

Marlene was too engrossed in her project to take offense at his slip.

"Go 'head," she said.

Roberts hesitated. What was so special about talking to a storekeeper? He had always bought at markets where you went in and took what you wanted off a shelf and then got checked out by a cashier. When you did buy something at a little store where there was a clerk, you told him what you wanted and he got it down for you and that was that. As simple as that.

"Look, Marlene," he said. "Why make such a big production of it? I just go in, see what's there and tell him what I want. Okay?"

"You just don't know nothin', do you?" she said severely.

She had been thinking back, remembering exactly how Negroes behaved in stores. It was difficult for her because though she had been present with them many times she had not really seen them. There had been no reason to notice and they always stood back until the white folks were through. But the pattern was so unvaried that she was able to evoke it. And it also helped to remember how Negroes acted around her father.

"In the first place," she said patiently, "you just don't say nothin' when you go in."

"I don't say anything?"

"No, sir!"

Roberts did not recall ever having heard "sir" used in quite that way before by a white person. He had heard it ironically, reluctantly, self-consciously and, on a few occasions, naturally, but Marlene was not sirring him in any of those ways, she was only using the word for emphasis.

"You just go in and wait till he asks you what you want," she continued.

"I don't get it."

"You are the dumbest white man!"

"What did you say?" Roberts demanded, stunned.

Marlene raised her hands helplessly.

"See?" she said. "You even get me mixed up the way you act. That's just what I say to somebody that's really dumb."

"Oh," Roberts said, understanding. "I get it. Negroes are expected to be dumb so it wouldn't especially mean anything to tell one he was. But when a white is dumb . . . Is that it?"

"Lordie," said Marlene. "We could starve to death 'fore you get to the store, the way we're goin'. Lookie, you go out and come back in like you were comin' into Mr. Treadwell's."

"Go out and come back in? Oh, come on, now."

"You got to start at the very beginnin'. You don't know nothin' at all 'bout how to act. Not one thing."

"Oh, hell. All right. Anything to humor you, Marlene."

He went outside and came back in feeling ridiculous. He looked at her expectantly.

"You done wrong already," she said disgustedly.

"What is it this time?"

"You ain't supposed to look at me."

She remembered clearly how nigras always looked down at the ground or off in the distance or anywhere except at the person they were talking to. She had taken that for granted in the past and so had not really noticed it, but now it was important.

"Not supposed to look at you?"

"You just stand there and wait till I ask you what you want. I told you that right at the very first."

He sighed and said, "But you didn't say not to look at you."

"I'm sayin' it now. You kind of look down at the floor, you know? All right?"

"All right."

He looked down at the floor, feeling more ridiculous than ever.

"You want somethin'?" Marlene demanded gruffly, trying to sound like a man.

Roberts was startled as much by the tone as the question but recovered quickly. He found he was concentrating despite his reservations.

"Yes," he said.

"Yes, sir," Marlene corrected. "An' try to talk, you know, Southern like."

"Yes, suh."

"Good. Now say what you want."

"Okay. Say, what do I want? We haven't decided that yet, have we?"

"Oh, 'vaporated milk, margarine, rice, stuff like that. I'll make you a list."

"You've got to have eggs and meat and fresh vegetables."

"How much'a them you think we can buy for fourteen dollars?"

"I don't know. Not much, huh?"

"Not near enough for as long as we're gonna stay. Now. Say what you want."

"I'd like some evaporated milk, margarine . . . Oh, hell, Marlene. I feel so silly."

She clapped a hand to her head as she had so often seen him do.

"I told you you got to talk more Southern like, Charlie! An' you looked at me again. I swear, I just know we're goin' to starve if we have to depend on you. You ain't never goin' to learn how to act at Mr. Treadwell's."

"The hell I won't!" he cried angrily, thinking, Now she's managed to make me want to go, and how the hell did I ever let her talk me into it in the first place?

"All right," she said patronizingly. "Go 'head. But just try to remember what I told you."

"Don't worry about me holding up my end," he said curtly. "Let's make the list."

They sat down at the table and made a list of the most inexpensive, wholesome and easy to prepare staples, with Marlene making the decisions. She had had far more experience than he at stretching a dollar, Roberts realized.

When they finished, Marlene hesitated a moment and then asked shyly, "Charlie, if they's any money left, will you bring me a sack of jelly beans? And lickrish?"

16

It was warm again next morning, for which Roberts was grateful. Even had the day been bitter cold he would not have been able to wear the coat he had stolen from Treadwell. He walked to the highway wearing the fishing pants and the oversize khaki shirt he had found in his room. Marlene had assured him Treadwell would not think it strange if the shirt was too large because Negroes often wore clothes that did not fit.

He had a sense of freedom at being away from the house but was apprehensive about his encounter with Treadwell. What if the man recognized him? That was unlikely because Roberts was certain his face had not been seen the night he broke into the store. But he might betray himself in some unanticipated way. He was not nearly so confident he could play a Southern Negro as he had led Marlene to believe. He was a lawyer, not an actor. He looked the role, however, he thought ruefully. Hair unkempt, face unshaven, clothes ill-fitting and shoes badly worn. Marlene had told him it was a good thing the shoes were cracking and unshined. They were expensive city shoes, not at all the sort a farm Negro would wear unless they were white hand-me-downs.

He had walked only a few yards up the highway when a peeling, slick-tired old pickup truck pulled off the shoulder ahead of him and its Negro driver called back to him.

"Hey, man, wheah you headin'?"

Roberts hurried to the truck. The driver wore a shapeless sweat-stained felt hat and bib coveralls over a faded wool shirt.

"I'm goin' to the store," Roberts said.

"Mistuh Treadwell's?"

Roberts nodded, not knowing how much of himself he dared reveal to the man.

"Things is cheapuh in town."

"Too far to go."

The man nodded.

"Git on in," he said, opening his door. "Ah'll carry you theah."

Roberts reached for the door handle on the passenger side and found it gone. The driver got out and stood waiting.

"Got to git in on this side," he said. "Doah don' wuk."

"Thanks," said Roberts.

He walked around and slid under the wheel and across the ruptured seat. The driver got in and looked at him sidelong as he nursed the engine into starting.

"You fum roun' heah?" he asked.

Roberts shook his head.

"Din think so," the driver said.

"Why not?" Roberts demanded edgily.

If he could tell, Treadwell would be able to tell.

"Ain' seen you befoah. Wheah you stay?"

"Back there," Roberts said vaguely.

"Unh-huh."

They were moving along the highway now, the truck's motor laboring. Roberts studied his companion. There was a straggle of wiry hairs on the man's face and the sweat stains at his armpits had a look of permanency. The inside of the cab reeked with a sweetish stench and Roberts wondered if it came from the truck or the driver, decided it probably was a little of each. Probably hadn't washed for days, Roberts thought, realizing he, too, needed a bath. During the cold weather he had not bathed every day. It was frigid in the bathroom, though the electric heater had helped, and they were short on soap. The man was concentrating on his driving, the wheel wobbling loosely in his heavy, scarred hands. His mouth was slightly open, giving him an oafish look.

Roberts wondered if he gave a damn about voting, or sending his children, if he had any, to a decent school.

No wonder they treat you like swine down here, Roberts thought. How do you expect them to show you any respect when you don't have enough for yourself to show a little intelligence? And take a bath once in a while? He felt a stirring of anger. Why the hell don't you take a little more pride in yourself, you stupid clown? You make it hard on all of us. They equate us all with you. They. What do I mean by "they"? he thought. White people, that's who I mean. And he was filled with shame. I'm playing their game. It's easier for them when they keep us divided. And God knows we were divided long enough. But no longer.

What did he care what white people thought, and how could he blame this man for being a victim? He'd been behind the eightball from birth, and his parents before him and their parents before them.

Roberts had thought things were bad in the North until he had come South and seen the real, naked pressure applied. In the North a man could fight back in some ways. Down here he was in a straitjacket.

But despite his shame, Roberts still was unable to think of the man sitting next to him as his equal.

"You from around here?" he asked in an effort to be friendly.

The driver nodded, keeping his eye on the road, nursing the wobbly steering wheel.

"You a farmer?"

The man nodded again.

"You ever have eggs or milk to sell? Fresh vegetables?"

The man turned to look at him, grinning and showing a gold tooth.

"Nah. Ah grows cotton."

The grin grew sly.

"You fum up Noth."

It was a statement, not a question.

"No," said Roberts warily. "Why do you think so?"

"Oh, no, you ain't fum up North. Not much you ain't."

"What difference does it make if I am?" Roberts demanded, thinking, Oh, Jesus, if this simpleton can tell, Treadwell won't have any trouble telling, too. Maybe I just won't go in. And something else in the back of his mind said, I should have said, "What diffunce do it make?", and he felt that it was a lucky break to have been picked up by this farmer, that this was a dress rehearsal which might keep him from disaster when he had to perform for Treadwell.

"No diffunce. You jus' watch yo' step with Mistuh Tread-well. He doan like no sass. You ack right, he all right."

"You mean as long as I know my place?"

"Thass right," the man said, oblivious to the irony in Roberts' question.

Then they were across from the store and the man got out to let Roberts slide across the seat. Treadwell was standing in the door, looking at them indifferently. Roberts was glad the storekeeper had seen him arrive with another Negro, and one obviously from the area.

He thanked the man and held out his hand. The man

looked at it, disconcerted, then gave a short laugh and shook it. He got in the truck but before leaving thrust his head out the window and whispered conspiratorially, "Hey, you ack right with Mistuh Treadwell, he treat you right, heah? Mistuh Treadwell, he's a good white man."

The shame Roberts had felt earlier returned, and in greater measure. They did stick together down here. The man wanted to help him, a stranger whose only bond was the color of his skin. He knows it's us against them, Roberts thought, even if he has been subjected to their brainwashing all his life.

When Roberts started across the highway, Treadwell had disappeared into the store. He was arranging cans on a shelf when Roberts entered. He glanced over his shoulder and then busied himself with the cans again. Roberts waited, looking down at the floor and churning inside.

Wait on me, you white son of a bitch, he thought.

When the cans were arranged to his liking, Treadwell stepped back and studied the effect. He turned, wiped the counter with a rag and then, at last, looked directly at Roberts.

"You want somethin', boy?" he asked with a civility lost on Roberts.

You're damn right I want something, Roberts thought. My fist right down your throat. And don't call me boy. Damn it, Roberts, don't lose your temper. Don't be a fool.

He choked back his anger, cleared his throat and shuffled a little, trying to remember every Negro servant and low comic he had seen in motion pictures, trying to put himself in the shoes of the Negro who had just given him a ride.

"Yes, suh," he said obsequiously, feeling completely unmanned and hating Marlene for having brought him to such a pass.

"Well, you come to the right place, whatever it is," Treadwell said pleasantly. "What you need?"

Roberts held out the penciled list with a hand which he managed to keep from trembling only with the greatest effort. Rage, not fear, caused his agitation.

"Unh-huh," Treadwell said, studying the list, a pleased expression on his face. "Ah can take care of all this for you. Yeah, Ah believe Ah can."

He began moving around the store filling the order, piling coffee, cans of condensed milk, a sack of dried lima beans, boxes of rice, canned beans, lard and other items on the counter. As the pile grew, Roberts began worrying about the cost. Would fourteen dollars be enough? If not, he'd have to forego something. Marlene hadn't told him which things were least important and he felt strangely inadequate.

"You not from around here, boy," Treadwell said.

"Yes, suh."

You white bastard, you call me boy just once more . . .

"You mean you are or you mean you ain't?"

"Ah mean Ah am."

He fought to keep his tone civil but apparently something resentful in it betrayed him. Treadwell stopped stacking groceries and gave him a sharp look.

"You gettin' smart with me?" he demanded.

You son of a bitch. I'll kill you. I'll smash your face the way . . . Watch it, you stupid bastard! You want to talk your head into a noose?

"Me?" Roberts said, feigning surprise. "No, suh! Ah jus' mean Ah'm fum aroun' heah. Ah stays with mah cousin. The one carried me heah."

That was damn clever of me, he thought, to remember how the man who had picked him up had used "stay" instead of "live" and "carry" instead of "drive." And for the first time in his life he realized with utter clarity and horror how clever Negroes who lived here had always to be.

"Yes, suh, boss," he said, looking at his feet. "Ah stays with him."

Treadwell relaxed.

"The "boss" did it, Roberts thought. It doesn't take much to make him feel big. No wonder he's stuck out in the country in a penny-ante store.

He felt immensely superior to Treadwell but the feeling did little to alleviate the outrage and humiliation of his position. He watched covertly while Treadwell added up the bill.

"Lemme see," Treadwell said at last. "Looks like 'bout twelve dollars, seventy cents. You got that kinda money, boy?"

Though the "boy" rasped his nerves like a file, Roberts humbly said, "Yes, suh. Right heah."

He dug the limp wad of bills from his pocket, relieved he had enough. Marlene had calculated well. He counted out thirteen bills, being careful not to do so too efficiently. Treadwell took them and counted them a second time.

"Thuhteen dollahs," he said. "You 'bout got this money wore out, ain't you? But it spends good as brand-new."

He looked at Roberts as if expecting a laugh but Roberts did not oblige him, taking refuge in a study of the floor at his feet.

"Tell you what Ah'm gonna do," said Treadwell. "Seein's it's a right nice orduh, Ah'm gonna round it off to twelve dollahs even."

Roberts sensed that Treadwell was waiting for a reaction and forced himself to respond.

"Ah sure do appreciate that," he said.

"You just tell yo'h cousin and all yoah friends Mr. Treadwell treats nigras right in his stoah, you heah?"

I'll do that, Roberts thought. I'll do that little thing.

"Anything else you need?" Treadwell asked.

All Roberts wanted was to get out, to leave Treadwell's loathsome presence, but he felt it would be running and he did not intend allowing Treadwell to make him run. The last white man who had made him run . . . Roberts tore his thoughts away from that.

"Is you . . . is you got socks?" he asked.

"Why, yeah. Ah 'spect Ah do. Right nice ones. Fo' bits a pair. How many you want?"

Would Marlene be angry if he spent her money on socks? The money was intended for food and it would be like stealing from her. Because despite her nonsense about the money belonging to the owners of the house it was hers. But he had stuck his neck out to come here and the groceries had cost less than expected. And Treadwell had knocked seventy cents off the bill, which was more than the socks cost.

"One pair," he said, realizing apprehensively he had pronounced the "r."

But Treadwell seemed not to have noticed.

"Size 'leven," Roberts added.

" 'Leven? You got a mighty little foot foh a nigra, boy. Ah think Ah can take care of you."

He went to the back of the store and returned with a pair of heavy white cotton socks, which he handed to Roberts.

"How you like them socks?" he said heartily. "Right nice foh only fo' bits."

They seemed large and Roberts examined them. They were size twelve and a half. Miles too big, Roberts thought, raging, and he didn't even ask me what color I wanted.

"Somethin' wrong, boy?" Treadwell demanded.

You're God-damned right there's something wrong, you miserable bastard, Roberts thought. I'd like to make you eat these God-damned socks.

"No, suh," he said, almost strangling on the words.

Treadwell opened the cash box, put the thirteen bills in it and took out a half dollar, which he put on the counter by Roberts' purchases. Roberts was reaching for his change when he remembered Marlene had asked for candy. How could he bring himself to deal with this clod again? But he had bought socks for himself and he would not be able to look her in the eye if he came back without the jelly beans and licorice she had asked for so shyly. It was, after all, her money.

"Mistuh," he said with great effort, "is you got jelly beans? An' lickrish?"

"Got a sweet tooth, ain't you?" Treadwell said with a grin. "Got one myself."

Treadwell dug under the counter for a small sack and filled it with jelly beans and licorice whips. He added it to the pile.

"How much it that?" Roberts asked.

"No charge."

"No charge?"

"You bought a nice orduh. Ah treat folks right when they treat me right."

Roberts felt baffled and confused, as he had so often with Marlene. Jesus Christ Almighty, he thought, how do you figure these people? He calls me boy, he sells me the wrong size socks and now he wants to give me something for nothing. I'll be damned if I'll take his God-damned conscience gift. If that's what it is.

The words of refusal were on his lips when he caught himself. He had managed to avoid disaster this long and he was not going to court it now. Instead of speaking, he ducked his head in thanks.

"You can have one a them to carry yoah groceries in," Treadwell said, nodding toward some empty cardboard boxes in a corner.

"Thank you," Roberts said, thinking, You son of a bitch, you're supposed to pack my order, not me.

He found a box, shook out a cockroach scuttling frantically across its bottom, piled his purchases into it and left, feeling not so much as if he were leaving a country store as fleeing a battlefield.

Treadwell followed him to the door and called after him

"Remembuh, now, you trade heah, Ah treat you right. Tell yoah cousin, too."

Roberts looked back over the box of groceries, forced a grin and whispered to himself, "I'll see you in hell first, you son of a bitch."

The box was heavy and awkward to carry. Roberts wished the man who had picked him up earlier would come along, or some other Negro. In his present mood he would not dare accept a ride from a white man though he doubed if a white man would stop to give a Negro a ride. He felt dirtied and physically ill from his encounter with Treadwell. He had been obliged to scrape and fawn and accept insults from an inferior without fighting back, and he was sick and surfeited with anger.

By the time he reached the house he was sweaty and exhausted, and throbbing with resentment. Marlene was wait- in the front yard and ran to meet him.

"Goody," she cried. "You got everything."

Then, seeing his set face, she became apprehensive.

"Somethin' go wrong?" she asked.

"No," he said curtly, continuing to walk toward the house.

"What you so mad about, then?" she asked, keeping pace with him.

"What the hell do you care?"

It was her fault, he thought bitterly, and she was white just like Treadwell and couldn't understand the humiliations to which he had been forced to submit even if he were to try to explain to her, which he did not intend to do.

"Charlie?" she said, full of concern. "There is somethin' wrong, ain't there?"

"I'm sorry, Marlene," he said contritely. "That bas . . . that Treadwell just rubbed me the wrong way."

"How you mean? Mr. Treadwell, he's right nice."

"To you, maybe. Not to a . . . not to me."

"What'd he do?"

They were in the kitchen now and Roberts dropped the box on the table and fell gratefully into a chair.

"He called me boy," was all he could think of to say, although the memory of the other indignities was still fresh and exacerbating.

Marlene laughed.

"Is that all?"

"God damn it, it's nothing to laugh about!"

He put his hand to his head and then laughed himself, though bitterly.

"No," he said. "That's not all. It was his whole damn attitude. The way he . . . I don't see how a Negro can stand to live down here. And the way he said nigra."

"He said nigra? I told you he was nice."

"Nice! What do you mean, nice?"

"If he wasn't, he'd of said, you know, that other."

"You mean nigger?"

Marlene nodded.

"I'd rather he had. The way he said nigra. If he went that far, why couldn't he bring himself to say Negro?"

She looked at him uncomprehendingly.

"It's the same thing," she said.

"The hell it is."

"It is, so. It's just the way we say it down here."

"That's what I'm objecting to, damnit. That you say it that way. There's something about the way you all say nigra instead of Negro."

"But it's the same," Marlene said stubbornly.

"Marlene . . . " he began, exasperated, "look, do me a favor, will you? Let me hear you say Negro."

"Sure. Nigra."

Roberts sprang to his feet.

"See?" he said. "Even you won't say it."

"But I just did."

"You did not. You said nigra."

"I said 'xactly what you told me to say. Nigra."

"I told you to say Negro."

"An' I did," she insisted.

Roberts pressed his hand on top of his head and said, "Damn it! Oh, damn it!"

Then he looked at her thoughtfully and said, more calmly, "Say knee."

"Knee? Why?"

"Just say it."

"All right," she said, shrugging. "Knee."

"Now say grow."

"Grow?"

"Yes, grow."

"Grow."

"Now put them both together."

"What you mean, put them together?"

"I mean say them together. One after the other. First knee, then grow."

"All right," she said, as if humoring a capricious child. "Knee, grow."

"Closer together."

"Knee grow."

"You did it!" Roberts cried triumphantly. "See, you can say it. You can say Negro. Now say it again. Negro."

"Nigra."

Roberts groaned.

"Oh, Christ!"

And then he began to laugh, forgetting how hot and weary he was and Treadwell's indignities. And Marlene laughed, too. They looked at each other and laughed until tears ran down their cheeks and then they sat down at the table and ate licorice whips.

17

Roberts went in to take a bath while Marlene put away his purchases. He had seldom felt so dirty. It was more than the dust and sweat of his trip to the store. It was as if his encounter with Treadwell had left him physically besmirched, and even the lighthearted interlude with Marlene could not temper it.

He could hear her singing at her chores as he soaked in the warm water and he thought again how little it took to make her happy and how quickly she recovered from even the most painful experiences. How ironic that this should be so, he thought. Negroes were supposed to be like that. That's what ignorant whites believed. Yet he was the one with the capacity for doubt and dread, not she. And he was glad she was as she was. It helped him, he realized, helped him immensely.

When Marlene finished putting the groceries away she started for her room but, in passing the bathroom, saw that the door, which opened out, was slightly ajar. She looked away, filled with embarrassment bordering on panic. What if she had looked in and seen him naked? She had seen nothing in her fleeting view of the bathroom except his head, dark-glistening shoulders and two knobby knees.

But as she stood poised to flee to her room before he might see or sense she had passed by and so compound her embarrassment, she remembered another door ajar many years ago, and her father in the cast-iron tub with clawed feet which had frightened her as a small child. She had come home from a visit with her cousin, Fay Marie, a visit which had been marked by a solemn discussion between the two of them and another little girl about the private parts of their fathers.

Marlene had never seen her daddy naked, and her mother only rarely, but both Fay Marie and the other little girl had seen theirs unclothed, Fay Marie once and the other girl several times. Both had agreed that fathers wore something strange and ridiculous dangling there, but Fay Marie said there was only one thing there and the other girl insisted there were two, of quite different shapes. And they had argued about the proportions of what they had seen. Fay Marie, who had had only a glimpse, said that it was very long, reaching almost to the knees, but the other girl, Marlene could not remember her name, out of the sophistication of repeated and more prolonged investigations, insisted it was much smaller. They had argued fiercely until the noise had attracted the attention of Marlene's Aunt Donna and although the aunt had not known the subject of the dispute the girls had dropped the subject and did not return to it.

But Marlene had remembered it when she came home and found her daddy had neglected to latch the bathroom door and it had swung open an inch or so. She had waited, unmoving and scarcely breathing, until he rose from the tub to dry, feeling terribly wicked without knowing exactly why except that Christians were not supposed to see each other naked and that there was some sort of unnamed punishment, whether earthly or heavenly or both she was not sure, for those who did. And she had been aware of something shapeless and silly-looking growing from a clump of tangled blackness and realized Fay Marie had been wrong.

Marlene had crept away undetected and a little disappointed both in what she had seen and in the fact there had been no punishment of any sort for having seen a man naked. And she had never again seen that part of a man, not even of the boy who had seduced her, because she had kept her eyes closed.

And now she felt the same curiosity about Charles Roberts as she had about her father, equally as sexless.

Nigras, she thought, are supposed to have great big ones, maybe as big as Fay Marie said her daddy did, and she wondered if it were true. All she had to do was stand where she was and she could find out.

She waited, and it was like waiting outside the bathroom at home all over again, standing back a foot or so and peering through the narrow opening. Then Roberts stood up to soap himself with one of the new bars he had bought at Treadwell's and at first Marlene was conscious not of his sex but of how thin he was, all bones and sooty juttings, and then she saw he was no different from other men, or at any rate other men as represented by her daddy, except that he was as black there as he was over the rest of his body.

Marlene felt somehow cheated, but nothing else, not a

first, because it was no different than looking at her daddy, though now she felt none of the childish sense of wickedness of that other time, only a sort of petty guilt for doing something she was not supposed to, and she might have stolen away from the door with hardly a second thought had not Roberts suddenly noticed the door ajar and, reaching out to shut it, saw the white gleam of an eye behind it and let out an outraged bellow and leaped from the tub, slamming the door and crashing flat on his back on the slippery linoleum as he did so.

To Marlene, the shout, the thunderclap slam of the door and the heavy thud of his fall were both accusation and indictment and, shame-filled and frightened, she fled to her room and, in her turn, slammed the door. She could feel the blush spreading over her entire body like something molten and then, despite her embarrassment, the thought of his fall obliterated all else and she pictured him leaping from the tub and his feet skidding out from under him on the slippery floor and him skidding along on his soapy back like the fat man she had once seen slip on a squashed rotten orange on a street in town, and she began to giggle. She could not stop and she flung herself on the bed and ground her face into the pillow and bit it, but still she giggled.

And then she heard the sound of bare feet slapping on the hall floor and her door was flung open. She turned on her side, her teeth still clenched on the pillow, and saw him standing there, dripping water and still covered with soap, a towel draped around his hips and held there with a death grip of one fist while the other was brandished at her.

"You . . . you . . ." he said furiously. "What the hell you mean doing that!"

His face was contorted with anger and embarrassment and Marlene stopped giggling.

"Doin' what?" she said innocently.

"You know damn well what!" he stormed. "What's the matter with you? Don't you know any better than to . . ."

"It wasn't my fault," Marlene protested. "You left the door open. I was just goin' by an' I couldn't help it if . . ."

"The hell you couldn't. You were peeking."

Peeking, she thought. That's the way she talked, the way children talked. Despite his rage she wanted to giggle again but she was afraid to, and beneath everything she was ashamed and apologetic.

"Did you get a good look?" he demanded, breathing heavily with outrage.

"Huh?"

"God damn it, can't a man have a little privacy around here? What kind of a . . . of a dirty-minded little trollop are you, anyhow?"

Marlene sat up.

"I am not either dirty-minded," she said. "Just 'cause I . . . 'cause I. I just wanted to see if . . . if . . ."

She felt herself blushing again. She could not say it. To talk about things like that with a man was bad enough, but to admit to him she had thought he was different from white people in that way was, if anything, worse. Christians did not talk about such things or even have such thoughts.

"See if what?" he demanded.

"Aw, you know," she said hesitantly.

"No, I don't know. Suppose you tell me."

He was angry, still, but in control.

"You do, too."

"Stop playing games, Marlene. What the hell are you talking about?"

"I ain't gonna tell you. I wish you'd just go on back and finish your bath an' leave me alone."

"You started this and I intend to get to the bottom of it. What the hell were you doing spying on me? Are you the kind of sick mind that gets its kicks looking at a naked man?"

"Lookie here, Charlie Roberts, don't you start sayin' nothin' like that about me! I never seen a man naked but one time before in my whole life. My daddy. When I was just a little bitty girl."

"That's a likely story! How did your belly get stuck out like that? Immaculate conception?"

She felt herself blushing again.

"I never seen him," she said in a low voice. "It was dark an' I . . . an' I had my eyes closed."

Somehow she was not as embarrassed talking to him about it as she might have expected. She was too intent on making him understand for it to seem to her like talking dirty. Nevertheless, she could not look at him as she spoke.

Roberts could see the memory distressed her and he was sorry he had attacked Marlene with her pregnancy. That was hitting below the belt in more ways than one. And obviously there had been nothing really ugly about her spying.

She was still just a child in many ways, with the curiosity of a child. But he was curious, too. She spoke as if she had had a specific reason for looking.

Though he was now uncomfortably aware of the fact only a towel covered his nakedness he was determined to find out what that reason was.

"What was it you wanted to see if not just a man's . . . " he insisted.

"Nothin'."

"Don't give me that."

Marlene sighed in resignation.

"All right."

She hunched up her shoulders and held her arms flat against her sides as if trying to make herself smaller.

"Nigras are supposed to be, you know, *different*."

"What do you mean, different? Different in what way?"

Marlene began growing angry. Was he trying to embarrass her or was he just too dumb to know?

"You know," she said, almost choking on the words because her throat felt so small, "bigger."

"Bigger? What the hell are you getting at?"

And then he understood and was embarrassed.

"Oh," he said.

He half-turned, as if put to flight, and mumbled, "Well, don't you ever pull a trick like that again."

But Marlene, having been more candid than she ever dreamed she could be, and relieved of much of her embarrassment by his, was not ready to drop the subject. She felt a compulsion to finish the conversation, to share with him her new-found knowledge.

"But they ain't," she said.

Roberts stared at her.

"What?"

"Bigger," she said doggedly. "You was just like my daddy."

"Jesus Christ!" Roberts said.

He tightened the towel around his waist and stalked back to the bathroom. Marlene put her face in the pillow and giggled some more. Neither mentioned the subject again at supper that night though the first few minutes of the meal passed awkwardly. Then they became involved in plans to augment the larder by fishing and forgot all about it.

In the morning Roberts broke into the garage in search of fishing gear and found a sheaf of long cane poles fitted with lines, hooks, lead sinkers and cork bobbers. Among the odds

and ends of old newspapers, magazines, tools, garden imple-
ments, flounder gigs, cans of drying paint and porch furniture, he found unexpected treasure: a peach basket full of
worn men's and women's clothing and half a cobwebby,
roach-ridden case of Dr. Pepper.

Marlene was much more pleased with the Dr. Pepper than
with anything else he found and announced they would
share a bottle every day as long as the supply lasted. Roberts
was grateful for the clothing, which included two old white
shirts, mended socks and a pair of patched but warm wool
dress pants.

Roberts had fished only rarely in his life and Marlene's
experience was confined to fishing for perch and catfish in the
creek near her farm home with worms and grubs for bait.
She and Roberts dug among the withered stalks in the flower
beds for worms without success and pried bark off rotten logs
for grubs with no greater luck. They searched the winter
grass for crickets and grasshoppers and found none, then
went to the beach and pursued fiddler crabs, which proved
too elusive until Roberts threw a heavy stick at them and
managed to kill several.

"I wonder if they're good to eat," he said, looking at the
crushed shells with distaste.

"Ugh," said Marlene. "Anyhow, it'd take 'bout a million
for one bite. We'd run ourselves poor tryin' to catch 'em."

"They should be all right for bait, though, shouldn't they?"

"I hope so."

They went out on the pier, stopping short of the end for
fear that if they went that far they might be visible from the
highway. The peninsula was not long enough to shield the
full length of the pier. They sat several yards apart, their feet
dangling, and watched the bobbing corks on their fishing
lines. Roberts hooked the first fish. Marlene had instructed him
to give a jerk when the cork went under to set the hook in the
fish's mouth and he did it with such enthusiasm that the
fish sailed into the air the length of the line, broke the rotten
cord and went flying over the pier to land with a splash in
the water.

"God damn it!" Roberts cried in frustration. "And did
you see how big it was!"

"Shoot, it was teensy."

"You're jealous."

"Jealous of that little ol' thing? Anyhow, you didn't catch
it."

She giggled.

"You should of seen your face when the line broke," she said. "For a minute I thought you was goin' right in after it."

"Were," Roberts said.

"Huh?"

"I thought you were, not I thought you was."

"Ain't that what I said?"

"Isn't, not ain't."

Marlene studied him, perplexed but not displeased.

"You tryin' to be my schoolteacher or somethin'?" she asked.

"I don't know. It's just that sometimes I feel the urge to defend the English language from you."

He said it good-naturedly.

"Do you mind?" he continued.

"No," she said, adding, "I 'preciate it. I wish I could talk the way you do, 'cept not so . . ."

She stopped and giggled.

"Not so what?"

"Prissy-like."

She looked to see how he was taking that and was relieved to see him grinning.

"I'm going after another pole," he said. "Try not to catch all the fish in the ocean before I get back."

"The Gulf of Mexico," Marlene said. "Not the ocean. This is the Gulf of Mexico."

"Whatever it is," Roberts said, grinning again.

He was returning with another pole when Marlene caught a fish. She jerked the pole and the small fish popped out of the water twisting at the end of the line. With a squeal, she raised the pole into the air, the fish dangling and swinging in a long arc. Roberts ran toward her, excited.

"Lookie," she cried. "I caught one!"

After several tries she managed to lower the fish to the pier in the middle of its swing on the long line and it lay flopping convulsively. Roberts lunged for it and Marlene cried, "Watch out!" but too late.

He seized the fish and felt a searing pain in his hand.

"It's a catfish!" Marlene yelled.

Roberts looked at his throbbing hand in disbelief. It was bleeding.

"What . . ." he said.

"He finned you," Marlene said. "I tried to stop you."

"I'll live," Roberts said.

He scowled at the fish.

"You little bastard."

"They'll fin the fool outta you if you don't watch out. Does it hurt real bad?"

"How could a tiny thing like that hurt so much?"

"Bigger'n the one you let get away."

"Mine was three times this size."

"That's what you say."

She showed him how to hold the catfish down with a foot while she worked the hook out of its mouth. She put a string through its gill and dropped it into the water and they returned to their fishing. In a few minutes Marlene caught another fish, a silvery one seven or eight inches long that made a strange croaking sound as it flopped on the pier.

"Oh, goody," Marlene cried.

"What kind's that?" Roberts asked. "Sounds like a frog."

"I don't know. But it looks good to eat."

She caught two more small catfish and another croaker before Roberts made his first catch. It was a dogfish, a small ugly creature, soft and slimy to the touch.

"Ugh," said Marlene. "What's that?"

"I don't know. Whatever it is, it doesn't look edible."

He extracted the hook and kicked the fish back into the water.

"Why'd you do that?" Marlene asked.

"We couldn't eat a thing like that."

"I know. But it was so . . . ugh. You should of killed it."

"You don't kill something just because it's ugh, Marlene."

She gave him a fond, almost maternal look.

"You sure are softhearted, you know? I don't believe you could kill a fly. Even if you did, you know, slap me that time you got so mad at me."

Roberts' face went stiff. Oh, no, he thought, I couldn't kill a fly. If she only knew. I wonder what she'd say if she knew.

"What's the matter, Charlie? You look so funny all of a sudden."

"What? Oh, nothing."

"Is it your hand? Does it hurt?"

"I'm all right. Let's get back to fishing."

They caught seven catfish, three too small to keep, and three croakers before Marlene decided they had enough for a meal. Roberts carried the poles and Marlene the string of fish as they walked back through the strip of woods. They were approaching the road when they heard the car.

"Listen," Roberts said, holding up a hand to stop Marlene.

"I hear it."

They stood transfixed as the car drew nearer.

"Get down," Roberts whispered, dropping the poles and kneeling behind a bush.

Marlene got down behind him.

"I hope it ain't . . ." she said.

"Ssh," Roberts hissed.

What if it's the people that own the house? Marlene thought. They'll find out we been there and call the police and have us arrested and everybody will see my stomach sticking out this way and know.

And Roberts was thinking. Is this it? Oh, Jesus, is this it?

They watched from behind the bush, holding their breath. The car went past their house and stopped before the one down the road.

18

Two persons got out of the car, a glistening black Thunderbird of that year's model. The man, of medium height, had on a brown corduroy cap with earflaps and tan duffel coat. The woman, slim and almost as tall, wore slacks and a matching coat, and had a bright blue scarf wrapped around her head. The walked through the front yard toward the porch.

"What are we gonna do?" Marlene whispered.

"I don't know."

Roberts whispered, too, though there was no reason for it. The man and woman were more than a hundred yards from them.

They were at the porch door now, and talking, but were too far away for Roberts to hear them.

Maybe they're only checking the front door and will go away without finding out the house has been broken into, he thought. Because if they find it has, they'll look in the other houses and I'll be running again. And Treadwell will remember me and give the sheriff a description and they'll have me pinpointed. I knew it was too good to last.

For suddenly, now that his refuge was threatened, it did seem good. Good perhaps only in comparison with being on the run, but good enough that the thought of losing it, apart from the danger, made an ache inside him.

"They can't get in," Marlene said. "Looks like the screen's latched. Maybe they'll just go on. Oh, I hope they just go on."

Why should it matter that much to you? Roberts wondered. It'll only mean you'll have to face reality a couple months earlier than you'd expected. You've got nothing to worry about.

The man went around the corner of the house, leaving the woman on the front steps, and Marlene said wretchedly, "Oh, shoot."

Should I hide here until they leave or take off right now? Roberts wondered. If I leave now I'll have more of a head start but if I wait I can get together some food and clothing.

But he knew what his decision would be, not a decision really because he had no choice. He felt absolutely immobile hiding behind the bush, knowing he would not, could not run until he had to.

"Hey, honey!" the man shouted from the rear of the house, his words clearly audible to Roberts and Marlene. "Come on back here! Somebody's broken in."

The woman ran around the house in answer to his summons and Marlene turned a stricken face to Roberts.

"They're gonna find out!" she gasped. "They'll look in our house and find out."

"Don't worry," Roberts said, trying to keep the panic out of his voice. "They won't do anything to you. You'll be all right."

"They'll call the police an' put me in jail. And everybody will see my . . . see my . . ."

"Will you stop worrying about that!" Roberts snapped, made edgy by his fear. "Nobody gives a damn about that. I wish to God that's all I had to worry about."

"Oh," she said, looking at him as if fully understanding for the first time the peril he was in. "Charlie, what are we gonna do if . . ."

"Do? Run. But not you. You've got nothing to worry about. I told you."

Damn them, he thought, damn their lousy white hides for coming here, and damn you, Marlene, for pinning me down and keeping me here when I could be far away now.

But even in damning her he knew it was in no way her fault he was here, that he had stayed because he thought he would be safe, and that if he had left he might have been caught long ago and maybe even be dead. What had he gained by staying but a few extra weeks of life, and now it would be starting all over again, the hiding, the running in dark places, the fear.

The front screen opened and the man and woman came out. They were talking in loud voices now and Roberts and Marlene could hear them.

"Let's check the Sprouses'," the man said. "Maybe they broke in there, too."

A sort of numbness spread over Roberts.

That does it, he thought. No point in kidding myself any longer. They'll take a look and the next stop, the sheriff's office.

"Did he say the Sprouses?" Marlene demanded urgently. "Was that the name he said?"

"What?" Roberts said absently. "What did you say?"

Instead of answering, Marlene leaped to her feet and began running through the trees toward the road, the string of fish dangling from her hand. Roberts half-rose to pursue her, then sank back, stunned.

What are you doing, something within him shrieked. Marlene, what are you doing? Not you. I never thought you . . . Not you.

There was more agony in him than anger that she should at last betray him. After they, for the first time in either of their lives, had broken through the barrier of color. For it was more than the running to betray him, it was white running to white. When she needed him color had not mattered. But now. What was it they called it, his people? The nitty gritty. When you got down to the nitty gritty, white ran to white.

After she crossed the road, Marlene slowed to a deliberate walk, moving toward her own house. The man and woman saw her when she reached the front yard and hurried toward her. Marlene waited for them, seemingly at ease.

How easy it is for her once she made up her mind, he thought. How could you understand people like that? And he watched, as if hypnotized, Marlene standing there so calmly and the couple approaching her and with each step bringing him closer to disaster.

"Hello," Marlene said, her left hand behind her back.

"Hello," the man answered suspiciously. "You from around here?"

"Yes, sir. I live here. In the Sprouses' house."

The man and woman exchanged glances. The man was fair-skinned with heavy, dark eyebrows. The woman was fair, too, and pretty. They were perhaps in their late thirties. Roberts hated them because they looked decent and civilized but probably were not, as far as he was concerned, because they were part of this state and its paranoia and because soon they would be the instrument of his destruction.

"The Sprouses' house?" the man said with just a hint of Southern accent in his voice. "I didn't know . . . Did you, honey?"

The woman shook her head.

"They didn't say anything to me about leaving anybody," she said.

Her accent was somewhat more Southern but not so marked as Marlene's.

"The Sprouses are in South America," the man said challengingly.

What the hell is she up to? Roberts wondered. If she's going to turn me in, why doesn't she do it and get it over with?

"Yes, sir," Marlene said. "I know. That's why they asked us to stay in the house. Me an' my husband. We're lookin' after it for 'em."

She doesn't intend to betray me, Roberts thought. She's trying to bluff her way out of it. And he was filled with shame and relief, the relief giving way to apprehension when he saw how the man and woman looked at each other and whispered together.

The man nodded at something the woman said and said, "This husband of yours, where is he?"

"He ain't here right now."

The man and woman looked at each other again.

It was a good try, Marlene, Roberts thought. And I hope some day I get a chance to thank you for trying. And apologize for doubting you.

"He had to go to town," Marlene said. "Somebody tried to bust in last night. He run 'em off but he thought he better report it to the police anyhow. In case they tried to, you know, come back."

Marlene, Marlene, Roberts thought. Bless your conniving, innocent little heart.

"They tried to break in the Sprouse house, too?" the man said with considerably less antagonism.

"They did break in ours," said the woman. "Didn't you hear them?"

"No, m'am. We sure didn't. If we had, my husband he'd of run 'em off. He's got this shotgun. I sure am sorry."

"That's all right," the man said. "It's not your fault you didn't hear them."

"I hope they didn't take nothin'," Marlene said.

"Wasn't much to take," the man said. "Just some groceries that didn't amount to much. But they broke a window getting in."

"You'll have to see about getting it fixed, Jack," the woman said.

"Damn," he said. " 'Scuse the language, young lady. I sure don't like the idea of coming all the way back down here just for a window."

"My husband, he'll fix it for you when he gets back," Marlene said.

My God, Roberts thought admiringly, and I once thought you were so dumb. And look how she keeps her hand behind her back so they won't see she doesn't have a wedding ring. And he wondered, was that part of it all cunning or was it because she did not want anyone to know she was pregnant but not married. Had she invented a husband out of cunning or shame?

"Not with real glass, though," Marlene was saying. "He'll, you know, put boards over."

"He will?" the man said gratefully.

"We surely do appreciate that," the woman said.

She turned to the man.

"What is it, honey? Oh. Oh, yes."

He reached in his hip pocket under the duffel coat and brought out a wallet.

"I want to pay him for his trouble," he said, taking out some bills.

"Oh, no," Marlene said, for the first time showing confusion.

Take it, Marlene, Roberts urged. We can use it. And then, No, don't take it. Not from them. We don't want their handouts.

"I couldn't do that," Marlene said. "I'm just sorry we didn't hear 'em bustin' in in the first place."

"Go on, take it," the man ordered, sounding as if he were accustomed to being obeyed and Roberts disliking him using that tone with Marlene despite the fact the man was only trying to be kind. "And maybe you can keep an eye on the place for us, too."

"No, sir," Marlene said, firmly now. "My husband would be right mad if I took your money. An' don't you worry none about your place. We'll look after it."

"Fine," said the man. "Fine. But I wish there was something we could do for you."

"Yes," the woman said. "Isn't there some way we could repay you?"

Yes, Roberts thought. Just go.

"No m'am," said Marlene.

"Well," the woman said indecisively, adding, "when are you expecting?"

"M'am?"

"Your baby."

"Oh. My baby. 'Bout three months."

"Your first?"

"M'am? Oh, yes m'am."

"I thought so. You're very young, aren't you?"

"Seventeen."

"You look even younger."

The woman reached out impulsively and touched Marlene's cheek.

"Don't you be frightened," she said. "There's really nothing to it. I've had three."

"Honey," the man said, "I hate to break up this girltalk but if we don't get moving . . ."

"All right," the woman said. "Are you sure there isn't something . . . ?"

"No m'am," Marlene said.

"Good-bye, then," the woman said. "I just know you're going to have a wonderful baby."

"Thanks again," said the man. "If you write the Sprouses, tell them the Larabees said hello."

"Yes, sir," said Marlene. "We'll do that."

She stood motionless watching them walk back to the car. Roberts watched, too. The man opened the door for the woman and after she got inside kissed her lightly on the forehead, to which she responded by patting him on the cheek, before closing the door. It was an affectionate and natural gesture which somehow angered Roberts. He did not know if it were because they were white and assured and their mere presence could force him to cower behind a bush or because they had all the things Marlene should have, Marlene who was standing there so thin and bulging with a child who would never know its father and possibly not its mother. Marlene who had just saved his skin. His black skin.

When the car passed out of sight he ran to her. She was clutching a hand to her breast, her face white.

"Marlene," he cried, wanting to hug her, "you were great!"

"I'm so scared," she said uncomprehendingly. "How come I'm so scared now and I wasn't before, not hardly at all?"

"It's a natural reaction. You'll get over it. Marlene, you should be on the stage. I never saw such acting."

"Actin'?" she said, a little color coming back into her cheeks. "I wasn't really actin'. Least it didn't seem like it. I felt like . . . like I really did have a husband. While I was talkin' to them, I mean."

There was a sadness in her face now that the fantasy was over.

"That lady," she said. "She sure was nice. I wish . . ."

I wish I did have me a husband like I said, like she did, who'd be nice to me and buy me a coat just like he had himself and drive me in a big car and open the door for me, and then I wouldn't be scared about the baby and I'd want him and we could visit and talk about our babies and she could tell me things I need to know.

And she felt disloyal to Charlie Roberts for not including him in her hopes and to her mother for thinking about getting help and advice from the lady instead of her. And she wondered if she had told the lady the truth, that she was not married, would the lady have taken her away with her and helped her have the baby and maybe afterward taken care of them both, she was so nice. But if she had done that, what would happen to Charlie, and anyway, she wouldn't have told the lady for the world because the minute she found out she wasn't married she'd have stopped being so nice and would look down on her, and for a moment, but only a moment, Marlene hated the woman for being rich and having a husband who took good care of her and children she could brag about instead of having to hide.

"Hey," Roberts said. "You all right now?"

She was looking better, he thought. Should he tell her what he had thought at first, and ask her pardon? No, not now. Not yet. Not ever.

"Unh-huh," she said. "I'm all right."

"You handled it perfectly. They won't even report it. I'm proud of you, Marlene."

"I wish I hadn't had to tell 'em those stories," she said. "But I guess I had to." She squared her shoulders as if marshaling her forces and said, "I better take in the fish an' clean 'em. Charlie, will you get the poles?"

"The poles? Oh, the fishing poles."

He went after the poles and put them in the garage. Marlene had already begun cleaning the fish when he got inside. She worked deftly, showing no repugnance as she cut off heads and pulled out entrails with a crooked bloody finger. Roberts, who had never cleaned a fish in his life, was repelled and fascinated.

And then, without warning, he began trembling.

"What's the matter, Charlie?" she said, full of concern.

He managed a smile.

"Remember how you felt after they left?" he said. "That's the way I feel now. It just hit me."

"Oh, is that all? I thought you was . . . you were gettin' the chills an' fever."

"I could really use a drink."

"You just sit there," she said, washing the fish blood from her hands, "an' I'll open a Dr. Pepper."

"Not that kind of drink. A real drink. Whiskey."

"Whiskey? I didn't think you was a drinkin' man. "

"I'm not. Usually. But I could really use one now."

"Shoot, we got some whiskey."

"We have?"

"In the dinin' room. In that china closet."

He went into the dining room and found the bottle and brought it back with him. He poured a stiff drink with a hand that still trembled a little and stopped in the act of putting it to his lips.

"You want one, Marlene?"

"Me? It's nasty."

She hesitated and added shyly, "Charlie? Would it be all right if I had me a Dr. Pepper? A whole one?"

"Of course. You've earned it."

He waited until she opened the bottle, then lifted his glass in a toast.

"To Marlene. For gallantry in action."

"What in the world are you talkin' about?"

Before answering, Roberts downed his drink in two burning, choking swallows, coughed and wiped his lips. The whiskey trailed fire into his stomach and he felt vastly eased.

"You may have saved my life," he said soberly.

"All I did was tell those people a story."

She wondered if that would be considered sin, like being pregnant without a husband only not so bad. And whether a big sin like doing what she had done that got her pregnant was so big that the little ones like telling stories didn't really amount to anything. That lady had been so nice she hated having lied to her.

"Charlie," she said, "we got any boards out in the garage?"

"Boards?"

"Unh-huh. To fix their window with. The Larabees."

"Fix their window? Why?"

"Didn't you hear me from where you was hidin'? I told 'em you'd fix it."

"You said your husband would fix it, not me."

"I ain't got no husband an' you know it," Marlene said, refusing to make a game of it. "The only one I got to do it is, you, 'less I do it my own self."

"Why does either of us have to?"

"I promised. That part of it wasn't no story."

"It really bothers you to lie, doesn't it, Marlene?"

" 'Course. Don't it bother you to tell a lie?"

"I don't know," Roberts said thoughtfully. "I suppose sometimes it does and sometimes it doesn't. There are times when it may be better to lie than tell the truth."

"You would think that," Marlene said without apparent malice. "Bein' a lawyer."

19

Marlene continued with supper, sipping contentedly from the Dr. Pepper as she did so. She gave no evidence of having come through a crisis, and Roberts wondered if perhaps she had not already forgotten about it but knowing she had not, just put it away because it was over with and she could do nothing further about it. So illogical and irrational in some ways, he thought, and so remarkably practical in others.

He felt almost fully recovered himself, and not too concerned about the possibility the couple might return without warning or might decide to report the theft and bring the sheriff down upon him. He did not know if it were the whiskey, but doubting that, or if it were Marlene's flexibility and resolute practicality rubbing off on him, thinking it possible, or if he had become passive and fatalistic, resigned to the certainty that whatever would be would be, for good or ill, and there was nothing he could do to change that. And this last he repudiated, for the Charles Roberts trembling for his life behind the bush in the wintry sun had been no fatalist. Passive, perhaps, but no fatalist.

Marlene fried the fish, complaining womanlike because there was no cornmeal to roll them in and later, when Roberts complimented her on how good they were, said diffidently, "They'd be lots better if we had us some cornmeal. I should of put that on my list. Next time . . ."

"Next time? There won't be any next time. I can't go back to the store. Not after . . ."

"Shoot, they won't say nothin' to Mr. Treadwell. Folks like them, they ain't goin' to stop in his store. That Mr. Larabee, he was in a hurry." She sighed. "Did you see how he opened the door for her? She never even put her hand out for the handle, like she knew all the time he was goin' to do it for her."

"Yes. I saw."

Poor kid, he thought. You want to have a man do that for you, don't you? But one never will.

The catfish had very little flesh on them and the croakers were full of bones, but because they had caught the fish themselves and because the meal was different from their normal fare, and also because they had survived near-catastrophe, they ate with more than usual relish. Marlene washed the dishes and Roberts dried them, and afterward he had another, smaller drink of whiskey and put the bottle away.

Later, sitting in the kitchen for warmth and companionship, with the portable radio playing in the background, they talked. Roberts tried to discuss the implications of the Larabees' discovery that the house was occupied but Marlene was no longer interested, having dismissed the possibility of danger, retaining out of the incident, and that vividly, only the memory of how serene and cared for the woman had been and how nice to her, and how casually yet proudly she had mentioned her three children. And she reminded Roberts that he must cover the window he had broken.

And Roberts again found his own confidence bolstered, or was he actually only being lulled, he wondered, by her unconcern, no longer considering her placidity mere ignorance or indifference but something valid drawn from a source he could not fathom and of which she herself was unaware.

"Them fish," she began.

"Those fish," he corrected.

"Those fish, they sure were good," she said.

"They were. We should have begun fishing a long time ago. Instead of just sitting here without trying to help ourselves. We've got to live off the land more, Marlene. You must know how to do that. You've lived on a farm."

She shrugged apologetically.

"We mostly raised just cotton. Daddy keeps some pigs an' a cow an' Mama keeps some chickens but that's about all. We got most of our groceries at the store, just like everybody."

"Didn't you have a vegetable garden?"

Marlene shook her head.

"We grow cotton."

Roberts remembered what the man who gave him the ride had said when he asked about eggs and milk. He grew cotton. Therefore he could not be expected to grow food.

"Doesn't anyone grow for the market down here?" he asked.

"Oh, sure. Some grow sweet corn and truck and all, or raise chickens or have, you know, dairies."

"Well, then, I'll just have to go out and look for them. You need milk and eggs and fresh vegetables. Though I doubt if I'll find any fresh vegetables this time of year."

"Look for 'em? I thought you didn't want anybody to see you."

"They won't."

"They won't?"

"No. I'll do my looking after dark."

"After dark? Oh. You mean steal?"

"I mean steal. Any objections?"

"I don't guess so," she said with a sigh. "But I sure wish we didn't have to."

"So do I."

Because it's dangerous, and because I may be stealing from Negroes without knowing it, he thought. I wouldn't mind if it were only from whites.

He did not go out that night because when faced with the reality of leaving the safety of the house he realized he was still shaken by the visit of the white couple, but he went out the following night, wearing the warm coat he had stolen from Treadwell and canvas work gloves he had found in the garage and taking with him, hopefully, a burlap bag which Marlene called a towsack.

He walked miles through the chilly night before finding a farmhouse and then was put to flight by a barking dog before he had an opportunity to try the barn. Near midnight he found a crib full of feed corn and filled his sack with as many of the flinty ears as he could carry. Later he got into a chicken coop and squeamishly twisted the necks of two chickens, thrust them in the bag and made his escape with five eggs warm in his coat pockets as lights went on in the farmhouse and someone came out shouting about that damn fox being at the chickens again.

He had mixed feelings about the chickens. They would be a welcome addition to the menu, but stealing chickens was such a *nigger* thing to do. There were so many jokes, condescending, sniggering jokes, about Negroes stealing chickens that he felt as if he were part of one of them, that he was not only stealing, he was also playing a humiliating role in a discredited farce like the shuffling Negro actors in old movies. But he got over that on the way home with his bulging sack, the provider bringing food.

He was away more than six hours and when he returned, exhausted from the walking and the unfamiliar tension of

thievery, he found to his surprise that Marlene had waited
up for him and had hot water on the stove for coffee.

She was ecstatic about the chickens but disappointed with
the corn.

"Shoot, Charlie," she said. "This is horse corn."

He looked at her wearily over the cup in his two hands.

"Horse corn? Looks like corn on the cob to me."

"It's for feed. The kind people eat is, you know, tender."

"Tell you what, Marlene. I'll steal a horse, we'll feed it to
the horse, and then we'll eat him."

"Eat a horse? I wouldn't eat no . . ."

She saw he was joking despite his fatigue and she smiled
at him.

"You can't help teasin' me, can you, Charlie?"

"Even if it is horse corn, we can eat it, can't we?"

"I don't know. Hey, I know what. I can grate it up and
make us corn cakes. You like corn cakes?"

"I'll try anything."

They fell into a routine. During the five days the fresh
eggs lasted, Roberts insisted Marlene have one every morning
for breakfast despite her protests that it was not fair to him.
"You need them," he said. "I don't." They fished every afternoon except those days when it rained or they could not
face the thought of another bony croaker, and on those nights
when Roberts did not go out foraging they sat in Marlene's
room with the electric heater on—Roberts left it in her room
now—Roberts in a chair reading and Marlene huddled in her
bedspreads listening to the radio. She would often interrupt
his reading but he came to welcome it. He did not care for the
books in the house but he preferred reading books he did not
like to not reading at all.

" . . . you hear me?" she demanded one night as he sat
reading *Gone With the Wind*.

"What?" he said, looking up.

"I swear, when you get your nose in a book it's like you've
gone deaf."

"Deaf."

"Deaf. I must of repeated myself a million times."

"Sorry. What is it?"

"I said, is that a good book?"

Roberts closed it, holding his place with a finger, and re-
garded the spine as if to see what it was he had been reading.

"It's all right," he said, shrugging. "For a fairy tale."

"What you mean, fairy tale? It's about how it was after the Civil War and all."

"I thought the people down here called it the War between the States."

"That's what it was. But it's called the Civil War, too. Anyway, it's supposed to be true. I mean how it was in those days."

"How it was with whom?"

"Huh?"

"The trouble with this book, Marlene, is that it's about the wrong people."

"The wrong people?"

"Everybody knows what the Southern whites went through. Or said they went through. Or are supposed to have gone through. But what about the Negroes, the slaves? They're the ones the Civil War was really about."

"But it does tell about the slaves. Least the moving picture did. I never read the book."

"It gives a false picture of the slaves. Oh, not completely. I'll grant there are some truths. But generally, it's the picture white people like to think is the way things were. Why, Marlene, this book makes it appear almost as if emancipation was bad for the Negroes. And that the good Negroes didn't want it."

"Well, it was bad for 'em. My daddy used to say . . ."

"How can you say freedom is bad? But you have a point whether you know it or not. Because they were never really freed."

"Aw, come on. They were, so. I took history."

"Not my kind of history. Tell me something, Marlene. You think Negroes liked the way things were before the Civil War, don't you? That their masters took good care of them and all that and they don't know how to take care of themselves, even today?"

"Well . . . yes. Everybody knows that."

"Who do you mean, everybody?"

He got to his feet and paced the bedroom, not angry with her despite her misconceptions but stimulated by the discussion and a chance to expound his views.

"I mean, you know, everybody."

"Do you mean to sit there and tell me I don't know how to look after myself, Marlene?"

" 'Course you do. But you're . . ."

"I'm what? Different? From whom? I'm just as black as any cotton-picker you ever saw."

"But you're smart. You're extry smart. You even been to college."

"Don't you believe there are plenty of other Negroes who're, as you say, extra smart? Who've been to college? And thousands more who'd go if they had the chance white kids do?"

"It ain't . . . it's not just nigras don't have the chance, Charlie Roberts. How about me? How could I go to college, even if I wanted to?"

And I wish I could, she thought, and maybe I could be smart like you, and make my baby smart, too.

"You have a point," Roberts admitted. "But not a big one. And you still haven't answered my question. Do you think there are plenty of Negroes who are smart?"

"No. Everybody knows nigras . . . " She stopped, her face showing how carefully she was formulating her answer, and continued, "Negroes aren't very smart. Mostly."

"That's a myth. Just like the myths in this book. It's because they haven't had the opportunities."

"Just because you're one it don't mean . . . "

"Jesus Christ, Marlene!" he interrupted. "I'm not saying it out of racial vanity. I'm saying it because it happens to be true. And not necessarily only of Negroes down here. Take yourself, for example."

"Me?"

"Yes, you. When I first met you I thought you were stupid. I thought you were the stupidest person I ever met."

"Well," she said matter-of-factly, "I ain't real smart. Not like you."

He stopped pacing and looked at her with admiration, almost awe.

"You know something, Marlene? You're the most honest white . . . hell, the most honest person I've ever . . . "

He sat on the edge of the bed and looked at her earnestly.

"You're not dumb, Marlene. Don't ever let anyone tell you that, not even me. You'll never win any scholarships but you're not dumb. You're just deprived."

"Deprived?"

"You've never had the chance to learn if you have any brains or not. You're exactly like the Negroes down here."

"What do you mean?" she demanded, angry now.

"Nobody ever gave them a chance. And nobody ever gave

you a chance. If you'd been born somewhere else, if your family . . ."

"Don't you say nothing against my family, Charlie Roberts!"

"I'm not talking about your family. I'm talking about the whole damn social structure, the power structure, down here. Don't you know what it's done to you?"

"What you mean, what it's done to me? It ain't . . . hasn't done nothing to me."

"Then you're satisfied with your life? The way it's gone?"

"Shoot, yes."

She looked at the bulge her stomach made in the spread.

"Least I would be if it wasn't for . . ."

"Then that's the worst thing of all! That you're content to grow up in ignorance and prejudice."

"I thought you said I wasn't dumb."

"You're not. But you're sure as hell uneducated."

Marlene sighed.

"It's been a long time since you talked mean to me," she said forlornly.

"I'm not talking mean to you, Marlene. I'm trying to help you."

"Less talk about somethin' else, then."

"No. This is important. Don't you realize how much better off you'd be if you had the same chances as other people?"

"You been to college and all and you ain't so good off."

Roberts laughed helplessly.

"Okay," he said. "Less talk about something else."

"Do you think I'd like to read that book?" Marlene asked, relieved.

"I suppose so. It reads well."

"You know somethin'? I didn't know it was a book, too, for a long time. I thought it was just a picture show. I liked the picture show a whole lot. Even if it was old. Hey, Charlie?"

"What?"

"I wish we had us a television."

"I'd rather we had a decent library. And a deep freeze. Full of steaks and vegetables."

"An' frozen dinners," Marlene said as if they were playing a new and exciting game, her eyes shining.

"We're just making ourselves hungry. Let's change the subject. Here. Want to read it?"

She nodded and took the book from him. He went to the frigid living room and returned with a best seller of five

years past and began reluctantly reading it. They sat for a
while in silent rapport which was broken by Marlene.

"Oh," she said, sitting up straight.

"What is it?" Roberts asked, looking up from his book.

"He kicked. Hard. He's a right stout baby."

"Stout? How can you say that? He must be skin and bones
on what you're eating."

"Stout means strong."

"I learn something every day, don't I, Marlene?"

He studied her face.

"You've changed your mind about the baby, haven't you?"
he asked.

"What you mean?"

"You don't hate it any more."

"I never did *hate* it, 'xactly. I just . . . you know."

"And now you want it?"

Do I want the baby? she wondered. What would I do with
a baby? No, I don't want it. But I feel sorry for it. That's what
it is. I feel sorry for it. It ain't its fault it's going to be born
without no daddy to claim it, and I'm going to try and eat
good and all so it'll be healthy and go to one of those places
like Charlie says so it'll have a good home.

And she thought about the baby growing up among strangers, and herself all alone in the world and having to go to
work without even finishing high school and she felt as deprived as Roberts had told her she was and her eyes filled with
tears.

"What's the matter, baby?" Roberts said gently, sitting on
the edge of the bed by her side.

She leaned forward and hid her face against his shoulder
and cried.

Why didn't my daddy talk like that, she thought, instead of
getting so mad and throwing me out of the house?

"Don't cry, Marlene," Roberts said awkwardly, patting
her shoulder and thinking, You poor kid, you never had a
chance and it's going to be worse for that poor little bastard
you're carrying. And you could be a good mother if you had
the chance, but you won't because it's too late for you just like
it's too late for that cotton farmer who gave me the ride and
for all the other Negroes and poor white trash down here, yes,
the poor white trash, too, and if somebody doesn't do something damn quick too late for all their children and their
children's children.

And he grew sad, too, thinking about the hopelessness and

the waste, and unexpectedly about a girl he had once loved and almost married but had not because he was not sure he wanted to bring another black child into a white world—or had that only been an excuse for avoiding responsibility—and yet feeling strong and in some way reassured because he was repaying Marlene in some small measure for having saved him the day the neighbors came and because she was white and he was black and she was leaning on him physically and emotionally and there was no nonsense about color. And he thought, If you were my daughter you wouldn't be here. I wouldn't let the world do this to you. And he wondered, would he be able to prevent it, for how many Negro fathers had been unable to protect their daughters, and their sons, against the world no matter how hard they tried because there were too many things going against them, and if he had a son or a daughter, though it was not likely now that he would, could he protect his child from all the hate and inequities he would have to face and knowing that even if he could not he would try.

"It's going to be all right, baby," he said. "When the time comes you'll leave and have your baby in a hospital. And every thing will be all right. You'll see."

But even though he knew things would not be as bad for her as she now thought because she was young and adaptable and, in her own way, tough, he knew things would not and could not be all right for her, ever, because she was doomed from birth just as the baby would be if it stayed down here.

Marlene leaned back against the bedpost, wiped her eyes and smiled.

"You know somethin', Charlie?" she said. "You're so skinny. I could feel every bone in your shoulder."

20

"You know what today is?" Roberts said, shelling the last of the corn.

"I ain't kept track," Marlene replied.

"Haven't," Roberts said automatically.

"I haven't kept track," she said, just as automatically.

"Day before Christmas."

"Day before Christmas?"

She jumped up heavily, being careful even in her excitement not to bump her swollen stomach against the table at which she was sitting.

"I forgot all about Christmas," she said. "First time in my whole life I ever forgot about it."

Her happy face grew regretful.

"An' we haven't got a tree or noth . . . anything."

Roberts sighed.

"I wish a tree was all we didn't have," he said.

"Charlie," Marlene said coaxingly, "let's have us a Christmas tree."

"What have we got to celebrate?"

"Aw, come on."

"What good is a bare tree, anyhow? We haven't anything to decorate it with and no presents. None of the things that go with a Christmas tree. Anyhow, it's kid stuff."

"Please."

He looked at her hopeful face and thought, Even with your big belly you're still a kid. And not the miserable-looking kid you were when I first got here.

He wondered if that were because he knew her now and was fond of her or because of what being pregnant did to a woman's face. And she had gained weight because he had become quite a competent thief and two or three nights a week brought home potatoes, chickens, eggs and, on one occasion, even milk. It had been a five-gallon can from a dairy farm almost three miles away and it had taken him almost two

194

hours to roll it back to the house. They kept it on the back porch in the cold and there was still some left, only a little sour.

The extra pounds helped, too, he thought. She was no beauty but if she ever learned to make the best of what she had as many other girls did she could be pleasant looking. Perhaps after she'd had the baby she could make something of herself and marry some decent young man and have a normal, happy life. But where could she find a decent young man in this part of the world, or have a normal life?

"Please," she said again.

"You know something, Marlene? You've become better looking."

She blushed.

"Shoot. You're just sayin' that."

"No. I mean it."

She smiled, pleased, then grew serious again.

"Can we, Charlie," she said, "can we have us a tree?"

"Why not?"

"Goody!"

They found a rusty hatchet in the garage and went across the road to the woods. Marlene selected a graceful pine sapling and while Roberts was chopping it down gathered sprigs of red-berried yaupon and tufts of moss. When they got the tree back to the living room they found they could not make it stand upright. They tried propping it up with books but it fell over immediately.

"We'll have to lean it against the wall," Roberts said.

"No, it wouldn't be like a real Christmas tree," Marlene said, so disappointed her eyes were teary. "It's got to stand up in the middle of the room."

"When I was a boy, we bought our trees with a stand already on it," Roberts said, remembering the trees and ornaments and presents of his childhood, and how his parents continued having one after he was big, even after he moved into his own apartment, and wondering if they had a tree up now, and if they expected that somehow he would get home for Christmas as he always had every year before.

"My daddy makes a thing out of boards," Marlene said. "That's what let's do. Make one out of boards."

"I don't know how. And we haven't any nails. I used them all boarding up the window next door. Remember?"

Marlene sighed heavily.

"I've got an idea," Roberts said.

Marlene brightened and waited expectantly.

"You know that milk can on the back porch? We can put the rest of the milk in jars and stand the tree up in that."

"That's a good idea! Charlie, you're so smart."

Marlene washed some empty fruit jars and Roberts emptied the remaining half-gallon of milk into them. They washed the can out with the garden hose and took it into the living room. When they stood the tree in it it fell over with a clatter.

"Shoot!" Marlene cried, vexed.

"We need something heavy in the can," Roberts said. "The tree's too top-heavy for it. But what?"

"I know! Sand. From the beach."

They carried the can to the beach between them, each holding a handle, and scooped sand into it. Then they found they could not lift it. They removed the sand a few handfuls at a time until it was light enough for Roberts to roll along the ground and then, panting and sweating despite the cold, he worried it back to the house and up the back steps.

When he got it into the living room he lopped off the bottom limbs of the tree and worked the trunk down into the sand. The tree leaned slightly but remained upright.

"Not much of a tree," he said critically. "I wonder if it was worth all the trouble."

"Yes," Marlene whispered. "Oh, yes. Now let's decorate it."

"With what?"

"Lots of things."

Marlene spent a euphoric afternoon making decorations for the tree. She fashioned chains from strips of old newspaper from the garage, making links by pasting the ends of the strips together with a mixture of water and flour gleaned from an almost empty canister in the pantry. She cut the tops and bottoms from tin cans retrieved from the trash and punched holes in them, and slit a can lengthwise, smoothed it flat and with kitchen shears cut out an almost symmetrical star.

She wound the paper chains around the tree in spirals and hung the tin disks from the limbs with string. She tried to prop the star among the needles at the top of the tree but it would not stay. She was ready to cry with vexation. Roberts, making his only contribution and feeling quite proud of it, punched a pair of holes in the center of the star, put string through them and tied the ornament to the top of the tree.

Then Marlene festooned the branches with streamers of moss and they stood back to admire the tree.

"You know, you're very good with your hands," Roberts said. "Instead of going to business college maybe you should think about putting that knack to use."

Marlene blushed, as she had when he told her she was not bad looking.

"That's just, you know, foolin' around," she protested. "It don't amount to anything."

"You'd have to live in a big city, of course," Roberts said, ignoring her protest. "And you'd have to study. Natural talent's not enough."

Do I really believe that? he wondered. Or am I just impressed that she can do anything at all and want to believe she'll be able to take care of herself later? As she is now, she's unemployable except as a waitress or something of that sort. And I'd hate to see Marlene end that way, like all the other ordinary, uneducated Southern poor whites. Because she's not ordinary. She has possibilities.

He had seen her mind open, in fact had caused it to open. And that was one of the major reasons, he knew, that he was concerned about her future. She was his creation. In a way, his child.

"I'd like to live in a big city," Marlene said. "Like Jackson or New Orleans or Houston. If I could just get me a job. But first I'm goin' to get my high-school diploma. No matter what."

She said the last fiercely.

"That's very sensible. You can go to school at night if you have to."

"I know. I just wonder who's goin' to take care of my . . ."

She bit her underlip as she often did when puzzled or troubled.

"But I guess I wouldn't be able to keep him even if I wanted to," she said disconsolately.

"I don't see how you could. Unless you took it home to your parents."

"No," she said with determination, shaking her head in emphasis. "I ain't never . . . I'm not ever goin' to see my daddy again till I can come home like a lady. An' . . . an' with my . . . husband."

"I thought you didn't care for the boy."

"Him!" she said scornfully. "I wouldn't marry him if . . . No, I'm goin' to get my diploma and then I'm goin' to business

college or like you said an' I'll find me somebody real nice
with a good job. An' I'll show him."

"The boy who got you in trouble?"

"Shoot, no. My daddy."

I wish I could take you home, Charlie Roberts, so you could
tell my daddy I'm not bad like he said and how I'm not
dumb and good with my hands and he'd have to believe you
because you've been to college and a lawyer and all, and even
with all your education and everything you like me and respect me and are sweet to me and that would make him sit
up and take notice, I bet; and she realized with a shock
which showed plainly on her face that she could not do this
because Charlie Roberts was black and her daddy would call
him nigger and throw him out of the house or worse, and her,
too.

And she could see her daddy insulting or hurting Charlie,
a smart, sweet man like Charlie, and she grew indignant,
which also showed plain on her face.

"What in the world is going through your mind?" Roberts
demanded.

She flushed and looked away so he could not see her face.

"Nothin'," she said guiltily.

She did not like lying, and especially lying to Charlie
Roberts. You did not lie to someone who trusted you and was
good to you.

"You were upset about something. It showed in your face."

"I was just thinkin' about . . . about my daddy."

"You can't carry a grudge inside you the rest of your life,
Marlene. It doesn't hurt anyone but yourself."

Listen to me, he thought. I've been carrying a grudge all
my life, and against a whole race. And it's helped me, not
hurt me. Kept me from being used by them. It was weakness
to let them use you.

"You used to," Marlene was saying.

"What?"

"Carry a grudge. Against anybody who was white."

"I still do. I have a right to."

"I'm white."

"What's that supposed to prove? You're dif . . ."

Jesus Christ, Roberts, he thought, nothing ever made you
angrier than to have some white man say that to you. But
why shouldn't he feel that way about whites? If you picked
a hundred white men at random and assumed they were all
against you, you'd be right ninety-nine times. But what about

the hundredth man? To hell with the hundredth man. It was better to hate one innocent man without cause than to trust ninety-nine who were out to gut you any time they had the chance.

And yet, supposing Marlene were the hundredth? If he had gone away from the house when he tried, still hating her, he would have missed something precious: the intimate knowledge of another human being, a good human being. For, he realized, he had never in his life known another human being, black or white, so well or felt so close. If she were his sister or his daughter, he could not know her so well. And when you knew someone that well, there was no race or color.

He had heard that said many times by both whites and Negroes, and he had had it preached at him from pulpits until he stopped going to church, and read it in books, and he had scoffed and said if all men were brothers the name of the white brother was Cain. It was, he had thought, the credo of the white do-gooder and the Negro Uncle Tom. Could he have been wrong? If he was wrong, it was only in hating and distrusting all whites, almost as wrong as the white men who hated and distrusted all Negroes, but not wrong in expecting a white man to prove himself before accepting him. Because if all men were brothers, it was up to the white brother to prove it, not the black brother. It was the black brother who was required endlessly to prove himself and, even when he had done it, nevertheless remained an object of scorn and injustice.

The white man claimed to have emancipated the Negro but he had not, and would not. And could not, until he emancipated himself. The Negro could not do it for him. And yet, this girl, Marlene, was emancipated. And he had emancipated her. And perhaps some day she would emancipate others.

And suddenly he wanted very much for Marlene to keep her baby and not let it be lost to ignorance and prejudice as Marlene would have been lost had he not stumbled upon her in this house. And if the baby were lost, he himself would be lost because it was the only legacy he had to leave if he should not have a child of his own. And this child of Marlene's could be a voice in the wilderness crying out the truths he had taught her.

"Marlene," he said, "I'm glad you want to keep the baby. Even if you can't."

"What in the world brought that up?"

Roberts looked at the tree.

"Christmas, I suppose."

"We made this manger scene at high school last year. I helped. You know, I just remembered. The art teacher said I was good with my hands, too. Just like you did. She wanted me to take art, only I took home economics."

She sighed and Roberts thought she was sighing about the lost opportunity until she said, "I wish we had us some popcorn."

"Popcorn?"

"Unh-huh. You know, to string together with a needle and thread and put around the tree. Like we do at home."

"We've got the corn I shelled this morning."

"You can't string horse corn. You need popcorn."

"It looks fine the way it is. I don't see how you did so much with so little."

"I wish my mama could see . . . You know, this is the first Christmas I ever wasn't home. I wonder if they've got a tree this year. Mama saved the decorations, you know, tinsel an' snow an' everything, an' lights, and every year we'd get them out and use 'em over and over again. An' after I was asleep Mama and Daddy would put my presents under it. Till I got too old. Then they just gave 'em to me when I got up. I wonder if they got a present for me this year."

She thought about the tree her mama and daddy would have at home with all the old decorations on it, even the tinsel they picked off so carefully every New Year's Day, and the colored lights going off and on, on and off, remembering how she would lie awake at night when she was a little girl wondering who it was turning the lights off and on, and she wondered if they had bought presents for her this Christmas despite what had happened and were waiting for her to come home and open them in the morning.

Maybe Daddy's not mad at me any more because it's Christmas and peace on earth and good will toward men and all, and if I go home he'll be glad to see me and tell me he's sorry how he acted and Mama will cry and I will too and then we'll open presents and Mama'll have a turkey in the oven stuffed with cornbread like she does, and cranberry sauce and sweet potatoes full of pecans and marshmallows melting on the top and punkin pie and mince pie both and when I can't decide which one I want she'll cut me a piece of both of 'em like she always does.

And for a moment she felt so strongly it was so that she

was on the verge of going to her room and packing her things and leaving. Then she looked down at the bulge of her stomach and knew her daddy would never forgive her for that, and if he saw her now with the evidence of her sin sticking out like a watermelon under the skirt she had to leave unzipped because it could no longer contain her, his eyes would get red with rage and this time when he raised his fist he would not hold off hitting her.

And anyway, she thought, what about Charlie? I couldn't just go off and leave him all by himself on Christmas Eve. Not when he's been so good to me, better than anybody in my whole life except Mama, and she couldn't do anything to help me like he's done.

But she did miss presents. She tried to think of something she could give Charlie for Christmas, or something he could give her, but they had nothing. If she had thought about Christmas in time, she might have made something. She did not know what but whatever it was, it would please him because he thought she was good with her hands. There were so many things he needed she wouldn't know where to start even if she could go to a store and pick out whatever she wanted. Socks and shirts and shoes and every other kind of clothes, and warm slippers and a robe and a watch and books. And all the things she needed. Bubble bath and a comb and brush and box candy, and shoes and stockings and a little radio with a thing you could put in your ear so only you could hear it and, most of all, maternity clothes. She felt like a sausage in her old skirt and with anyone but Charlie she would be embarrassed because it wasn't even zipped and the tail of the old man's shirt she wore was all that covered her hip where the skirt gapped open. And she remembered the matching coats of the couple who owned the house next door and thought about how nice it would be if she and Charlie had coats like that for Christmas.

"I'm goin' to roast that chicken we got left for Christmas dinner," she said. "And sweet potatoes."

"Not sweet potatoes again!" Roberts said with a groan.

"Or would you rather have it tonight?" she said, not paying attention to him.

"Christmas dinner. And maybe tonight I can find a little something special to go with it."

"You're not going out tonight? Not Christmas Eve!"

"We don't take holidays in the stealing business, ma'am."

"But it's Christmas Eve! It's, you know, wronger to steal

on Christmas Eve. Anyway, you ought to stay home tonight."

"You really think of this place as home, don't you?"

" 'Course. Don't you?"

It was not home and could never be, this lonely place in alien country, but it was not the trap it might have been, either. He could not have borne it were it not for Marlene and because of her, though this place was not home, it had a kind of warmth and sweetness he had known nowhere else. And he knew that if he ever got out with his life he would remember her and this place with tenderness and nostalgia.

"Not exactly," he said slowly. "This is no life for me, Marlene. I couldn't stand it, except for you."

"You didn't just stay here to help me 'cause you're sorry for me?"

"I'm not that self-sacrificing. You know that, Marlene, I'm an angry, bad-tempered bastard."

"No, you're not. You were when you first came but now you're right nice."

"Only because I can't stay angry around you. You're so . . . hell, so uncomplicated and innocent."

She looked down at her stomach and he caught the look.

"Yes, innocent," he repeated. "Even with that. If you hadn't been innocent it probably never would have happened."

"I wish you could have told my daddy that," she said ruefully. "It wasn't what he had to say about it. Charlie," she continued earnestly, "I know you're staying here partly to help me, no matter what you say, but it ain't . . . it's not the real reason. How come you never told me the real reason? I know it's somethin' you did, somethin' real bad, but you never told me just what."

"It's better you don't know. It might complicate things for you some day."

"I wish you'd tell me."

"You have enough problems of your own. I want you to leave here with nothing on your mind but your baby. And forget I ever existed."

"You think I could do that?" Marlene asked quietly. "After you been so good to me?"

"Well," Roberts said uncomfortably, "remember me but keep it to yourself. How would it look if anyone knew you'd spent all this time living in the same house with a . . ."

"A man?" she finished for him. "If they knew you, they wouldn't think nothin' of it. Not anything wrong."

"Even a *Negro* man?" he said gently.

"I keep forgettin' that," she said. "But I wouldn't tell anybody anyhow. Honest."

"No. It's better you don't know."

They had their usual simple supper, with Roberts insisting Marlene drink a large glass of milk even though it was turning sour.

"You need it," he said, "and you've got to drink all you can before it spoils."

Because it was Christmas Eve, he opened the can of chocolate-covered bees which had remained untouched during their weeks in the house and, before Marlene's horrified eyes, ate one.

"Not bad," he said, pretending to enjoy it. "Have one."

"Ugh," said Marlene.

After the dishes were put away they took the electric heater into the living room where the Christmas tree was but it was too small to temper the cold in any way. They moved the tree to Marlene's room, where it looked larger and more resplendent.

The radio stations were all playing Christmas carols and thoughts of home filled Marlene and Roberts with melancholy nostalgia. By chance they sighed simultaneously, looked at one another as if awakening from naps and smiled.

"What were you thinkin' about, Charlie?"

"Home."

"Me, too. The way it was before . . ."

"It'll be that way again," he said, knowing he lied and knowing nothing could ever be the same again for him, either.

She shook her head.

"But I don't care," she said defiantly. "I'm gonna have my baby an' keep him if I can but whether I can or not I'm goin' to get my high-school diploma an' I'm gonna go to some kind of other school. An' I'm gonna make somethin' of myself like you want me to an' some day I'll meet me a nice sweet boy an' get married. An' then I'll go home and I'll tell my daddy, 'I want you to meet my husband.' An' that'll show him."

"Hear, hear," said Roberts, applauding.

Marlene flushed with pride and embarrassment.

"Let's sing some carols," she said. "So it'll really be like Christmas Eve."

"All right. If you can stand my voice."

"When I was little and sang 'Silent Night,' you know what

I sang?" Marlene said. " 'Stead of 'round young Virgin' I
sang 'brown young Firgin.' It was I don't know how long
'fore I quit thinkin' there was this nigra, this Negro girl in
the manger with the Holy Family. Named Firgin. Like,
you know, their washerwoman or somethin'. Only I never
could understand how they could have a washerwoman if
they were s'posed to be so poor and all."

"And when I was little I thought they were all Negro,"
Roberts said. "And I remember how angry I'd get when I'd
see pictures showing them as white."

"You sure must of been a mean little boy."

"I was. And I grew up to be a mean man."

"No. No, you didn't."

"There's quite a few people who'd argue that point with
you."

"I'd like to see 'em try!"

For a moment she seemed genuinely angry, her normally
placid face stern and her eyes glinting. Then she relaxed
and said, "Come on, let's sing. How about 'Oh, Little Town
of Bethlehem'?"

They sang it and all the other carols they knew, her voice
immature but pure and sweet, his strong but off key.
And somehow the effect was deeply satisfying to both of them.

21

On a frigid afternoon five days after the New Year, Marlene turned from the stove in dismay.

"It went out," she cried. "We must of run out of butane."

Without stopping to put on their heavier clothing, Marlene and Roberts went outside to check the gauge. The tank was empty.

"What are we gonna do?" Marlene said, close to tears. "We can't cook or keep the kitchen warm or nothing. And it's all my fault."

"Your fault? Don't be silly."

"It is, too. I should of kept track of the gas. I'm used to butane stoves an' you're not."

"It wouldn't have done any good to check the gauge. It would have run out eventually whether you checked it or not."

"But I could of, you know, tried to save usin' the stove so much if I'd kept track and known we were runnin' out."

"It's cold out here. Let's go inside and see if we can think of something."

Back inside, Roberts put on his heavy jacket and Marlene put on the terry-cloth robe over her sweater. Though the kitchen had not yet had time to grow really chilly, the absence of heat from the oven made them both feel colder than they actually were.

"You ever notice if any of the other houses have fuel left?" Roberts asked.

"I don't rightly remember."

"I'd better have a look right away, then."

"I'll go with you."

The tank beside the house next door was a quarter full.

"What a break," Roberts said, relieved. "How long will this much last?"

"I don't know. It's not as big as our tank. Way we been usin'

205

the stove, 'bout a month or somethin'. Not any more'n that."

"No longer than that? Maybe there's more in the other tanks."

One of the houses had no butane. The other had half a tank.

"Between the two of them it should see us through until you have to leave," Roberts said when they were back in their own house.

He did not like putting it into words. He knew Marlene must leave to have her baby and that he must leave, too, to have, as it were, his baby. For he could not stay here indefinitely any more than Marlene could and, though he was not bound to so rigid a nine-month schedule as she, he must eventually face his own realities. Neither of them, he knew, had been truly facing their realities. Marlene, despite the fact that she now accepted the baby as something real and inevitable, and even schemed endlessly on ways to keep it, did not really accept the fact that having the baby would force her to leave her haven and go out into the world. And he, though he fully understood and accepted the fact that he must leave, if not when Marlene did then certainly before the owners of the house returned for the summer, had refused to think about it except when caught unaware by memories or nightmares.

"How we gonna get the tank to our house?" Marlene asked. "It's right heavy."

"We don't move the tank. We move us."

"You mean move out of our house?" she demanded, incredulous.

"Right. It's simpler that way."

"We can't move," she wailed. "I love our house."

"It's not ours," Roberts said gently. "Not really."

"It's ours more than any of the others. We live here. An' I love it like it was our very own."

She looked at him imploringly.

"Don't make me move, Charlie."

"What can we do?" he asked helplessly. "We have to have a stove."

"We could maybe cook over there," she said hopefully, nodding toward the window overlooking the house next door.

"We need the heat, too. I know the stove doesn't get the kitchen really warm but it does take the chill off."

Marlene sighed wretchedly. Her despair touched him deeply.

"Okay," he said. "If we can move a tank we will."

"You think we can?" she cried eagerly. "It's heavy. But I'll help."

"No. Not in your condition."

"I could show you what to do, at least. How to connect it up and all."

"Fine, Marlene. That would be a big help."

There was a rubber-tired wheelbarrow in the garage and, among the tools in a metal box, the pipe wrench Marlene had said he would need. The wheelbarrow did not move easily.

"If it's this hard to push empty, how am I going to manage with a tank of gas on it?" Roberts said anxiously.

"Maybe if we oil it? There's an oil can."

"It isn't just that. The tire makes it hard to push. It needs to be inflated more."

"We can pump it up."

But there was no pump. Roberts oiled the axle, which helped some, but the wheelbarrow still resisted his efforts.

"It's the tire," he said impatiently. "Maybe I can get it off."

"They wouldn't like it if you did that, Charlie. This here is a real expensive wheelbarrow. I never saw one this nice before. The one we had, it just had a plain iron wheel."

"Would you rather do without a stove, or move next door?" Roberts demanded a little testily.

"I'm sorry, Charlie. I guess we've got to, huh?"

When Roberts could not pry the tire off he sent Marlene into the house for a sharp knife and sawed laboriously through the tough rubber. There was objection to this in Marlene's face but she did not give voice to it. With the tire removed, the wheelbarrow rolled easily. Roberts felt vindicated.

He pushed the wheelbarrow through the winter-killed grass to the house next door. Marlene closed the valve on the tank and Roberts uncoupled it with the pipe wrench. The connection was stubborn and it took all his strength to unscrew it.

"Now comes the tricky part," he said.

Fortunately, the wooden rack on which the tank rested was several inches higher than the wheelbarrow and he was able to nose the wheelbarrow under the rack. With Marlene helping him by guiding the tank, he was able to roll the cylinder onto the wheelbarrow without mishap. It was not as heavy as he anticipated but was nonetheless quite difficult to manage because of its size and shape.

It was not quite centered on the wheelbarrow and teetered awkwardly. Roberts was forced to accept Marlene's help in sliding it to a balanced position.

"You all right?" he asked anxiously.

" 'Course. I didn't push very hard."

It was hard work wheeling the tank over the grass and Roberts stopped often to rest. Marlene wanted to help but he would not permit it. He allowed her only to steady the tank with a hand as she walked beside the wheelbarrow. By the time he reached the house he had taken off his coat and was drenched with sweat. Marlene made him put his coat on and rest until he stopped sweating.

"You want to catch your death?" she demanded.

While he was resting she took the wrench and, over his protests, uncoupled the empty tank, which was a good deal larger than the one with which they intended replacing it.

Roberts rolled the empty tank off the rack and out of the way. When he nosed the wheelbarrow and its load up to the empty wooden rack he found to his dismay it was too low to slide the barrow under, yet, because of the thickness of the planks, was an inch or so higher than the new tank.

"Damn," he said. "If it was just two inches lower."

"Maybe we can lift it. It's just a teensy bit too high."

"That teensy bit is just a teensy bit too much. We've got to find some way to get the wheelbarrow up enough so I can roll the tank off."

"I bet we could lift it that far," Marlene insisted.

"No. I don't want you lifting anything."

"What are we gonna do, then?"

"I don't know. Maybe . . . Marlene, go get a couple of boards out of the garage."

She brought two short planks and when Roberts pulled the wheelbarrow out of the way put them on the ground along-side the rack. Roberts was unable to roll the wheelbarrow onto them though he pushed with all his strength.

"It won't work," he said. "We'll have to try something else. Get the boards out of the way."

When she had done it he pushed the wheelbarrow up to the rack again.

"Marlene, you think you can hold it steady if I let go for a minute?" he asked.

"Sure. What are you gonna do?"

"Maybe if I get my back under it I can lift one end enough to roll it on."

Marlene held the handles of the wheelbarrow while Roberts got down on his hands and knees and backed under a protruding end of the tank. He raised himself gingerly until he felt the tank against his back, then began lifting with his arms and legs.

"I think I'm getting it," he grunted.

He raised the end of the tank several inches but instead of rolling off the wheelbarrow onto the rack it began to slip.

"Marlene!" he cried.

She dropped the handles of the wheelbarrow and sprang to seize the other end of the tank. The wheelbarrow toppled over and for a moment she stood there with the end of the tank cradled in her arms, the other end on Roberts' back.

"Let go and jump back!" he cried. "You can't hold it."

"Yes, I can," she cried, feeling the weight of the tank pulling at her shoulders and deep inside her body. "You'll get hurt."

"Try to put it down, then. And I'll try to straighten and let it roll off."

She started to bend and the tank slipped out of her arms. Roberts tried to lunge free but was not quick enough and the tank pinned him to the ground across the back of his legs at the knees.

"Are you hurt, Charlie?" she cried, pulling desperately at the stubborn cylinder.

"I don't think so," he said. "I just can't move. If I could just turn around a little and push."

"I'll roll it off you."

"No," he said. "You'll hurt yourself."

But instead of obeying, she strained and heaved and the tank moved just enough for Roberts to pull one leg free, twist and push the tank off with his free foot.

As he did so, Marlene fell to the ground, weeping with frustration.

"Just when we almost had it," she moaned.

Roberts scrambled to his feet, then dropped to his knees beside her.

"Are you all right?" he demanded.

Marlene looked at him dumbly for a moment.

"I don't know," she said. "I feel kind of . . . funny."

"Did you hurt yourself?"

"I don't know."

She felt pulled and torn inside but she did not know if what she felt was pain. It was a kind of stirring fullness.

"You're as white as a sheet," Roberts said. "I'd better get you inside."

"But the butane."

"To hell with the butane. I'll take care of it later."

He helped her to her feet and she stood there clumsily, her knees unwilling to remain straight and her big stomach a grotesque burden suddenly too cumbersome to support.

"Charlie," she said. "Charlie. I feel so funny."

He picked her up in his arms and despite the burden was not conscious of weight, only of urgency and concern.

"There, there, baby," he said. "You'll be all right."

He carried her up the back steps and kicked in the screen door but had to put her down a moment to open the kitchen door. Inside her room, he put her in bed and piled covers on her and brought the electric heater as close as he dared.

"There," he said. "Is that better?"

She nodded and smiled wanly. Night was close and her face was pale in the gathering shadows.

"I'm sorry, Charlie."

"Sorry. About what?"

"I didn't hold the butane."

"It wasn't your fault. I was a fool to let you . . . I only hope . . ."

"What?"

"How do you feel now?"

"Like . . . I don't know. Like something's, you know, busted inside."

He hurried to the light switch, turned it on and came back to her side.

"The baby," he said. "Does it feel like the baby?"

"I don't know what a baby feels like. 'Cept when it kicks. It just feels like . . . I don't know."

"Maybe something hot," Roberts said distractedly. "There's soup left. I'll go to the house with butane and make you some."

She smiled faintly.

"It's funny the way you say make some soup," she said. "You mean fix some."

"If you think that's so funny you must not be so badly off," he said hopefully. "Will you be all right while I'm gone?"

" 'Course, I'm fine. You know how to turn it on? The butane?"

He shook his head and she gave him instructions.

Roberts emptied a can of tomato soup into a saucepan and walked through the frosty night to the last house which still had butane.

Marlene lay in a cocoon of warmth and looked up at the ceiling trying to analyze her strange sensation of lassitude and numbness. The baby can't be coming, she thought. It's more than two months too soon and besides I don't hurt. It's supposed to hurt something awful and it's just the opposite. Maybe the baby's killed. Maybe when I pulled on the butane it did something to the baby.

She wanted to laugh with relief and weep in despair, for if the baby was dead she did not have to worry about giving it away or having to raise it without a father, but she would have lost something which was hers alone, not hers alone exactly because somehow it was Charlie's, too, because he had helped her and told her what she must do and she owed it to him to have this baby. He would be mad at her if something happened to the baby, especially after he had told her not to strain herself and she hadn't listened.

She reached under the warm covers and pulled up her skirt and thrust her palms under the stretched elastic of her torn underclothing and felt, under the smooth, distended skin of her stomach, life.

Oh, thank you, Jesus, she thought. He's alive. Now I can still do like Charlie wants me to and go some place where they'll take care of me and the baby and maybe let me keep him and some day Charlie will come see us and he'll see how good I raised the baby and be proud of me. And maybe I could even have a house like this one and I could keep house and go to school at the same time and Charlie could live there, too, if he wanted to, and I could keep house for him and the baby both and he would help me see the baby grows up smart like him instead of dumb like me.

And she pulled her hands back from her belly and grew sad because she knew people would not let her live with Charlie because he was a Negro and they didn't know he was like a daddy to her, better than her real daddy, and that it didn't make any difference what color he was and she was because she had forgotten all about color until just now and they wouldn't understand how it was with her and Charlie not even counting color because people had ugly minds and they would think all kinds of ugly things, not knowing how good he was and how sweet and how they had never even thought about that kind of thing, not even the time she had peeked into the bathroom to see if it was true what they said about Negro men and he had caught her peeping and got so mad and bawled her out.

When Roberts returned with the hot soup and brought it to her bedside in a bowl she threw her arms around his neck and so startled him he narrowly avoided drenching her with it.

"Hey," he said wryly. "What's got into you? When I left I thought you were ready to pass out."

"He's alive! Our baby."

"Our baby?"

Marlene laughed aloud.

"If you could see your face," she said. "I mean, I feel like it's as much yours as it is mine on account of . . . well, you know, how you worry about me and it and everything."

"Eat your soup," he said, moved.

She was not hungry but she began eating from the bowl in his hands because he wanted her to.

"Charlie," she said, the spoon poised over the bowl, "maybe some day, a long time from now, after I've had the baby and everything and maybe have a good job and he's big enough to say mama and things like that I'll write to you and you could . . . And I might even be married by then and I'd tell him, my husband, how you helped me . . . I could tell him, couldn't I even if I'm not s'posed to tell anybody else about you . . . and he'd want to meet you and thank you 'cause if it wasn't for you he wouldn't have a wife and baby, maybe. And you could, you know, visit."

"It doesn't work that way, Marlene," Roberts said. "Even if I . . ."

"Shoot, I wouldn't marry anybody that would be against you on account of that."

"It's not only that I'm a Negro. You can't seem to get it through your head that the sort of trouble I'm in is going to . . ." he groped for words that would not disturb her ". . . restrict my movements."

And he added to himself, I wish to God that's all it would do. But she's right, the way she almost always is in that direct, uncomplicated way of hers. I do feel as if it's my baby, too. I've got a big investment in that child.

"But we can write each other?"

"Yes," he said, without really being sure even of that.

After a few swallows of soup Marlene stopped with the

spoon halfway to her mouth. A slow tremor ran the length of her body and her mouth twisted with pain.

"What's the matter?" Roberts cried. "What is it?"

"Oh, Charlie. It hurts somethin' terrible."

Within an hour she was having hard labor pains. She moaned and sobbed and thrashed about under the covers and during the pain-free intervals apologized to Roberts for carrying on so. He wiped her face with a damp towel and stroked her hand, holding it tightly when the pains hit, and made helpless, soothing noises.

"Oh, Charlie!" she cried in the midst of her pain. "Do something! Help me!"

"I don't know what to do, baby," he said, feeling ineffectual and implicated.

Yes, I do know what to do, he thought. She needs a doctor. If she doesn't get one she's going to die.

But how could I get a doctor? There isn't even a phone here. But there's a phone at Treadwell's store. Maybe Treadwell could get a doctor in time. But you're afraid to go there, Charlie. You're going to sit here and listen to her screams and possibly watch her die, her and the baby you claim you care so much about.

"Oh! Dear sweet Jesus!" Marlene cried. "It hurts. It hurts me so bad, Charlie. Why does the baby hurt me like this? I hate him."

She was babbling now and the words ran together.

Roberts wiped her face and said, "There, there, baby."

"What's gonna happen?" she asked weakly, lucid for a moment. "How will the baby . . ."

"You need a doctor," Roberts said, getting to his feet. "I'm going after one."

To hell with it, he thought. I won't sit here and watch her suffer and perhaps die. Treadwell doesn't know I'm a wanted man. I'll make sure he gets a doctor and then just fade away. I was on the run when I came here and I can be on the run again. And this time it will be easier because the heat is off. It was so long ago.

Who are you kidding, Roberts? They'll get you sooner or later. Then why not sooner, if it saves Marlene? At least it won't be useless.

Deep inside he knew he was deluding himself, that he was not a hero and was going not only because it had to be done but also because he thought there was a chance he could find help and still get away. But at a deeper level he sensed, rather than knew, that once he left the house he was doomed, that he had perhaps always been doomed, that though his time-table had not been so rigid as Marlene's, something waited that had to be met. She had her appointment with birth and he had his with . . . And she was coming early to her appointment and he . . . and he. Who could tell?

"No," she cried, reaching for his hand. "Don't leave me! I'm scared!"

"I am, too," he said gently. "But I've got to."

He bent over and kissed her fleetingly on the lips.

"Good-bye, baby," he whispered.

Good-bye, Marlene. You poor sweet kid. You ought to be in a hospital somewhere, with your husband making nervous jokes in the waiting room, instead of lying here alone like an animal. But you're going to make it, you and the baby, too. Because you're tough and you've got something in you that won't quit and you'll raise the baby that way, too, and maybe somewhere, some day I'll know about it.

He stopped at the door and turned back.

"Good-bye, Marlene," he said.

"Don't be long. You'll come right back, won't you?"

"Sure. I'll come right back."

I wonder if she knows, he thought.

Don't be gone long, Charlie, she thought. I wish you didn't have to go at all. I want you here when the baby comes, more than I want the doctor. You've got to be here so you can see my baby and my baby can see you. I wonder if they can see when they're born and when they grow up remember it.

She tried to remember when she was born but could go no further back than four, when she got the hat with the little pink ribbon on it and she wondered what had happened to that hat and why her daddy had got it for her it must have been for church because she could remember sitting in church with it on and listening to the preacher and she remembered how he had frightened her shouting about hell and if it was a girl she would buy her a hat with a pink ribbon on it but of course it was going to be a boy and she would name him Charles and then a pain lashed through her and she thought of nothing but hurt.

22

Roberts trotted along the highway dragging in searing breaths of chill air and trying to think not of what might await him at the end of his errand but only of Marlene, alone and in labor, struggling to bring a fatherless child into a world without future. But a child more his own than any other would ever be.

He reached the store more quickly than he expected. The darkness which wrapped the store made it seem larger than it was, and ominous.

It's only a two-bit country store, Roberts told himself, and the man in it is only a two-bit country storekeeper. Just remember to act like a nigger and you'll be all right.

He waited at the door until he had caught his breath, then knocked and listened. Each rap hurt his cold-numbed hand through the old work glove, and he took it off and blew on his knuckles. There was no sound from the back of the store. His knock had been too timid. Now he breathed deeply and hit the door again, harder, cursing the pain, the cold, the darkness and Treadwell. He put his ear against the door and thought he heard sounds deep within. Then he heard an inner door open and footsteps shuffling across the floor and Treadwell's sleepy voice crying, "Don't have to bust the door down. Ah'm comin'." And then, closer and less sleepy, "Who is it?"

"It's me, mistuh," Roberts said.

"Me?" Treadwell said from inside the door. "Who the hell is me? An' what you mean knockin' on a man's door this time of night?"

Treadwell opened the door as he spoke and stood silhouetted in the opening in a spill of light from his living quarters. He was barefoot and in his underwear. He thrust his head forward to peer at Roberts.

"What the hell you want?" he demanded, shivering.

Before Roberts could answer he thrust his face closer, so

215

Roberts could smell the reek of his sleep-soured breath, and said, truculent but less disapproving, "Don't Ah know you, boy?"

The "boy" did not bother Roberts. He scarcely heard it.

"Yes, suh," he said. "Ah was in here once. Mistuh Treadwell, there's a girl needs help down there . . ."

"What girl? Get the hell inside. I'm freezin' my tail off."

Roberts slipped inside and Treadwell closed the door behind him. Roberts was conscious he had been mixing Southern dialect and his normal speech and that Treadwell had not seemed to notice it.

"Now, what is this all about?" Treadwell demanded. "What girl, where at?"

"In one of them houses down there. By the watuh."

"Shady Cove? They ain't nobody in them Shady Cove houses. Not this time of year."

"Yes, suh. This girl. She's about to have a baby."

"What the hell she doin' in one of them houses? Must of broke in. An' how the hell you know so much about it, boy?"

Will you shut up and listen, Roberts thought. God damn it, she needs a doctor fast. Be careful, Roberts, don't lose your temper. You need him.

"Ah was just passin' by. And Ah heard her yelling. And she told me to run for the doctuh."

"You gonna have yourself a long run. Nearest doctuh's . . ."

"Would you phone him, mistuh? She's bad off."

"Ah don't know if Ah could get the doctuh out this time 'a night for a nigger girl, less he knows her."

You dirty, dirty bastard, Roberts thought.

"But if you're sure she's real bad off Ah'll try. You sure?"

"Yes, suh. Real bad off."

"They'll do it ever' time," Treadwell said, grinning. "Have their baby in the middle of the night. White, black, don't make no difference. Right in the middle of the night."

The son of a bitch is human, Roberts thought grudgingly. But why doesn't he get on with it and phone the doctor instead of standing around making small talk.

"Ah'll put us on some coffee an' phone," Treadwell said. "You look half-froze."

"Ah think you better hurry," Roberts said desperately.

"Oh, you do?" Treadwell demanded. "Look here, boy, you seem awful bothered 'bout this just to be somebody happened to pass by. You sure it ain't your woman in that house?"

I'll have to tell him, Roberts thought. Or he'll stand there all night.

"No, suh," he said flatly. "She's white."

"White? Why didn't you say so?"

"You didn't give me a chance," Roberts said, not talking Southern at all.

Treadwell eyed him speculatively.

"Where you from?" he said.

"Mistuh, can we talk about that later? She's real bad off."

"Okay. Ah'll call the doctuh. But you just wait right here. Ah want to talk to you. Yo heah?"

"Yes, suh."

Treadwell walked to the back of the store and, with his hand on the doorknob, said " 'Member what I told you, heah? You wait right there."

He closed the door behind him. Roberts waited an intolerable moment, then walked quickly but quietly to the front door, opened it carefully and stepped out into the night. Treadwell would never be able to find him in the darkness. If he took the trouble to look.

Roberts took a few steps and stopped dead. How could he be sure Treadwell was actually calling a doctor? Why had Treadwell shut the door behind him if that was what he intended doing? What if he was calling the sheriff, instead? Marlene wouldn't get the help she needed. If he left now he would never know. But what good would it do for him to hang around, whether it was the sheriff or the doctor Treadwell was calling? If it was the sheriff, he was done for, and perhaps Marlene, too. If it was the doctor, he might reach Marlene in time and she'd be all right, and he himself would have a chance to get out of the area by the time they started looking for him.

But he would never know. He would always feel he had left the job unfinished, that he might have failed Marlene when she needed him most. He knew he could not go until he was sure help was on the way.

And Treadwell wouldn't leave me by myself if he thought anything was really wrong, he thought, reassuring himself.

He went back inside the store as quietly as he had left it, thinking, When Treadwell comes back I'll just stick to my story about hearing her scream, Uncle Tom him a little until I know if he's called a doctor, then go.

Despite his resolve, during the minutes Treadwell was gone Roberts had repeatedly to fight down a panicky urge to

slip out into the night again and get as far away as he could.
And another part of him was anguished because no matter
what happened he would not be with Marlene when she had
her baby. She should not have to have her baby among strangers. A member of her family should be with her. And he
was her family.

He blew on his hands and stamped his chilled feet and at
last Treadwell returned. He had slipped on shoes, trousers and
an overcoat with a ragged hole in one elbow. He had a steaming cup in each hand.

"Here," Treadwell said, holding out one of them. "Have
yo'self some hot coffee."

Roberts was dumbfounded. He had been prepared for anything but hospitality. Was Treadwell playing games with
him?

"Did you get the doctuh?" Roberts asked, not reaching out
for the proffered cup.

"On his way."

Roberts sighed with relief.

"Thank you, suh. Ah guess Ah bettuh get on home. Mah
cousin, he . . ."

"You forgettin' somethin'?" Treadwell demanded. "Ah told
you Ah wanted to talk to you. Here."

He thrust the coffee at Roberts and Roberts took it reluctantly.

"Now. How come you told me you was from 'round here?
You from up Nawth, boy."

Jesus, thought Roberts, is that all that's bothering him?

"It's because I didn't want to get in any trouble," he said
with a false air of candor. "I really do live down here now.
With my cousin. And he told me if I acted right I'd be treated
right."

"Yoah cousin's a smart nigger," Treadwell said. "You pay
attention to him, you be all right. Even if you are from up
Nawth."

"Thank you, sir," Roberts said, you white trash son of a
bitch. "I guess I'll be getting on back."

"You bettuh stay," Treadwell said. "Show the sheriff which
house."

"The sheriff?"

God Almighty, he did call the sheriff!

"Yeah," Treadwell said comfortably. "Figured fastest way
to get the doctuh here was have the sheriff carry him."

He sat down on the counter as if preparing for a leisurely, cozy chat.

"Drink yoah coffee," he said. "Be half an hour till they get here. Mighty fine thing you done comin' for help. Ah had you figured wrong at first an' Ah admit it. Thought you just another uppity nigra but you a real good boy to do that."

Roberts did not hear the words. All he could hear was the massive thumping in his chest. The sheriff was coming. He had to get out. He turned blindly toward the door.

"Hey. Where you goin'? Ah told you the sheriff wants you to show him which house."

Still moving toward the door, Roberts looked back over his shoulder.

"I have to go," he said, his voice shaking with urgency.

"An' I say you ain't," said Treadwell flatly.

He slide over the counter to his feet.

"What you in such a hurry for, boy?" he demanded. "Somethin's real funny. Real funny."

He put his cup down, reached Roberts in two quick steps and grabbed him by the upper arm. Roberts pulled free and sprang toward the door. He had it half-open when Treadwell grabbed him again and pulled him back inside. Roberts wrested free and pushed Treadwell away.

"Hit me, will you, you black bastard!" Treadwell cried. "Ah show you to hit a white man!"

He hit Roberts in the mouth and drove him back against the door, slamming it shut. Roberts was not conscious of any pain or of any fear of Treadwell, only of the need of getting away. Blindly, unaware of the blows Treadwell was raining on his back, he turned and tried to pull the door open. Treadwell hooked an arm under his chin and wrestled him back to the middle of the store, where both fell heavily. Treadwell was on his feet first. Roberts began scrambling for the door on his hands and knees. Treadwell sprang for the counter and as Roberts fumbled at the doorknob he looked back and saw Treadwell clambering over it.

"Stay 'way from that doah!" Treadwell shouted. "Ah'll blow yoah black head off!"

Roberts flung the door open at last and ran out into the darkness. He heard feet pounding behind him and a voice filled with hate calling out for him to stop and suddenly he was reliving a familiar nightmare.

The white man was chasing him through the night and he had never known such fear, had never known such fear was possible. "Stop, you nigger! Stop, you black bastard! Ah'll show you to come down here an' make trouble." Run, run. Get away. He'll kill you if he can and nobody will care. Not down here. Open season all year round on Negroes down here. Now you know how it is down South. You wanted to know and now you do. Now you know what it feels like to be a nigger. Why didn't you stay North where you belonged? Run, gasping, tasting panic and fear thick as slime. Into the alley, quick, quick, maybe he won't see you. Run, faster, faster. But the footsteps and the hate and the threats follow. And the alley ends. And you turn and there is the white man, his face so ugly with hate and violence you want to faint and you hate yourself for your terror because he has seen it. He draws back his fist and you feel it smash into your eye like a firebrand and you go sprawling in the dirt and garbage of the alley and he kicks you and yells, "Nigger!" And suddenly you realize there is only one white man, not the half-dozen who dragged you from the march and beat you, just one white man and you, and you find your courage and your manhood and you get to your feet and you hit back and you fight all over the alley, bouncing off the ground and the brick walls without feeling pain, and suddenly you sense his weakening and he is no longer calling names but fighting for his life and then you see the fear in his eyes, the same fear you had in yours earlier, and something inside you shrieks in cruelty and blood lust and vengeance and you hit and hit, and the face goes bloody and beseeching and you keep hitting and cursing until there are no features left to hit, just a ragged blot of flesh and you let go and it slips to the pavement and you bend over and listen to its heart and when you realize it is dead you know a moment of exultation because you have killed the monster at last and you have shown you are a man and had your private revenge for every murdered and beaten and spat-upon Negro and you feel the blood pride of having at last stood and fought back and killed, yes, killed, and then you know dread because you have killed a human being. But you have learned that a white man could make you run for your life and feel like a nigger and you swear no white man would ever do that to you again.

But here you are running again, Charlie Roberts, and it is a white man chasing you.

He stopped and turned and shouted into the chill, dark air, "Come and get me, you white son of a bitch," and saw too late that Treadwell had a gun and heard an explosion and felt a smashing blow at his chest and fell to the highway, thinking, Why don't they fight fair? and then, Marlene, and then, nothing.

Marlene chewed her knuckles and the sheet and thrashed about in the disordered covers sodden with her sweat and water.

It hurts, Charlie, it hurts and I'm scared. Help me, please help me. Hold onto my hand. But Charlie's gone. Where are you, why don't you come back? Gone when I need you. I hate you, Charlie, you claimed you liked me and you're gone and the baby's coming and you left me all alone. Mama. Oh, Mama. Make him come back. Make Charlie come back. I'm dying, Mama, I'm dying and Charlie ain't here and what will happen to my baby with him gone?

Stupefied with pain, she did not hear the sheriff's car stop in front of the house and was only dimly aware of the front door being forced open and of men and voices in her room. She listened for Charlie's voice among them, as if from a great distance, but did not hear it and she looked for him but her eyes would not focus and she saw only a blur of movement and heard, the words meaningless to her, a voice say, "Why, Ah seen this little lady befoah," and another, "Too late to move her. She's about to pop right now." And then there was one last great pain dragging out of her in an excruciating dangle and then a complete absence of sensation and dark melting weariness and she thought, Oh, Charlie, I must be dead.

And then, she did not know how much later, low voices sank into her stupor like pebbles in a still deep pool and with as little meaning.

". . . in mah stoah, must of been foah, five months ago."

"All that time livin' by herself, can you imagine. Wonder how she managed, poor little thing."

"She goin' to be all right?"

"Tough as shoe leather, that little lady. And the baby. Healthiest premature I ever delivered."

"Funny 'bout that nigger. Ah wondah. . ."

"He hadn't come for help, she never would have made it. Too bad you had to go and shoot him, Tread."

"Hell, Ah told you, he was comin' for me. Crazy nigger."

What are they talking about? What nigger? What do they mean using that word, anyhow? Charlie don't like it and I don't neither. He'll throw them out of our house if they don't watch out. What are they doing in our house, anyhow? Big as you please like they owned it.

She opened her eyes slowly, as if something would shatter in them if she were not exceedingly careful.

"She's wakin' up," a voice said.

She looked toward the sound without moving her head and saw three men standing close together, one with a bundle in his arms, regarding her. There was something about them grotesque and frightening and she wondered if she were having a bad dream and then she knew what was wrong. The faces which loomed over her were pasty white, like Mr. Doughface, and they seemed all wrong, all pale and cold.

"Charlie," she called weakly.

The men looked at one another and one of them stepped closer, the one with the bundle, and held it at her.

"Already have a name picked out for him, have you?" he said. "You've got a fine little boy, young lady. He's going to be all right even if he is ahead of time."

Oh, she thought, my baby, I've had my baby, my dear sweet baby and I'm alive, and she took it in her arms and felt it warm against her like a prize she had won for having endured so much pain, and she kissed it and wanted to hold it up for Charlie to see. But Charlie was not there.

"Where is he?" she asked. "Charlie?"

"Who?" the man asked. "Who's Charlie?"

"He went for help," said Marlene. "An' he promised to come right back."

"I wonder does she mean the nigger," the man said.

"She must mean the nigger."

"This Charlie, he a nigger?" said another man, the one wearing a badge that winked at her when he moved.

"Where is he?" she demanded.

"Ah 'spect he's dead," the sheriff said. "Mr. Treadwell here, he had to shoot him. He was comin' for him."

"Dead!" she shrieked.

Oh, dear sweet Jesus, they've killed you, the doughfaces have killed you. They've killed my sweet Charlie and now you'll never see the baby and I haven't got anybody.

"Don't take on so," Treadwell said. "Ah couldn't help it. He was comin' for me."

"You killed him! I'll kill you, kill you!"

She tried to get up but the baby was in the way and she was too weak and she fell back, staring.

"Doc, you don't reckon . . ." Treadwell said, profoundly disturbed.

"No," the doctor said. "Baby's all white. Bet my bottom dollar."

Marlene began to cry.

"Why did you do it?" she said, sobbing. "Why did you kill my sweet Charlie?"

"Listen at her," the sheriff said. "Talkin' that way 'bout a nigger."

"Never would of thought it," said Treadwell, shaking his head in wonder and disgust. "A sweet-lookin' little thing like her. Looka here, Marlene, that's your name, ain't it, what you mean carryin' on like that 'bout a nigger? Who was this Charlie?"

She stared at him.

Who was Charlie? He was a man. What are you? I hate you. I hate your white face. Mean, hateful, stupid white face. If Charlie was here he'd . . . But Charlie's dead and I won't ever see him any more. And you did it. And I won't let you talk about him like that. Not about my sweet Charlie. You think you can scare me talking like that but you can't. Not you or anybody else. Not ever. I'd explain to you about Charlie but you're too dumb. You're all too dumb.

She looked at her baby. It was white, too, like Mr. Treadwell and the others, and for a moment she almost hated her baby and then she realized it was not the baby's fault he was white, and that just being white did not make it dumb and cruel like the others, and he never would be that way, not if she could help it and she could help it, and he was going to grow up sweet and good and smart like Charlie and maybe wherever Charlie was he would know about it and not be mad at her because she got him killed trying to help her.

"Ah asked you a question, Marlene," Treadwell said angrily. "Who was that Charlie?"

And anger and some of the hurt drained from her and she thought, You're so dumb I feel sorry for you.

And she looked at him with great wisdom and tolerance and she said gently, "He was my daddy."

Have You Read These Bestsellers from SIGNET?

☐ **FEAR OF FLYING by Erica Jong.** A dazzling uninhibited novel that exposes a woman's most intimate sexual feelings. . . . "A sexual frankness that belongs to and hilariously extends the tradition of **Catcher in the Rye** and **Portnoy's Complaint** . . . it has class and sass, brightness and bite."—John Updike, **New Yorker** (#J6139—$1.95)

☐ **PENTIMENTO by Lillian Hellman.** Hollywood in the days of Sam Goldwyn . . . New York in the glittering times of Dorothy Parker and Tallulah Bankhead . . . a 30-year love affair with Dashiell Hammett, and a distinguished career as a playwright. "Exquisite . . . brilliantly finished . . . it will be a long time before we have another book of personal remembrance as engaging as this one."—**New York Times Book Review** (#J6091—$1.95)

☐ **THE FRENCH LIEUTENANT'S WOMAN by John Fowles.** By the author of **The Collector** and **The Magus,** a haunting love story of the Victorian era. Over one year on the N.Y. Times Bestseller List and an international bestseller. "Filled with enchanting mysteries, charged with erotic possibilities . . ." —Christopher Lehmann-Haupt, N. Y. Times (#E6484—$1.75)

☐ **HARRIET SAID by Beryl Bainbridge.** An explosive shocker about little girls . . . here is the horror of child's play mixed with erotic manipulation and evil possession. "A highly plotted horror tale that ranks with the celebrated thrillers of corrupt childhood."—**New York Times Book Review** (#W6058—$1.50)

☐ **DANCING MAN by Edward Hannibal.** From the author of the one-million-copy bestseller, **Chocolate Days, Popsicle® Weeks** —a novel that touches the most intimate emotions—a love story, moving and unforgettable. (#W6205—$1.50)

THE NEW AMERICAN LIBRARY, INC.,
P.O. Box 999, Bergenfield, New Jersey 07621

Please send me the SIGNET BOOKS I have checked above. I am enclosing $_____(check or money order—no currency or C.O.D.'s). Please include the list price plus 25¢ a copy to cover handling and mailing costs. (Prices and numbers are subject to change without notice.)

Name_____

Address_____

City_____State_____Zip Code_____
Allow at least 3 weeks for delivery